The Sol Empire
Volume 7
Telepath
Nightmares

Vic Broquard

The Sol Empire Volume 7 Telepath Nightmares
First Edition
Copyrighted © 2021 by Vic Broquard
ISBN: 978-1-941415-88-7

Thank you to my colleague, Lisa Walker, for her many useful suggestions and corrections.

What isn't fictional is the work that Humanity and Inclusion (formerly Handicapped International) is doing to help those who have suffered:
http://www.hi-us.org

Published by:
http://www.Broquard-ebooks.com
Broquard eBooks
1055 Brandy Lake Rd
Woodruff, WI 54568
author@Broquard-eBooks.com

For Morgan and L. Ron Hubbard

Table of Contents

Chapter 1 Why Me?

Three Months Later, August 1, 2369
Chicago, Sol Empire

"How can you lose ten million people? Helpless people at that," yelled Lin Dho, the CEO of Galactic Expansion (GPan) for the Sol Empire. The Heart of Gold deep space exploration ship had landed on Bella only to find its population had vanished.

From my Empress throne, I glared at him. Armless people aren't helpless. Handicapped, yes. Is he insulting our personal assistants?

He flushed. "All right, physically challenged."

"That's better. Now then, I was there with the Third Invaders."

"If they've tricked us again, Empress Parkinson, I swear I'll send our whole fleet to blast their Home World to oblivion!"

The tall, thin man's face drilled his intention into me. I didn't need telepathy to know he meant it. My daughter published her translation of the Third Invaders' Bella experiment document months ago. Only now had GPan visited that world expecting to find the ten million armless humans.

My throne room occupied the top floor of a refurbished skyscraper. Mei Hui, my personal assistant and standing on my right, adjusted my long hair. Off to my left, Hans Klein (my fiancé) and his personal assistant, Shu Ying, stood. A half-dozen security guards hovered around the outer walls and main doors. To my far right, various ambassadors often sat, in particular Katya Binsk and her personal assistant Li Feng. But

Katya, the Third Invader ambassador, had been recalled to the Jafari home world and hadn't yet returned. Both Lin and I glanced at her empty chair. I realized Lin had meant his words for that Third Invader.

"I was there. The Third Invaders were undoing their experiment. In the beginning, they created two different mutations: one for males and one for females. Rather than attempting to create two independent mutation cures, we both thought it wise to subject the Bella women to the male mutation and then create a single cure. That was the plan."

Tenseness lifted from his body. I continued. His surface thoughts suggested he'd wanted to target his rage onto Katya, their ambassador. With her gone, he found no target.

"When I visited Bella, I detected traces of what happened. I've already reported this to Admiral Carr. I believe the First Invaders, the Alitos, kidnapped all ten million humans. They amputated the arms of the fifty Third Invaders who worked to keep the people supplied with the necessities of life. Those men killed themselves—"

CEO Lin Dho interrupted. "Makes sense they would."

I frowned, but continued. "I've had Admiral Carr searching for the Alitos home world. No luck. I've had our Senior Investigator, Ward Tilman, searching Earth records for anything about these First Invaders. They were here millennia ago. All he's found are vague references to a short, porcelain-skinned, thin-armed people. Neither the Sixth Invaders nor the Third Invaders know the location of the Alitos home world."

"Did they kill the Bella humans?"

"I don't believe so. They took the women's stashes of lip disks. Why take those if they intended to kill the women?"

CEO Lin Dho nodded. "These rogue robots—your Telepath Squads haven't detected any of them here in Chicago."

"Four were flushed from Admiral Carr's fleet. Sure glad they didn't infiltrate the CEOs of our corporations."

He flashed the briefest of smiles. "Thank goodness for that. The Senate is established. I assume Senate President Egan Ivar has contacted you."

I nodded, and he left.

Hans said, "Molly, I'm so bored. When I joined the Telepath Squad, I envisioned—"

"Lots of action. I know. They've got you assigned to protect me, dear."

"I'm going nuts, and it's only the second month. One hundred eighteen more months to go. Oh, gods! I'll never make it."

I smiled. "Dear, when I have the twins, you'll be plenty busy."

"But I know nothing about babies," Hans said.

Both our teenaged personal assistants giggled. Shu Ying said, "Don't worry, Hans. You'll learn fast enough, but we'll be doing most of the work since neither of you have arms."

I said, "Hey, arms aren't necessary to care for babies. Look at the videos we have on our computers. We'll do as much as we can. That is, when we're not stuck here in the throne room. I'm already bored, too. I miss Katya."

Hans said, "So do I. We used to play telepathic guessing games to pass the hours in here. But I sensed how scared she was when they ordered her to return to her home world. Just glad she took Li Feng, her robot helper Sam, and the Third Invader Bazyli Dorek with her. It *is* frightening to be like this. When does it get easier?"

I shrugged my shoulders. The doorman announced my next visitor.

"Senate President Egan Ivar."

The Mars Colony man marched into the throne room. Short. A muscular build that looked odd in his sky blue suit.

"Empress Parkinson, good to see you. The Senate compiled this list of obsolete or invalid laws we want cancelled. I hope you won't veto them. If you do, I have enough votes to override you."

Posturing. For once, Mars Colony wasn't just in the background, taking Fourth Place to Pylon and Brussels, our two Earth-sized worlds in the Empire.

"I'm sure many previous laws should be abolished. Congratulations on becoming the Senate President."

I didn't tell him why I thought the big three worlds didn't want to be seen as the Senate Leader. Too many had been killed or mutated in terrorist attacks. Mei took the document from Egan.

He asked, "Is the official total still four rogue robots flushed from our space fleet and none discovered here on Earth?"

"Yes. Hans," I nodded to him.

Hans said, "That's the official total as of today. Zero found on Pylon and Brussels. Next week, Telepath Squad Two plans to visit Mars Colony and the others in our Sol system. After that, they'll visit the more remote outposts of our empire."

"That's a relief. Why do we need so many more Telepath Squads? I can't imagine what a rogue robot would want here on Earth, let alone Mars and the others. Protests are popping up against the creation of the Telepath Squads."

"People? The corporate leaders?" I asked.

He nodded. "No rogue robots found on Earth. CEOs are nervous about all these telepaths. Privileged information. Spying. You understand."

"Secrets." I laughed. "I know all about that. Old story."

"A heads-up, Empress. As soon as the rogue robot threat is handled, the Telepath Squads won't be needed. I bid you good day."

4

As he left, the doorman announced our next visitor.

"Geneticist Dr. Eve Burkey."

I relaxed. My younger sister, still wearing her white lab coat, didn't smile as she entered. I sensed something ill. My clone looked all of her forty years, while I still looked twenty thanks to the genetic mutations. But she wore her black hair short.

"Hi, got the latest genetic tests back. I wish I could bring better news," she said.

"Any good news at all?" Hans asked. "We're bored out of our minds. No one said the Telepath Squad would be such a bore."

Eve chuckled. "Just you wait, big boy, til the twins get here."

Hans laughed.

She continued. "The genetic mutation cure for the other telepath members will work as expected. I've had to undo one; she had a family emergency to handle."

I relaxed. "Thanks, Eve. I worried the cure might not work this time. That's a relief. Still, I hedged in their contracts by saying we may not be able to undo their mutation."

"Always a wise precaution with these mutations," she said. "Hans, we'll have a special cure for you next month. By Halloween, you'll look like your old self. For the bad news. Lara and I haven't found a way to undo your mutations, Molly. Nor Katya's. Yet. That mammoth dose of the mutation agent you received did a job on your DNA. It's so dominant that every time we insert a change, your DNA rejects it. At least in our mice test subjects. Lara said not to give up all hope. Your new clone bodies are developing nicely, thanks to that new technology we received."

"Whew. You had me worried there for a minute," Hans said. "I can't endure this for much longer, unless this telepath job perks up. But, Eve, I don't feel right taking a million credits a year for doing nothing. I wanted to work on computer systems or study the geology of other worlds or look for rogue robots, not sit here listening to diplomats drone on all day."

"You could always take online courses. Study genetics?" Her grin suggested a tease.

Hans groaned. "I almost flunked beginning biology in high school. *Nein, danke dir.*"

"Any word from Katya?" Eve asked.

"No, but Ambassador L'Grina went with her. I'm sure she'd let me know if Katya ran into trouble," I said.

Hans added his observation. "She's scared to be out in public on her own. Just like I am. We're still getting used to being nearly helpless. No offense, Molly."

"None taken. You've only had a couple months to get accustomed to living without arms. It takes time and practice doing things," I said.

We chatted a bit before Eve left.

"We can't even play cards while sitting here," Hans complained. "Wonder if I could get permission to explore the rock quarries south of here?"

"You're not getting me to assist with *that!*" Shu Lin said. "No way am I going to walk over rough ground in these heels. And you can't do it by yourself. Put that notion out of your mind. We're supposed to be perfect Galactic Dolls."

Just then Ambassadors L'Grina and Katya Binsk entered along with Katya's assistant, Li Feng. Her helper robot rolled along behind them. Bazyli Dorek brought up the rear.

Katya's red eyes told much. A wave of grief flowed from her. The tautness of Ambassador L'Grina's grey face added to the solemnity. The women walked to their usual chairs off to my right and sat.

"Glad you're both back," I said. "What happened?"

Ambassador L'Grina glanced at Katya and spoke for her. "Worst possible outcome. Katya is now the one and only

6

Jafari telepath, making her incredibly valuable. They are allowing her to remain on Earth until she and Bazyli have their babies. They are betting that since this mutation is so dominant, their children will be similarly endowed. Bet you can guess the rest."

Katya cried. "They want me to make eight more Jafari babies like me. That's still four egg cycles at least. My body won't make a new egg pair for about fifty years, They're dooming me to live like this for another two hundred years or more! They won't let me swap into my new clone body when it's ready."

At that, Katya broke into tears again. Since a Jafari often lived two millennia, I understood her anguish and why the fifty Jafari men on Bella terminated their lives.

Bazyli wore a blue suit. His reddish skin contrasted with his tall head, modified while a child. From what little I knew of Jafari society, this suggested he held a high social status. He rested his hands on her shoulders.

"There, there, Katya, it'll be all right. We can make this work. It's only a short time for us. Really it is."

His soothing voice almost mesmerized me. It calmed Katya, while Li dabbed away the tears. We knew he was an elementary education teacher and that they knew each other from childhood. Their mating two months before, seemed a stroke of luck for Katya.

He said, "I'm charged with helping Katya until we've met the Home World's goal of eight telepath children. That's several hundred years, if her biology hasn't changed. She's the most beautiful Jafari ever. I have a natural ability to calm children."

He didn't say it, but I picked up his afterthought. *Almost impossible to keep Katya calm.*

Hans said, "Katya, Eve just reported your clone body is maturing on schedule. It will be ready."

"But they won't let me swap into it." She wailed. "Not until I produce eight more Jafari telepaths. Damn this skyscraper's barrier walls. Otherwise, I could jump off and end this nightmare. I don't want to be a glorified spy."

"Oh, Katya, dearest. Don't say such things. You're beautiful and one of the most important Jafari ever." Bazyli's soothing words calmed her again.

"Wonder if Eve can keep my clone body alive for four hundred years?" Katya said.

***

That night when we returned to my home in northern Chicago, Eve dropped by.

"I heard you were back, Katya. Wanted to give you a hug."

After Katya explained what had happened, she asked, "Can you keep that clone body for four hundred years or more?"

Eve laughed. "Hardly, but I can grow another one when the time is right. How can you let them dictate how you live your life? That's not right."

Katya countered. "Often, women are still things. Objects, you call them. Your corporations dictate how you live yours. I feel helpless. How am I going to care for a baby, let alone eight of them? If only they hadn't put such tall barriers around the edges of the skyscraper roofs..."

It's one thing for me to face perhaps another forty years like this, but quite another for Katya to face many centuries as an armless telepath. I felt helpless to change futures, but I was determined to try.

***

CEO Lin Dho met in secret with ten empire-wide CEOs.

"It's working, gentlemen. The meddling Parkinson woman is out of the way. Playing Empress. Sits on her throne all day doing nothing."

Another CEO laughed. "Just what we wanted. Unfortunate she still has the ear of Admiral Carr."

"Ear?" another said. "He's enthralled. Does whatever she says. How long can we keep her from meddling?"

Lin Dho shrugged. "More worried about alarming number telepaths. Close to fifty. Carr keeps pushing for more. They must go."

On that, they all agreed.

A new CEO asked, "Can't we just arrange for an unfortunate accident for Parkinson?"

Lin Dho said, "Don't be stupid. Many have tried kill her. They've failed. She keeps getting mutated back alive. Plus, she's worse than angry bulldog. Nothing stops her from finding who tried kill her. Way she has Admiral Carr wrapped around her finger, hell to pay if she's murdered."

"But she doesn't have any fingers..." another joked.

The men laughed.

Chapter 2 Taking Care of Business

Late August, CEO Lin Dho and I appeared jointly before the full Senate. I began the meeting.

"I've called for this special session of the Senate. Our empire continues to expand. We've just added a new world called Bella. It's a world rich in minerals and potential. But it brings two critical problems to the fore. First, we need an empire-wide procedure for finding personnel to colonize these worlds. More cargo ships and crews are needed to support our expanding empire. I'll let CEO Dho discuss those details.

"The second problem almost happened on Bella. As you know, their ten million humans vanished. I got a sense the culprits were the First Invaders, the Alitos. However, Admiral Carr and Senior Investigator Tilman can't locate their world. I've requested assistance from those on Cass-C—their ID division, the Senators, and the many ambassadors. I hope to have a lead soon.

"But the question is how do we deal with another people who inhabit a world we discover. Bella's civilization had just entered an industrialization era with steam engines and basic electricity. Should we leave such populations alone? Let them develop in their own unique way? Should we try to provide some guidance to these populations? Hands off. Hands on. If we interfere, we risk altering their culture."

A senator spoke up. "You mean like what happened centuries ago during World War Two when we interfered in some South Pacific cultures?"

"Precisely. We risk making them dependent upon us for their survival. Perhaps the destruction of their native culture. For example, during my brief stay on Bella, organized religion played a vital role in the underpinnings of their society. I know religions are a distant past for us, but they dominated Bella society. Just how far can we allow our corporations to go when colonizing worlds that are already populated. Some cultures could well be far more primitive such as the one on Ross 248 back in 2330—where we 'sky people' murdered whole villages just to mine cargos of rare earths."

Someone laughed. "You mean we should enact a total non-interference policy? Like in that ancient TV series Star Trek."

"Isn't that taking it a mite too far?" another senator said.

"She has a point," said Senate President Egan Ivar. "We need to address this and provide guidance for Galactic Mining and GPan."

Thus began a serious discussion, one long overdue. Weeks passed before the Senate sent me legislation to sign. They'd been thorough, contacting many other budding empires of the Federation of Planets and those on Cass-C.

As I read the document, I smiled, though no one could see it because of the lip disk. I had actually succeeded in making a real difference. On a new world with inhabitants, we would allow them to decide how we'd interact with them. If they asked for assistance, we'd provide it in return for some mining rights. If they didn't want us there, we'd leave that world alone, though we'd keep it under our protective umbrella so another empire couldn't attack them. The new legislation became known as the Parkinson Rule. Yes, I was pleased.

Since we weren't at war with anyone, I had very little else to do but serve as the empire's figurehead. True, many ambassadors visited with me, discussing potential trading ventures, but I referred them to the appropriate corporation

CEO to work out the details. My idea of empress duties differed from theirs.

***

At the end of August, a situation arose that demanded my attention, though it wasn't part of my obligations as empress. Hans reported it to me.

"Molly, a telepath has gone missing. Connor O'Grady. I assigned him to assist Galactic Robotics. A member of my squad."

I perked up. "Details?"

Hans shrugged his shoulders. "Dunno. Ward just called me. Someone found his personal assistant unconscious near the MTES. He said not to worry; he's on the case."

"Well, I *am* worried. I feared this would happen. Telepaths are incredible assets. The unscrupulous will do anything to get their hands on one. Two months and already one has been kidnapped."

"We don't know that yet. Do we? You're speculating."

"Have you tried telepathically contacting Connor? I don't know him, so I can't."   "*Ja*, just as soon as Ward called. He wanted me to see if I could locate him. *Nichts*. Like he just vanished."

"I'm paying Ward a visit. Come on, Mei. We're off to see our Senior Investigator."

"Mr. Tilman's office?" she asked.

***

When I held that post, I'd trained him. Already he and his staff had uncovered surveillance video showing two giants abducting Connor. A discarded rag tested positive for chloroform. These two giants were not citizens of our empire, and their spaceship departed New O'Hare Spaceport less than twenty minutes after the abduction.

His staff alerted Earth's space fleet, but the ship dropped into hyperspace after it cleared our satellite bands.

12

Further, by the time I arrived, Ward had found the ship's registration was falsified.

"Fast work, Ward. We've lost Connor, right?" I said.

He sighed. "I worried about this happening. My worst nightmares come true. I'll send out a Federation-wide alert. If anyone spots Connor O'Grady, we'll eventually know. Might take years, Molly. I've already spoken to Admiral Carr. He's agreed to assign guards to all telepaths 24/7."

I thanked him and left. He and his staff had been thorough. I couldn't think of anything else that could be done, but that he'd put out such an alert gave me hope. Every reputable authority within the Federation of Planets would keep an eye out for Connor. In time a clue would come, if not his rescue.

Also, Hans and I set our wedding day and chose Halloween. Trick or Treat would be our theme.

***

September brought a strange event to my attention via a video call from Galactic Defense CEO Yasha Petrov.

"Satellites and ground-based systems have recorded ten of the strangest anomalies I've ever seen. Over the Atlantic. As you can see from these frames, it appears to be raining ice cubes."

I watched thousands of smallish blue cubes falling into the ocean. Baseball sized, perhaps. Not hail. I had studied Earth Science. Hail tended to be roundish, but these were perfect cubes, as though they came from some monstrous ice cube tray.

"What is that? Can't be hail," I said.

"We don't know. I sent out ships, but the cubes melted before they arrived. At least that's their conclusion. Either that or the cubes sunk to the bottom of the ocean."

"Any idea what they were? Where they came from? Weird weather phenomenon? Perhaps a defective climate control system?"

I suggested what I would investigate first had I been on the case.

"I've had a team analyzing them. One theory suggests the cubes are super dense, based on the estimated size and splash made when they landed. Another theory says it's an as yet unknown anomaly in our weather control system. There's more. I had my resident astrophysicist correlate all known observations of the cube rain—our name for it. Here's the supercomputer 3-D rendering. It is suggestive."

I watched, fascinated. By compiling data from dozens of systems, the video showed what might be the underbelly of a strange spaceship. At the bottom of the video frames, a line indicated the dimensions. The rain of cubes came from distinct sections, which spanned over a thousand feet long by a hundred wide.

Being a licensed spaceship pilot and navigator and having traveled extensively within the Federation, I was familiar with a myriad of ship designs. This fit none I'd ever seen. I relayed this to him and discovered this was his main reason for contacting me.

Yasha Petrov sighed. "I rather hoped you might have seen a ship that could fit the simulation. Seven ships continue to monitor that section of the Atlantic. They should be able to detect any attempts to poison our ocean or an invasion of some weird species, like those worms that struck Peoria some years back. Empress Parkinson, if these cubes represent anything harmful to us, I'll let you know at once."

"Thanks. Yes, it's the strangest thing I've ever seen. Any idea how many cubes fell?"

"Millions is our best guess. An accurate count isn't possible. We don't have that kind of tech. Yet."

14

I watched the simulation for an hour after the call and took it home with me to study further. Now I had something to help allay the boredom.

***

Mid-September, the Third Invader Admiral Irenka Bronislawa paid a surprise visit to my throne room. Her taut face suggested major trouble. After introducing her to our assistants, she explained.

"We have human-form robot problems on Fantasy World. Somehow, we missed a few, and they've begun taking over the facility. I've talked to Admiral Carr about this and have his agreement to send one of your telepaths to help us root out these fiends. But I must clear it with you, per his orders. Home World will pay ten million of your credits for the brief help of a telepath."

Ambassador Katya looked up. "I'll volunteer!"

Only months ago, one of those robots ripped her arms from their sockets, almost killing her. A light touch on her mind yielded her idea of getting a merciful death this time.

Admiral Irenka Bronislawa laughed. "I knew you would, Ambassador Binsk, but no. You are the most valuable Jafari in the galaxy, and you're pregnant with perhaps more telepaths. Home World would never agree."

"Hey, what about me?" Hans spoke up.

I knew how bored he was as my throne room telepath. The job drove him nuts with boredom.

He looked at me. "You can make all the wedding plans. Whatever you decide is fine with me. Here's a chance to really matter. As a telepath."

I couldn't resist his pleading face. Nor could I deny him this opportunity to use his telepathy skill. Besides, Eve had his cure about ready. In a few more weeks, she'd undo his armless Galactic Doll mutation, returning him to a normal male. I

15

knew how much that meant to him. This could be his last chance to use his telepathy to help others.

"Okay, Hans. You have my permission to go. Just don't get yourself killed. It'll be hard to hold the wedding ceremony if you're dead."

He laughed. The relief on the Admiral's face spoke volumes. I felt a sense of accomplishment in bringing our two races together. Again.

His assistant, Shu Ying, asked, "Do I go with him?"

I sensed how ill at ease she felt in the presence of the red-skinned Jafari.

"No, not unless you want. He can take his robot on wheels."

"Great. Thanks," she said, her relief visible to all.

"When do we go?" Hans asked.

"Now. Bring your robot. Stop by your place and pack a bag. Meet me at your spaceport as soon as possible. Oh, Roz Kowalksi says hello to everyone and wants you to visit when this mess is over."

Memories returned. I wondered how that scrappy dwarf fared. Scruffy. He's one powerful dwarf. Yes, I want to visit them, too.

Chapter 3 Plans

Voice 1 said, "Those despicable Jafari went too far."

"How so?" a second voice said.

"That old human colony on Zeta Tucanae-C. The one they call Bella."

"Oh, yeah. Where males are beasts of burden," Voice 2 said. "What a strange experiment. Has the experiment reached a conclusion? Do those mutated bodies keep their beings properly imprisoned? Better than the ones devised on Sol-C?"

"I believe the beings are more solidly locked into those mutated bodies, but now the Jafari have mutated the women who run the colony. The females are as helpless as the males!"

"What? How can that society survive? How can homes get built? How can food be raised? Last I heard, they'd just invented steam power from coal." Voice 2 said.

"Our observation flyby showed a few Jafari men keeping things going. I think it's time we intervened. I liked how well the beings were imprisoned by these mutated bodies, but the Jafari have gone too far. They should have ended their experiment," Voice 1 said, "and let Sol-C humans take over."

"We should bring this to the Council. Perhaps we could help them develop telepathy and telekinesis like we have. Then they wouldn't need arms to survive."

"Aye," Voice 1 said. "That is easily done, but the mutation will take time. How do we keep them alive that long? How would these primitives adapt to our society? They can't speak our language, let alone read it. No way to train them."

"Best let the Council decide," Voice 2 said.

Sometime later, the voices reappeared.

Voice 1 said, "The Council decided we can't take care of ten million helpless humans. And they can't risk freeing that many prisoners without having bodies in which to lock them back up. It's best to deposit them on their original home world. Since the cargo ship hasn't been used in millennia, a crew is repairing it now."

Voice 2 said, "I have orders to install a cloaking device on the ship and to verify all systems are operational. We make things to last."

Voice 1 chuckled and said, "The Council is sending a flotilla of ships to retrieve the humans. Make sure the tech still works or we'll be in dice with the Council."

"Those human bodies make perfect prisons, but now that species has proliferated like black flies."

"What I find interesting is that we haven't provided a prisoner drop to that penal colony in close to two millennia," said Voice 1.

"Well, I can't believe they removed all their criminals," Voice 2 said.

Voice 1 said, "Perhaps they have. Just look at how many penal colonies have sprung up in this quadrant of the galaxy. Humans everywhere."

**

Mid-September, Ru Renshu, the CEO of Galactic Mining (GMin) Empire-wide, flew to Cairo to meet with Akil Aten, the local CEO of Galactic Robotics. Olas Mans, the empire-wide CEO of Galactic Robotics, accompanied Ru.

Ru said, "This better be worthwhile..."

"Sh. Not a word must leak about our trip. Too many spies. Damnable telepaths," Olas said.

Once the Air Liner landed, CEO Aten met them with open arms and a broad smile. His thin frame contrasted with his black mustache. He put a finger to his lips and motioned for them to follow him. Before long, the trio of pyramids grew larger until the EMAC landed near the entrance of one. The three men picked up powerful lanterns and headed into a tunnel. Once deep inside the Queen's Chamber, both newcomers gaped.

Two sample human-form robots stood inert against a wall. Various plans and drawings covered a large table. CEO Akil Aten spoke first.

"Please, sit. Now safe to talk. No tech can overhear us. Phones have no reception. Thank you for coming. Here are the promised two prototypes. This one is indistinguishable from a human, while this one resembles those that the Sixth Invaders used to attacked us."

CEO Ru Renshu said, "Excellent work, Aten. The robots machines Empress Parkinson brought us make for more efficient mining. Hence, Galactic Mining builds them as fast they as can. Are you claiming these robots can increase production tenfold over that?"

Aten said, "Perhaps more. They look like us, but have twice our strength and can work nonstop. They need a recharge every week."

Olas Mans said, "With these new robots, Ru, your mining ships won't need any humans. Their salaries alone will pay for these machines."

Ru said, "Perhaps a hundredfold increase. Shame GPan hogged many of the exploration robotic devices Parkinson brought us. Still, let them find new worlds. Then with these, we extract valuable resources at fraction of current costs."

Olas said, "But there's just one small problem. Parkinson's Telepath Squads. I did get rid of the telepath who was snooping in our offices. But..."

Ru said, "Yes, they must go. They can detect our new robots."

"Think of the incredible security these Warrior Robots can provide," Aten said. "Heck, our ground forces barely defeated them in the Sixth Invader War. Once the telepaths are gone, GR goes into production mode. Which type should we focus our resources on first?"

Ru asked, "These have ID chips in them, don't they? We can't afford more robots attacking humans."

Aten chuckled. "But of course. I'm confident Galactic Defense will purchase an army of these soldiers. They'll save GD billions of credits."

Olas said, "What about making some human-forms available for purchase by citizens of the empire? We could make additional trillions of credits doing that. A human-form in every household providing both security and handling domestic chores. People will pay for them. Think of the covert surveillance they could provide."

"Can get actual manufacturing cost low enough so average person afford one?" Ru asked, pulling on his chin.

"Once we get Galactic Manufacturing involved, I believe so," Olas said. "But first, the Telepath Squads must go."

"How Admiral Carr respond these robots?" Ru asked. "He insisted have Telepath Squads."

"We must convince Lin Dho first. Once he's onboard, he'll handle the Admiral," Olas said.

Aten broke in. "Sirs, one more thing. The Warrior Robots have a built-in drone control mode. While each can handle the battle in front of it, we've installed an override. An operator who has a total picture of the combat can control the robots. Microcosm versus macrocosm. All bases covered with our new Warrior Robots. That will be a key selling point for GD. We took that approach based on studies of how General Blythe, Parkinson's sister, handled initial combats with the Sixth Invader robots. Once the telepaths are gone, we can set up a demonstration for Yasha Petrov, GD. Seeing is believing."

"And buying," added Olas. "Another thing, do we want and need a helpless empress running the empire?"

"No," Ru said. "But GD and GPan have all say on that. Best put hint in Lin Dho's ear."

"And Yasha Petrov's too," added Aten. "With an army of these invincible Warrior Robots, we don't need an empress. Say, have you heard anything more about the Bella situation? Last I heard, Parkinson wanted to bring ten million armless mutants here. What would we do with that many useless people?"

"I heard they had vanished by the time the GPan ship arrived at Bella. They're not our problem, thank goodness," Olas said. "Okay, I'll see what I can do about Lin Dho. Until we get rid of the telepaths, maintain absolute secrecy."

Aten laughed. "No one pays attention to us in Cairo, anyway."

With that, the meeting ended.

***

In January and while Empress Parkinson dealt with birthing, the heads of several empire-wide corporations met with Lin Dho, CEO Galactic Expansion, and until last year the unofficial leader of the empire. GPan had always been the leader since the corporate world takeover back in the early twenty-first century.

"Look, Lin," Olas said, "the need for these Telepath Squads is long over. They didn't find any rogue robots anywhere. Only those four in Admiral Carr's fleet. It's costing us tens of millions per year. And we get nothing."

Ru added, "Besides, challenge keeping information secure. Corporate spying."

"Any evidence telepath spying?" Lin asked. "I worry about that. Admiral Carr convinced me rogue robots threaten us. After year, I no sure they are."

"Unproven spying allegations from Mars Colony and Ganymede Association of Moons," Ru said.

"Enormous protests from Pylon and Brussels CEOs after Admiral Carr demanded they allow the squads to land and search for robots," Yasha said.

"I thought they may secede from Empire," Lin said. "And every CEO complains about their share of Telepath Squads' cost."

Ru said, "Only fair divide cost among all corporations. GPan and GD can't pay whole bill. Don't have need for them. Telepath Squads can be disbanded."

"Their contract duration is ten years," Lin said. "But we cut it short. We save on salaries of their personal assistants, too. But we must pay the cost of restoring their bodies."

"Is that expensive? Or possible?" Ru asked.

"We've already undone one. If the others work same, cost minuscule. If we have to clone them, that's another story. However, we've found telepath useful on our deep space exploration ships. When discover inhabited new world, telepaths indispensable. I may alter some squad members' contracts. Not everyone has linguistic bent."

Ru said, "Okay then. Let's get rid of squads soon."

"Understood. Gentlemen, we have another problem. With all new worlds we discover, finding colonists from Earth become most difficult. We are left with many low IQ people. Millions of them," Lin said.

"Can't they be used?" asked Olas. "Didn't Parkinson claim drugging people over sixty caused their dullness?"

"We've tried that. Too dumb. Accidents and disasters result. Yeah, she did. Few believe her on that point. Hasn't been proven. These people do handle routine things for Galactic Housing. Cleaning and basic repairs. Trouble is, they can't deal with new things. We don't dare take many more competent people or there won't be anyone to staff Med centers or be our staff."

"Can we import other aliens? Like we did with the giants and dwarves?" Olas suggested.

"We need their loyalties. I worry new aliens not be loyal to us," Lin said. "Only alternative is take new colonists from Sol's colonies, Pylon, and Brussels. But that gives those worlds more power."

"But don't they already know we're scraping the barrel's bottom?" Olas said.

"Point taken. I worry one day Pylon or Brussels have more power, more say in our affairs than us."

"Surely, not, Lin." Olas frowned.

"Hey, all Earth-based corporations are facing severe qualified-worker shortages," Yasha Petrov of GD said. "What about paying families to have more children?"

"How so?" Lin asked.

"For example, a family leader's pay goes up by ten percent for each child they have. There's no evidence that children from low IQ families inherit their dullness."

Lin smiled. "I like it, Yasha. As long as it's not compounded. We base each increment on original base pay. But would it apply to giants and dwarves or just humans? And what about everyone else in empire? Would apply to those on Pylon?"

"Tough questions," Yasha said. "It's our population we're concerned about, not Pylon, dwarves, and giants. But others might call it discrimination. I see your point."

"Call it pilot program tested on Earth first. If works, we extend it empire-wide," Lin said. He nodded his head once, ending further discussion of the matter.

Chapter 4 The Unexpected

Hans returned mid-October a wealthy man, a satisfied man. He'd helped Roz uncover two human-form rogue robots. Fifty soldiers enjoyed using their blasters. Further, he helped them set up UV light sources that revealed synthetic skin. Now Roz had a way to identify robots on her own.

When he returned, he underwent Eve's genetic cure. Thus, when we married on Halloween, he looked like he had while a university student. Neither of us could ever forget our wedding anniversary. He still watched over us in the throne room for another two months before Katya and I took our maternity leave. I admit seeing Bazyli just as pregnant as Katya shocked me.

Winter came to Chicago. Because of the new planet-wide climate control satellites, I discovered mild winters. Perhaps Chicago had lost its Windy City attribute. Days drifted by. Honestly, I had very little to do as Empress. Only the perceptions of lives growing within me kept me from the boredom attacks that infected Hans.

New Year's Day we sat around my living room. We'd given our personal assistants the day off. As pregnant as we were, we dared not stray far from a bathroom. Katya, who hadn't had a child before, complained about many difficulties.

She said, "I swear I gotta pee every couple minutes."

Bazyli said, "No, dearest, it's about every forty-five. Patience. It'll happen soon. I hope. This isn't fun for me either."

"Not soon enough for me. I can't endure this eight more times just to make Home World happy."

24

"Only four more times. With luck, next time I'll have one, too."

Hans laughed. "Glad I'm not Jafari. I don't see how any of you can deal with this."

"We look like blimps," I said, bringing a round of chuckles, lightening the mood.

Someone telepathically touched me.

'Molly? Is this you? Have I finally found you? Dante. Dante Gallo from Bella.'

I sent back, 'Dante? Wow. Yes, it's me. How did you find me? What happened to you and everyone on Bella?'

"Quiet, everyone. Dante Gallo from Bella is contacting me."

'What a relief. I sensed this must be your plant. The others started searching for new baby bodies. I searched for you.'

'You're welcome to one of mine. We thought we'd lost all ten million of you. What happened? Katya and Hans want to hear your thoughts too.'

With a bit of tuning, Hans and Katya picked up Dante's thoughts. His tale unfolded.

'When my body sleeps, I often don't. That's how come I know as much as I do about what happened. We were sleeping, though I was very worried about our women and how they might adapt to the loss of their arms. How could food be grown? Anyway, I sensed vapors entering the house and tried to wake. Thought someone left something on the stove. But my body refused to cooperate. Waist-high, tiny armed, white aliens walking into my bedroom. Bleached skin. Enormous eyes. Telepaths for sure.

'They levitated my body and floated it outside. It hung in space for a time, along with everyone else in my extended family. Hundreds of my neighbors, too. A dozen aliens floated us into a huge ship. A door shut. Darkness. I lay on a cold floor.

'Motion. I guessed we must be flying somewhere. Maybe to Earth so I could find you, but no. The door opened, and aliens floated us out, depositing us on another floor somewhere. I heard two voices talking but couldn't see them.

'Voice 1 said, "Those despicable Jafari have gone too far."'

He related the conversation between the two aliens, who communicated via telepathy and on which Dante eavesdropped.

'They wanted to bring our situation to some council. One suggested we could develop telepathy and telekinesis, but they couldn't keep us alive long enough for that to happen. They deposited us on our home world. I wondered why they kidnapped us in the first place. That was before I realized they didn't mean Bella, but Earth. They used an old cargo ship. Something about human bodies make perfect prisons. I didn't follow that part.

'Then came the cold. Intense cold. I, me, froze. Couldn't move. Couldn't think. Crushing pressure. Then, lights out; turned off my awareness. Blackness. I can't pierce it. Something must have happened, but I can't remember.

'Next thing I'm falling. I can't move. Can't see. But I'm solid, like I'm in a freezer and descending. I sense I make a splash and that many more splashes followed. Then, a slower descent. I'm getting warmer. I said a prayer to Santa Maria. I hate the cold.

'When I can move again, I soar up and see a bright, warm, yet foreign, world. I sense thousands of others waking up. Where am I? Took some doing and prying into many minds before I learned this is Earth. Find Molly. That became my goal. Find her and find freedom. Learn everything. Here I am at last.'

'Well, I'm glad you found me,' I sent.

'Hey, if I get a baby body here, can I learn whatever I want? It's not like Bella, is it?'

I chuckled. 'Nope. Dante, you can study everything you desire. '

Katya said, "It was the Alitos that kidnapped Bella's ten million people. The First Invaders are still active. I must report this to Home World. Too bad he doesn't know where they took him. The location of the Alitos world remains a mystery."

***

A few days later, Dr. Levitsky from Home World arrived. She gave Katya and Bazyli a thorough checkup.

"Your pregnancy is textbook. But we'll soon see," she said.

Next, she inspected the baby gear our personal assistants bought for us. Blankets, clothes, and a mountain of diapers.

"It's not our standard apparel, but they will do," she stated.

Now we waited for our trips to the Med center.

***

On January 10, 2370, I had Donata and Wendel. I let Hans name the boy. Dante chose the baby girl, and I let him name her. Both had long black hair for a baby, distorted feet, and no arms. A day later, Katya had a daughter, Anka, followed by Bazyli giving birth to their boy, Cyryl. Their bodies were reddish like all Jafari. Both had Bazyli's hair and blue eyes.

Dr. Levitsky gave both Jafari babies a complete checkup, including taking DNA samples for further study.

"Is she healthy? Is he okay?" Katya asked.

"Yes, both are normal. It's my guess both will develop telepathy. But will they be long-lived? Who knows? We're in uncharted space, Katya. Your body shouldn't produce another pair of eggs for fifty years. As you know, Home World insists

27

you provide eight Jafari children before you body swap into your clone."

"But that's at least two hundred years," Katya wailed.

"Jafari never had a real telepath before. You're incredibly valuable. The only reason Home World allows you to stay here with Parkinson is to learn all you can about doing things without arms. You'll have your feet full with these two. I'm off to Home World. Have to get these DNA samples studied."

Talk about a learning curve. Whew. We four worked harder than ever before caring for the four children. We watched the few videos in which others showed how they dealt with babies. And I insisted Bazyli, Hans, and our assistants allow us to experiment and figure out how to handle our babies. Our lives consisted of nursing, burping, and diapering with just enough time to eat. I let others handle cooking. For a few weeks, chaos reigned. By mid-February, life settled down into some kind of routine.

***

During one break when all four babies slept, Katya said, "I never knew how intimate having a baby is. We're so close. Despite the hassle, it's wonderful bringing new life into the world. They're so tiny and dependent on us."

Hans said, "That is an understatement. It's incredible being a father. But how are we going to raise them? Role models? Children look up to their parents and try to emulate them. They will be as handicapped as you are. They'll need role models. Is it fair for Bazyli and me not to be handicapped like they are? I want Donata, Wendel, Cyryl, and Anka to have someone to mimic. Molly, when your new clone is ready later this summer, maybe you shouldn't body swap. We have to think of the kids and how to raise them."

Katya cursed. "I hadn't thought about that. You're right. We don't have original DNA for the kids. We can't provide

28

them with clone bodies that are normal. They're facing a terrible life." She cursed again. "I can't let Anka and Cyryl face that alone."

Another curse followed. Bazyli's face paled.

She said, "We're stuck like we are, aren't we?"

I sighed. "Yes, for a time, I think that's best for the kids. Don't you?"

"Yeah," she said. "What about raising Cyryl and Anka? They are Jafari. Do we take them to Home World and try to raise them there? So they know what their Jafari heritage is?"

Bazyli said, "I've already checked on that. We're to stay here. I'm to be their scholastic teacher, and Molly must teach them life skills using their feet. Good thing I'm a teacher."

Katya glared at him. "I doubt it's an accident they sent you to me."

He flushed.

***

May Day, our maternity leave ended. Kids in tow, we headed into the skyscraper. Our assistants carried the children and bags of diapers, while Bazyli lugged four cradles. After taking our usual positions in the throne room, Ambassador L'Grina appeared.

"You're back. Missed you. Kids healthy?" she asked.

Proud parents showed off Donata, Wendel, Cyryl, and Anka.

"Sorry I couldn't see them sooner. Away on an assignment. Things are—"

"CEO Lin Dho," the bass voice of our doorman announced.

"Ah, you look well. I heard your children are healthy. I have news I think you'll like. Considering."

He didn't say considering what. Lin sounded serious, but I didn't pry into his mind.

"I'll get straight to details. First, need for Telepath Squads is over. No rogue robots beyond four in Admiral Carr's fleet. As Hans Klein attests, have enormous protests from many worlds, even though Admiral Carr demanded they allow squads to land and search for robots.

"In fact, I thought they might secede from Empire," Lin said. "And every CEO complains about their share of Telepath Squad cost. Corporation leaders and Senate agrees. Disband all Telepath Squads. Hand out their cures.

"However, telepath most helpful on deep space exploration ships. But you know about that, Empress Parkinson. I interview those who might like to alter their contracts. But not everyone has linguistic skill. And we don't need hundred. Perhaps six."

I said, "I know some counted on making millions of credits, but at least they'll have banked a million for this past year. Let me know if cures don't work."

"Of course, Empress. Next, everyone's agreed to solution of critical problem Earth faces. Finding colonists from Earth to settle discovered worlds is impossible. Can't use low IQ people. We tried. Accidents and disasters resulted.

"Rather than opening our doors to massive immigration from other Federation worlds, we try another approach. We promote families having more children."

I laughed. "They limited my parents to one child."

Lin smiled. "Two centuries ago, that solved overpopulation. Not today. Program agreed upon to increase family leader pay. Pay goes up ten percent for each child they have. If have ten children, head of household's pay be double.

"At moment, it pilot program on Earth. If works, we extend empire-wide. You'll soon see big promotion on Galactic Entertainment. Don't worry. We're making it retro-active. No family left out."

"What about families where both work?" I asked.

"One with larger salary gets boost."

"You've thought of everything."

He smiled. "Finally, your term of being Empress is complete. Now you step down and care for your growing family. We thank you for your service to Sol Empire."

I didn't see that coming!

"Er, how soon do you want me to leave? Is someone taking over my position? Are we electing our executive leader?"

His brows rose. "We hadn't decided on replacement. I hadn't thought of holding election. What great idea. You can leave today. We did okay with no empress while you on maternity leave. If more ideas, send them to me. An election. Interesting."

He left, continuing to mutter about holding an election for my replacement.

"No Telepath Squads? What the heck is going on?" Hans asked. "Well, I admit I did nothing for my credits. He has a point. But what are they going to do for a real job now?"

"Dunno," I said.

"What about us?" asked Mei Hui, my assistant. "Are we losing our jobs as Personal Assistants?"

Shu Ying said, "Let's get you home. Then, we can go to GMed and see what our employment status is. We should have received some official notification, don't you think?"

Li Feng said, "We should have. Even if we lose our jobs as Personal Assistants, we're now official Galactic Dolls. They'll have other positions for us. Don't you think, Empress Parkinson?"

"Bright. Attractive. Caring. You'll have new worthwhile positions in no time."

Ambassador L'Grina followed us home. After our assistants left to check on their own jobs, she spoke up.

"Lin Dho got to you before I could. I heard they were planning to dump you and the telepaths. I intended to warn you. I would have called, but I wasn't sure what the situation would be with four babies."

"Thanks," I said. "He took me by surprise. Wasn't doing much at all, anyway. I'm making an appointment with GMed to get my lip restored."

Ambassador L'Grina said, "I've more news. Seems Galactic Robotics wants to make human-form robots again. That might be what's behind their disbanding of the Telepath Squads. What about you two? Has Eve and Lara found a way to restore your bodies or is the clone route the only option?"

I sighed. "Not yet. We're stuck with the clones. But..."

Ambassador L'Grina prodded. "But what?"

"Our kids. There is no original DNA from which to grow a clone. Without a mutation cure, they're stuck this way. She's already taken DNA samples from all four babies. Like Katya and me, their DNA is messed up."

"So?" She teased with a coy smile.

Katya slumped. "We must stay like we are to be their role models. Moral support. Show them how to do things."

"They're making more robots?" I asked, changing the subject. "What for?"

"My sources don't know. They think once the telepaths are gone there'll be a big news conference about it. Don't think Admiral Carr likes it. Last time I spoke with him, he suggested he might purchase the contracts of several telepaths, making them permanent members of the space fleet," the Ambassador said.

For a moment, Hans perked up. Then, his jaw sagged. "I would jump at the chance to see the geology of other worlds—my dream job—but there's Donata and Wendel to think about. I can't just leave Molly to care for them. That's not right. Why more robots anyway?"

32

I knew I needed to have a long talk with Hans about this. I felt awful knowing the kids and I were holding him back from doing what he dreamed about—astro-geology.

Ambassador L'Grina said, "I'm sorry my people got your people off on the wrong foot with robots years ago. But robots can be useful. They can work in environments we can't. They're cost effective in the right situations."

"As long as they're identifiable," I added.

***

That evening, my sisters, Eve and Celeste, dropped by. Excitement illuminated their faces.

"The good news," Celeste said, "we're both getting married."

"Woo hoo. Congratulations. Have we met them?" I asked, as they hugged me.

"My Greg is a zoologist," Celeste said. "After we get married, we're moving to Domes where he can study the alien creatures. Wanda and Otto are coming with us. I'm moving my therapy practice to Domes. I'm tired of fighting the corporations who don't want people to become free and who denigrate us every chance they get. Besides, the rest of our sisters are on Domes. It's time I raised a family, too."

"Sam is a botanist, working on developing new medical cures," Eve said. "We're moving to Domes. But I've another reason for leaving even if I wasn't getting married. As you know, I gave a copy of the cloning machines and documentation to GMed. They're already abusing the tech, making clones of the top executives. Worse, they're experimenting with genetics. Trying to make super-men. I want no part of that. Plus, I just got a destroy order from the Jafari. Katya, they want me to terminate your clone body, which should be ready in a few more months."

Katya gasped. Tears trickled down, but she said nothing.

33

"Don't worry, Katya. I won't do it. I'm moving my whole lab and your clones to Domes, and I'll keep them there in secret until you need them."

"Thank you. Can you keep it alive for hundreds of years?" Katya said. "They won't let me escape this body until I've given them eight more telepaths. And that's likely several hundred years."

Eve laughed. "I've no idea. I'll keep monitoring the body once it's in a stasis pod. If it deteriorates, I'll clone a new one. I'll train someone to take over for me as insurance against something happening to me."

"How can I ever thank you? Can I pay you for its cost or something? Moving to another planet must be expensive."

Eve suggested a small amount for the needed supplies for the stasis pod. "Actually, we're hoping to use Molly's spaceship for our move, if she'll fly it for us."

I laughed. "You don't have to ask twice. That'll be my wedding present for you two. But you'll have to load the ship. I've misplaced my arms."

That brought a chuckle from everyone. We spent an hour discussing their wedding and moving plans.

After they left, Miss Ivy Worth called on me. Now twenty-one, she looked fabulous as a Galactic Doll and a member of Hans' Telepath Squad. Ivy's round face held a tinge of red, contrasting with her waist-length brunette hair. Her mellow voice always riveted my attention. She delayed her medical studies when the ad for volunteers went out and she jumped on it. She told me then, "I feel driven to save people, like a higher power wants me to save lives. It's something I must do. That's why I'm becoming a doctor. But I want to help save people from these rogue robots." After becoming an armless telepath, her therapy sessions uncovered her former life as Dr. Phil Raven, the inventor of these rogue human-form robots.

34

"Molly, excuse me for coming by so late, but have you heard? They're disbanding the Telepath Squads!"

"Come in. We've heard."

"But we've only found four robots. Where's the other hundred plus robots? How can they do this to us? We signed ten-year contracts."

"Sit. Let's chat," I said. "We're still grappling with the suddenness of the change. They dismissed me as empress, too."

Hans said, "I have the babies to think about now. But, yeah, that's what I'd like to know. Where did the other rogue robots go? What are they planning? This whole Telepath Squad thing has been mismanaged. If you ask me. All I did was sit beside Molly looking for robot visitors. Boring!"

Ivy giggled. "I wasn't bored. They had me visiting dozens of ships, checking crew members. More challenging than I imagined. Couldn't have done it without my Personal Assistant. Still, it's been rewarding. I think I'm more able to live independently, but now I will have to. My assistant lost her job, too."

"We lost ours," Hans said. "Are you able to manage on your own? How soon are you getting the mutation cures?"

Bazyli brought in a tray with tea, pouring each of us a cup, before heading back to the kitchen.

While Katya and I levitated our cups to sip, Ivy had to use her toes. "I wish I had more than just telepathy. At least, I can manage simple things with my feet. Molly, I want to help save people's lives. I'm not sure I want the mutation cure yet. We've not captured a single murderous robot. To undo all this now seems wrong, but they want me to get the cure soon."

She paused and sipped. "Can I ask you both a very personal question?"

I nodded, and she continued.

"Your massive mutation—it can't be undone, right?"

35

"At least not yet. My sister and Lara are working on it."

Hans said, "They're not too hopeful. Clones are their best way to become normal again."

"That's what I thought. Does your telekinesis powers make up for no arms? More or less?"

I snickered. "Yes, but we still use our feet as much as possible. People rather freak out when they see things moving on their own."

"But having that ability—it lets you be more independent, right?"

Hans smiled. "You can say that a thousand times over. You should see Molly and Katya handling the babies."

"Can you execute fine motions with it? Like cutting up an onion?"

"Onions give me headaches," I said. "But yes, though it takes practice, just like any skill."

"And you got it from a massive overdose of the usual mutation agent?"

"Yes. Why this interest?"

She sighed. "I hate leaving an important project incomplete. We've not stopped the rogue robots. And they need to be stopped before more people get killed. I'm sure they'll kill again. I can't let that happen, but I'm too helpless without my personal assistant. If I had your ability to move objects, I might become a doctor, too. Once the robots are stopped, I'd need a clone body. Unless Dr. Eve Burkey finds a cure."

"She can undo your mutation, but check with her soon. She's getting married and moving to Domes."

"Oh, my! I will. Thanks for everything. Both of you. Bye for now."

After she left, Hans said, "There goes one gorgeous woman."

I hip-bumped him. We laughed.

The next day, the Empire's Senior Investigator Ward Tilman called.

"Just wanted to alert you. In the process of wrapping up the Telepath Squad, they've discovered two more have gone missing. Missy Tweed and Elie Mc Pierson. Last seen dates are shaky, but my people are on it. More when I know anything further."

Chapter 5 Babies and Robots

June 15, 2370

"Well, that's that. Sisters, their husbands, and possessions to Domes," I said, as Hans and I flew my EMAC from New O'Hare Spaceport home. We had ferried them.

"I'm amazed, dear. Had my doubts, but you really can pilot and navigate without telekinesis. Lost that bet to Katya. Know I couldn't do it."

I grinned. "Before I could move things, I found it very challenging. I almost flunked out. But I swore it wouldn't defeat me."

Memories of trying to pass my final pilot's exam flashed. The simulator tossed my body around like a rag doll in my first attempt. Even the second try failed. But I made it on the final try.

"So, now we are on our own. All your sisters live on Domes."

I sighed. "All but my son, Bernardo. But he's so darn busy with his downtown restaurant we never see him."

"I'm glad we're still here. The grade school is within walking distance. It's a good one, I'm told. Good for Donata and Wendel. With all the tech on this world, life will be easier for them."

I laughed. "Don't forget we've another baby on the way come January."

We landed behind our ranch home. Katya stood at the backdoor waiting for us.

"Come inside. Got the news on. Plus, I've got news too," she said. "Glad you're back safe and sound. Kids are fine."

"Thanks for watching them," I said.

"Molly, you'll never guess what's happened to me. I'm pregnant again. That shouldn't have happened for another fifty years!"

"Wow! That is news. Is Bazyli—"

"Yes, he's carrying my second. We think we'll give birth in January, around your time, too. How weird is that?"

Bazyli walked up, a baby in each arm. "Unheard of. For a Jafari. Should never happen. Can't happen, but it has. Doc's all over it. Something to do with the mutation, she thinks. Me, I don't know what else it could be. But we must make babies."

I said, "Right. We must make babies. This is good news. Katya might not have to wait two hundred years to get her arms back."

Hans laughed. "We're doing just like the GEnt ad promoted. Have more children. Makes good sense, if we're to help colonize the new worlds GPan's discovering. Heck, they're finding more worlds than we can populate. So much for over-population issues."

"GEnt is sure promoting it," I said. "The ads are on billboards downtown. Saw them from the EMAC."

***

Years shot past us. Of necessity, my ever-growing family absorbed my time and energies. Taking care of one child challenged us, but each year added another precious life, not only to my family but also to Katya's.

March 2371 Franz joined us, while Katya and Bazyli added another two. In May 2372, I had Bonny, while Katya and Bazyli added another pair. July 2373 Hugh came. Katya and Bazyli added two more to their family.

For a few days, Katya celebrated. She'd done as Home World demanded: had eight telepaths. She anxiously awaited her chance to body swap into her clone body and get her arms and life back. Didn't happen.

A screech pulled me into her bedroom. I watched the doctor leaving.

The doctor said, "Babies are just fine. Not to worry."

"Gods! We're pregnant again," Katya cried, after her medical doctor left. "I can't swap now."

Katya cursed and yelled after the doctor, jostling the nursing babies. The two began crying. Bazyli rushed in to settle them back into position.

"Calm down, Katya. It must be a mistake," he said.

"It can't be a mistake. Molly, I'm pregnant again. I know we must make babies, but this has gone too far. They promised me I'd only have to bear eight telepaths. We're about to have even more! This can't be happening. I should only have a pair every fifty years. What's happening to me? We must make babies. But this isn't possible. I'm a Jafari, not a rabbit human."

"Yeah, I know we must make babies. I'm pregnant too. But Hans and I can't keep up with five now. We're spending all our time caring for our children. I don't know how you and Bazyli can manage eight, let alone ten. It's not natural."

Sometimes a word can trigger a reaction. My saying "Not natural" jarred me into the present time moment. In that instant, I realized I had been in a mental fog for the last five years! Life had been an ever-increasing challenge of using my feet to change diapers, pick up toys, clean up, cook, and nurse. Hans and I had gone from one emergency mess to the next, collapsing into bed at night, too tired to even talk. Unending days merged into one long, unthinking fog. In that instant, I woke from the mental blackout.

"Good god! Something's going on!" I said.

Katya looked at me, likely surprised by my outburst. "But we must make babies."

She looked confused for a moment. "But I've already met Home World's goal of telepaths."

"When they're done feeding, Bazyli, leave us," I said.

As soon as we were alone, I said, "Katya, I will run a bit of therapy on you. Close your eyes. Now repeat 'must make babies' several times."

She did that. "I feel tired. Must make babies."

"What do you see?"

"A grey-white cloud around my head is all. It's nothing. Must make babies."

I asked her a volley of questions, such as what she sensed in the cloud and if she in bed or standing? A yawn came.

"Oh, in bed. Sleeping."

"Excellent. When was it? Can you date it?"

"Before Anka was born. Before all this started."

"Good. Now go through the incident and tell me what's happening, what you're seeing as you move through it."

Katya yawned. "I'm sound asleep. Must be dreaming. I see or feel or sense—not sure what word fits—this incredible, beautiful light or energy or something. It's so pure, glorious. Then it's gone. I want it back. I try to hold on to it."

On the next pass through the incident, words appeared.

"Oh, I hear words in my mind. Like telepathy. Over and over. Must make babies. Must make babies. I want to make them. I need to make eight. Then I can get my new clone body and be whole again. Yes, I want to make babies."

She opened her eyes wide and sat erect. "It happened again. No, it happened ten successive nights, one after the other! Molly, this is an implant. Someone's implanted me." Katya laughed long and hard.

"Wait, this happened before we ever heard GPan wanted everyone to have more children. Who could have done this? Am I the only one implanted?"

My own eyes rose. I felt a huge yawn coming and couldn't suppress it. In doing so, I pulled out of a white mass

41

centered on my head. As it moved off me, I spotted the words: must make babies.

"No, I've been implanted too. I've blown it off me. End of our therapy session. I'll check on Bazyli and Hans. Perhaps they've been implanted too. Could your people be behind it? Ensuring you'd have the eight telepaths they wanted?"

"Could be," she said. "Well, perhaps not. They already had my full cooperation by denying me the new clone body until I gave them eight telepaths. You know how much I want to be whole again. How did they get into my bedroom to do it to me? You always lock your doors at night."

"Dunno."

We found Bazyli in the kitchen trying to feed eight children, while Hans struggled to deal with five of ours.

He asked, "Katya, can you handle all eight at once?"

"Molly wants to run a short therapy session on you. I can manage for a short time," Katya said, though from her facial expression, I don't think she believed herself.

After getting him sitting on their bed, I had him close his eyes and repeat the sentence a few times.

"Can you recall when you first heard it?" I asked.

"Sure, when Katya heard from Home World. She must make eight telepaths before she can abandon this body for her new clone one. So, yeah, we must make babies."

I had him say it a few more times and watched a fog surround his head.

"What are you seeing?" I asked.

"Oh, a whitish thing."

I knew I had him. With a few more passes, the implant blew. He'd been affected the same times as Katya had. Made sense since they lived and slept together.

He rushed into the kitchen, laughing. "We've been implanted!" he said. "Oops. You need help."

"You think?" Katya said. Her eight older children had lunch splattered over their faces and clothes, as did she. "I don't know how we can care for that many children. They're supposed to come fifty years apart, not like you human rabbits."

Hans grinned.

"Bazyli, look after our five kids for a bit. Hans, come with me."

"Yes, dear. Gladly. It takes both of us to handle all five, you know. How are we ever going to manage a sixth? What's this implant thing all about?"

A half hour later, Hans laughed. He'd erased the implant, and we rejoined the others. Bazyli had our children cleaned up as well as half his own.

"We've all been subjected to a 'must make babies' implant," I said. "From what I've heard when we're at the Med Center, the implant has been widespread. Many women are having their sixth child, just like we are. It reminds me of the implanting that the Sixth Invaders used on us decades ago when they were trying to conquer Earth. I wonder what L'Grina has to say?"

"Now that you mention her," Katya said, "I haven't heard from Ambassador L'Grina since Anka was born. Could they be behind this?"

I struggled to get my phone out with my toes. "Call L'Grina."

It went to voice-video message. I left her a note to call or come visit us. I wanted facts.

That night, she appeared at my door.

"Hi, Molly. Sorry I've not been by sooner. Had my own hands full," Ambassador L'Grina said. "Making babies of my own. Decided it was time, too. This is my daughter L'See, four, and son, G'Nor, three."

"Welcome! Come in. We're in the living room. Ignore the mess. With this many children around, well..."

"Gee, Mom. She doesn't have any arms," L'See said.

"Is that a Third Invader?" G'Nor asked, pointing to Katya. "She no arms too."

Donata walked up. "I'm Donata. I'm four. You must be a Sixth Invader cause your skin is grey. Do you really have six fingers?"

The kids gathered around the new children, leaving us adults to chat.

"I don't know why I started my family. Maybe you two rubbed off on me. Anyway, I've been busy with these. Have a third one at home. She's too young to bring with me. My mate is watching her. I see you've been even busier than I have. Do they possess your abilities?" she asked.

My initial theory of who originated the implant blew out the door. Knowing L'Grina as I did, a large family was the last thing she desired so early in her long life. When I got the chance, I put her through a short therapy session.

The key: repeat must make babies many times. That charged up the implant, making it easily spotted. In short order, L'Grina blew through it, laughing all the way. Thank heavens the implant contained no pain or heavy unconsciousness.

"We've all been implanted? My god, Molly. Your entire world is implanted. I admit we have the tech to do that, but it would take us about six months to cover your world. Last I knew, your people had just discovered implant tech. This implant wasn't complex at all. Any ideas who's behind it? Crap! I didn't want a family yet. I'm too young."

"What about me?" Katya said. "I wanted my arms back. Instead, I've reproduced twenty missing arms."

"You're pregnant again?" L'Grina asked. "That's not possible. Is it? I thought fifty years. Well, it's messed up Sixth

44

Invader reproduction cycles too. I should have had ten years between children, not two. Could your people have done this to us?"

"Not that I know. Yes, we have implant tech, but our biggest devices might cover Chicago in a few days. The power demand is huge. From what we've determined from our collective implants is that they did it about ten nights in a row, likely covering the planet. The power consumption exceeds the output of half our fleet. Not possible. Who has such power plants?"

L'Grina looked at Katya who looked at her. In unison, they said, "The First Invaders!"

"Well, it makes sense in a twisted way," I said, explaining what Dante had told me when he found me. "They needed baby bodies for ten million people in a hurry. Kind of overkill now. Say, could such an implant cause your bodies to alter their usual reproductive cycles?"

Ambassador L'Grina said, "What an intriguing question! It's worth investigating. Say, if blowing the implant like we did gets rid of that compulsion, then it should be years before I need to breed again."

Katya laughed. "How about fifty years for me? But after this, I don't care if it's millennia!"

Ambassador L'Grina said, "On a lighter topic, are you planning on getting one of these new human-form household robot helpers that GEnt keeps advertising? With three children running underfoot, I'm sorely tempted."

I sighed. We'd been in such a fog for the past years, I hadn't kept up with the news. "With six and with zero arms, we're considering it." I lied.

Katya said, "Bazyli, that's what we need."

***

In September 2374, I gave birth to Calli, our sixth. Katya and Bazyli had another pair, making their total ten. While in the

Med Center and alert this time, I discovered their policy had been to inject each new mother with a low dose of the Galactic Doll mutation agent, just enough both to make sure we kept our body's perfect forms and to repair any damage the pregnancy may have done. No wonder I always felt super sleepy after giving birth.

None of us became pregnant. I credit that to the erasure of the subtle implant. We hoped that Katya and L'Grina's bodies had reverted to their usual reproduction periods. Katya's doctor reported this news back to Home World.

With the fog of the implant gone, we could reach clearer decisions. Before we could, the Third Invader doctor returned bringing orders from Home World.

She said, "We thank you for your service, Katya, but we can't expect you and Bazyli to care for ten children, even if they are telepaths. We'll take them back to Home World."

Katya screamed. "You can't take away all my children! I'm their mother. Bazyli is their father. You can't do this."

"Compromise. You keep Anka with you. Bazyli will bring the other nine children back to Home World and care for them. We'll provide domestic assistance. Your children will get the very best care Home World can offer, along with the best education."

I suspected Bazyli had arranged this. He spoke up.

"I'm willing to care for nine of our children, Katya. And you and Anka can come visit them anytime. But the eight youngest need more care than we can give them ourselves. This is in our children's best interests, don't you think?"

I hated to see a family broken up. While Katya could handle one by herself, she couldn't ten children. She gazed at her children and sighed.

"Okay. That's probably best for the younger ones. Anka wants to go to school with Donata and Wendel. It's best she stays with me. But I can visit them anytime I want, right?"

The doctor said, "Yes, anytime. Just let us know. We can alert the children to their mother's visit."

Katya's eyes watered as she and I watched the doctor and Bazyli pack up the nine children's things. One by one, she pressed her body into each departing child, kissing each on their forehead.

"Mommy will come visit often," she called out as they left our house.

"You can lend me a hand with my six, Katya."

"But you don't..." Her sad face cracked a brief smile. "Yes, I'll help as much as I can. For Anka's sake, I won't body swap into Eve's clone. Not just yet. Wouldn't be fair to her."

A week later, Bazyli brought Cyryl back. His face seemed redder than normal.

"Cyryl wants to stay with you, Anka, and the Parkinson family. He's become a handful."

Katya smiled. "All right. Good for you, Cyryl. Go tell Anka, Wendel, and Donata the good news. Thanks, Bazyli."

"Thank Cyryl. He caused everyone massive head pains until we agreed to bring him back. He's more than we can handle. Good luck with him."

Chapter 6 Ivy's Decision

June 2371
Domes

Ivy Worth and her Cass-C robot helper, Tom, landed at the spaceport on Domes. She stood outside a gigantic transparent dome, taking in the sights and smells of an alien world. With Tom rolling along behind and pulling her bag, Ivy headed to the entrance. Sign insude read: information and housing. Just what she needed.

"Hello. How do I find Dr. Eve Burkey. She's gotten married, but I don't know if she's changed her last name or not. She's just moved here from Earth."

The teen typed into her computer. "Ah, Dome Ten. Take Tunnel Six. That's down the central plaza and to your right. Follow the signs. When you get to Dome Ten, check in at the information booth. They'll help you."

People ambled along the plaza. Kiosks offered hot meals. The rarity of an armless Galactic Doll with a robot on wheels drew stares. Ivy understood their curiosity. But her face still warmed as her heels clicked along the ceramic floor. Her telepathy picked up the gawkers. She accepted their interest, but detested their pity. While life without arms was hard, she'd done this of her own free will. The day she identified the rogue robot in the cruiser had been the proudest of her life.

Side passages appeared at regular intervals. She walked past 42nd Street. A cross sign read Main Street Plaza. Roofless buildings lay side by side down these streets. Six large signs hung from the dome far above her head. The one labeled

Tunnel One Spaceport pointed back the way she'd come. Another directed her right to Tunnel Six.

Soon, she approached the sloping side of the dome. Ahead, a ten-foot tunnel-like dome exited through the side of the giant overhead dome. At its entrance, signs read: To Dome Ten. Wait for transport.

Confused, she glanced around for someone's help. An electric cart whirred towards her from far down the tunnel. The cart slowed as it passed her. It turned around and whirred to a stop in front of her as though waiting for her to get in. Tom steadied her as she climbed up. The robot hoisted her bag and pulled itself up and onto the back. It only had one button on its front side and no steering wheel or levers.

"Should I push the Go button? What do you think, Tom?"

"Try it."

She maneuvered a foot and pushed it. At once, the cart began the journey. It picked up speed, bobbing her waist-length brunette hair behind her.

The same clear material formed the tunnel's walls. As far as she could tell, the floor was also ceramic. Based on the duration, the number of other carts passing them, some carrying people, and the speed of the cart, Ivy concluded miles must separate the individual giant domes.

When she arrived, a woman smiled. "About time a cart arrived. Let me help you with your things."

Ivy resisted the urge to say no and deflected the pity flowing from the woman. "Thanks."

With that, the woman hopped on and left as though in a hurry. Ivy noted the sign read: Tunnel One To Dome One. Ahead in this dome, she saw another plaza and information kiosk.

Ten minutes later, she had Tom knock on the side of the entrance to Suite 901. A voice said, "Come in."

Ivy entered, followed by Tom pulling her bag.

"Oh, hello. We've met. Once, right? Ignore the mess. My new lab," Eve said, pausing her work of unloading a crate of lab equipment.

"Yes. Ivy Worth. Telepath Squad One. Well, I used to be. They've disbanded us."

"Welcome to Domes. Didn't the genetic mutation cure work for you? Tea or a sandwich? Sit where you can."

"Tea, please. Okay, a sandwich. I've not eaten for hours. I came to see you."

Over tea and a snack, Ivy explained the purpose of her visit.

"My goal has always been to become a medical doctor and help save lives. To make a real difference. But I just had to help people by finding these murderous rogue robots. I found one, but it escaped the cruiser."

"Well done, Ivy. Silly CEOs. With the squads disbanded, now is a good time for those robots to reappear."

Ivy changed the subject. "I know Molly and Katya got exposed to a massive dose of the normal telepath Galactic Doll mutation agent."

Eve laughed. "Massive doesn't describe it. Don't tell Molly, but my estimates suggest she received the equivalent of ten thousand doses."

"And that has caused the significant enlargement of several endocrine glands in their heads. Molly told me about the severe headaches she endured and erased later. And their new ability, telekinesis, appears tied to those gland changes."

"Yes, that's my guess. I'm not a medical doctor, but her last medical scans suggested as much," Eve said.

"That's my conclusion, too. I'm here because I want to volunteer for some experiments. I'd like to prove increasing the size of these glands leads to telepathy and telekinesis. From a medical point of view, this could be a vital

50

breakthrough. Instead of handicapping people just to increase their skills, perhaps a specific alteration to their genes could be made.

"We could not get a hundred volunteers to become armless telepaths to save our empire from the rogue robots. Only fifty. And I understand why. No one would choose to be as helpless as we are. But having telekinesis would offset a lack of arms. Since I'm already mutated, I'd like to be a test subject for further mutations before I get the cure. Also, my original DNA is on file. If anything goes wrong, I can opt for a clone body."

Eve smiled. "Admirable intention, Ivy, but as you know, it's illegal to experiment on humans. Lara and I work with mice until we're darn sure of the result. Only then are we allowed limited trials on criminals or terminally ill people."

"I understand that. And I agree in principle. What I propose is an 'accidental' exposure. Under controlled circumstances. Otherwise, we won't know what it takes to create the correct mutations."

"But, Ivy, if we did something like that, your body might die or worse, you might end up like Molly. We haven't been able to invent a cure for her."

"I read your article. Their DNA now has self-correction streams in it that prevent cures from working. Fascinating article. Almost makes me want to go into genetics instead of medicine. Think of what we could learn. Besides, I've watched them. I think with telekinesis I could be a capable doctor even if I didn't have arms. If nothing else, let me work as your assistant for a time. See if I like genetics."

Eve twisted her hands. "Well, all right. Lab assistant for now. There's much we don't know about genes. Have you got a suite assigned to you yet? We don't have any of those Sixth Invader helper machines on Domes."

"No. But I've got my Cass-C helper robot, Tom."

51

Eve helped her through the application process, requesting she be assigned the suite next to hers. If the armless woman needed help, she'd be close at hand.

***

During the ensuing weeks, Eve found Ivy a bright student, albeit rather helpless in the lab. One day, Ivy hit upon key data.

"I've studied your file on Molly. It's clear with successive mutations, even identical ones, the required dosages kept increasing. It's like those people who give themselves small doses of poison until their body can tolerate a large amount which would kill a normal person."

Eve smiled. "Precisely put, Ivy. That's what's going on with these genetic mutations. Before Molly's massive exposure, she needed six normal doses to bring about the usual mutation you received with one dose.   I kept warning her to carry a dozen doses around in case of an emergency."

"And look at what's happened to her brain in this latest scan. Tom, bring up Case 1022 beside Molly's."

The two images appeared.

"So?" Eve asked.

"Look at the folds. The surface area of Molly's brain must now be double that of a normal person. Her brain has grown and used a folding process to accommodate the additional tissue inside her skull."

"I noticed that, but does it matter?" Eve asked, annoyed she'd never pursued this avenue.

"Well, perhaps. Molly should have more brainpower than before, whatever we mean by that. Perhaps brain growth is also a key player in developing telekinesis. Wait a minute! Eve, you're a telepath too. I can sense it."

The color faded from Eve's face. "Please, never tell a soul. Yes, some of us naturally possess telepathy. We've kept it a secret all these years to avoid being kidnapped or forced into servitude or sold into slavery. I heard three telepaths have been abducted this time, though I predicted more would be lost."

"I promise. But do you have a scan of your brain for comparison?"

Eve grinned. "Yes, my glands are a wee bit larger than the normal average, if that's what you're thinking. Between us, natural telepathic ability is closely tied to the spiritual being themselves, not to their bodies. Yes, we've proven if you increase the size of these glands, limited telepathy manifests, but at a terrible cost. Plus, we've never been able to pin down just what genetic markers are involved in the gland growth. It's quite a complex problem."

Ivy said, "Okay. Another thing. Have you documented the gland changes in Molly's brain versus the number and strength of the mutations she's endured?"

"No, that's not my area of expertise. That might yield important clues. I have all her scans. Might take a while to locate them. Things got rearranged with the big move. Do you know how to quantify the data?"

"I had basic theory in one class. I'm sure we can figure it out," Ivy said, a note of confidence in her voice.

***

A month passed before Ivy had the data analyzed. She kept her curses to herself. Should have taken me a few days.

"I've put it in a graph. Folds percentage on the left, successive doses on the right. I had to plot the doses logarithmically. Seven versus ten thousand."

Eve laughed. "Right. Say, it looks more like a straight line."

"Yes, I've plotted the least squares fitting line. It is linear. The more the dose, the more the folding. What's missing are the actual effects of the increased folding. Higher

53

IQ? Better mental processes? Can't say. No data. Unless Molly told you stuff."

"No, she hasn't. About here in the chart, she went to study at Soros University on Cass-C and spent six year studying just about everything except genetics."

Both laughed.

Ivy said, "Most can't handle medical studies."

"Before this point, Molly wasn't interested in advanced studies. Curious, isn't it?"

"Yes. I suspect to get even larger brain volumes the skull must enlarge a lot. Perhaps evolution will come to our aid," Ivy said. "Molly's brain must have been under enormous pressures during that last mutation because her skull stayed the same size."

"Because of the folding?"

"Precisely. Her brain grew in size, doubling its folding to accommodate the larger overall size. Fascinating."

Eve laughed. "But it doesn't help us undo her mutations or regrow her arms."

"Er, no. Not really."

***

Ivy knew Eve would never let her experiment on herself. She set to work arranging an "accident." Given the setup of the domes, poison gases had to be vented. She couldn't just release ten thousand aerosol doses in her room. But they had bio-containment suits and spacesuits. She chose the bio suit.

Next, she had Tom measure out the dosage. Ivy replicated what Eve believed to be Molly's exposure. To do that, she handled the math conversion from injected serums to aerosol doses.

She rigged up an exhaust tube to the lab exhaust fan. At the right time, Tom would activate its blower, sucking the mutation agent out of the bio suit, expelling it outside the dome. Getting into the bio suit challenged Ivy and Tom.

54

Together, they struggled for an hour getting her into it and the tubes hooked up. As soon as her feet slipped into the suit, she became helpless, dependent on Tom, following her sometimes-confused instructions.

"Remember, Tom. Give it fifteen minutes before you activate the blower. Then, fetch Eve. Show her what we've done and have her tabulate the results."

With that, Tom pressed the injection button. The yellowish gas filled the helmet. Ivy inhaled deeply. Her world went black.

Robots follow orders to the letter. Fifteen minutes later, Tom turned on the exhaust fan and observed the gas being sucked out of the helmet. The robot rolled off to find Eve.

"That foolish woman! What has she done?"

"She has logged all the data there," Tom droned in its monotone. "I detect she is still alive."

"Watch her. I'm going for help."

Her husband, Sam, joined her in the lab. Together, they got Ivy out of the bio containment suit and onto a medical cart. Sam wheeled her into Eve's lab. After initial tests, Eve reached a conclusion.

"She's in a mutation coma. I'll hook her up to life support. This new machine feeds the body the chemicals it needs as it needs them. Neat breakthrough in stasis pods, Sam. Give me a hand."

Per Ivy's instructions, Eve scanned Ivy's brain every day at the same hour. While she wasn't sure what Ivy could glean from the scans, she followed the woman's orders, since this was an "accidental" genetics experiment. Even if asked, Eve couldn't say what they might learn from the experiment.

Early August, Ivy showed signs of waking. Eve disconnected her from the stasis pod and summoned Celeste. She presumed Ivy would need serious therapy sessions, since Molly woke with an intense headache.

***

Ivy shrieked. "Iee. My head's exploding!"

She lay on the pod, covered by a sheet, the IV device still inserted into a leg vein, just in case. Celeste and Eve sat beside the pod and watched as Ivy's body shot up into a sitting position. The washcloth that Eve had used to wipe Ivy's forehead flew up and pressed against Ivy's head, as though an invisible hand did it.

"You're awake. Celeste's here, too," Eve said.

"My head's exploding. I can't take it. The pain!"

"I'll try a light massage," Celeste said in a soft voice.

"That's helping a little. Don't stop. Oh, Eve, did it work?"

"Don't know yet. You've been in a mutation coma for two weeks. That was a stupid thing to do, Ivy. You could have died."

"Molly didn't. Didn't think I would. Now we have more data. If only my head would stop throbbing. I'm thirsty."

A glass of water sitting on a medical stand shot through the air up to Ivy's lips.

"Oh! Cool," Ivy said, and guzzled the water. "It worked. Telekinesis, that is."

"Come on," Celeste said. "Let's get you dressed and fed. Then, therapy sessions."

A week of therapy sessions passed before the terrible head pains vanished.

After thanking Celeste, Ivy said, "I have telekinesis for sure, but now I must learn how to use it."

Celeste said, "Yeah, you're a bull in a china shop as the saying goes."

Ivy wanted to study the collected data right away, but Eve insisted she take time to learn to better control her new skill.

At one evening's supper, Eve said, "It's downright spooky seeing everything moving about without seeing anyone's hands doing it."

Ivy giggled. "I'm getting better at it. Since I can do finer motions now, I might be able to be a doctor using this skill. Won't need a clone body."

Next day, she began her extensive study of the collected experiment data. Days later, Ivy reached a definitive conclusion.

"Eve, look at the results. I think you were off in your estimate on how much exposure Molly and the others had. My dose was ten thousand fold. Based on the graphs, hers must have been closer to five thousand doses. My brain shows even more folding than hers does. I wish we could run IQ tests."

The following week, Eve and Celeste put Ivy through several tests.

"We already know a person's IQ goes up based on the number of therapy hours they get," Celeste explained.

"But my increase would suggest I've had a thousand hours. That's not possible," Ivy pointed out. "The mutation must have increased my IQ a hundred points."

She added, "My hearing is more acute, as is my sense of smell. I think my vision is sharper too, but how can we tell that? We should have put me through a whole battery of tests before the experiment. Ah well."

Eve said, "Well, there's no going back, Ivy. Your body is stuck like this. I've no idea if I'll ever be able to undo the changes you three underwent. Should I begin a clone body for you?"

Ivy sighed. "Wish my feet were normal. These heels are impossible. But no. Not yet. I will continue my education as a medical doctor. Only if I can't perform will I swap into a clone body. I'm sure with practice I can manage as I am."

"Okay, then. You should pay a visit to the Immigration Office and fill out your forms. You'll need them to arrange for a permanent suite and status."

The next morning, Ivy found the Immigration Office, but only after taking a trip back to Dome One. Her feet throbbed from the long hike looking for the office. One thing she noticed: no suites had doors. Not only were ceilings absent, but doors too.

"Oh, hello. Didn't see you coming in, but I heard you. Heels," a middle aged Galactic Doll with long black hair said. "Have a seat. I'm Janine Le Clair, Immigration Officer."

"Wow! You look just like someone I know. Molly Parkinson."

"Small world. She's my sister. How is she? Haven't seen her in years."

After relaying some news, Ivy said, "I'm here to make everything official. I'm in a temporary suite next to Dr. Eve Burkey."

"Yes, I'm aware of that. Do you want to become a citizen of Domes?"

"Exactly. How do I do that?"

"Don't suppose you have any skills. Other than telepath?" Janine said, filling out a document on her computer. "It says you were a member of Telepath Squad One. Obviously, you're a Galactic Doll."

"Oh, that gig is over now. They've disbanded us. Ended our crucial work."

"What was that?"

"Finding those murderous rogue robots. I've lost count of how many people they've killed. I joined to help eliminate them. Now, I'm resuming my studies. Soon I hope to be a medical doctor and help people in need."

Janine paused in her typing and looked up. "A doctor, you say? Not sure how you can manage that, but that's the single-most critical skill we need here on Domes. We only have one Medical Center and two doctors. I'll get you assigned to them right now. If you find you can't cope, come back. We'll see what other things you might be able to handle. School teacher, for example."

A 3-D printer powered up. Janine reached around and grabbed the new ID card, affixing it to a clip and neck chain.

"Here's your temporary ID card. Clever tech. Got your image from that camera up there." She pointed. "I've opened a bank account tied to your ID card. The computer will soon show us your account balance back on Earth. How much of it do you wish transferred here? All of it?"

"Yes, please."

"No going back, then."

"Not for me. Is that all I have to do?"

Janine chuckled. "Nope. Okay, immigrant. Here's the situation. We have about fifty thousand people living on Domes today. Ten domes are operational, but workers are always bringing more domes online. Our population is at a critical point, genetics-wise.

"The High Council encourages everyone to have as many children as they can afford to support. They recommended each child you have has a different father. Widen the overall gene pool. That's the goal. They don't care who you mate with: man or woman. Here on Domes, every man knows how critical the gene pool is if we're to survive. When you're ready for another child, just ask any man. 'Course, men love sex anyway. Between you and me, pick attractive, fit men that at least you like.

"Also, on Sunday evenings, singles meet in the plaza for a dance social. As an unmarried person, you must attend at least two socials each month. The various Domes take turns sponsoring the dance. The week's location is posted in every dome's main plaza. This is your chance to meet other single men and women.

"While the High Council wants our population to grow as rapidly as possible, they discourage single parenting. It's not illegal. Rather, we prefer to raise our children in two-parent situations."

"How do they know who's attending?"

"When you arrive, someone'll swipe your ID card. Between us, there aren't that many singles left, but we have newcomers like yourself arriving often. Now then, you should report to the Medical Center. Already Ann's texting me about your qualifications. I told her to hold her pants. We need more doctors. The Med Center is in Dome One at the far end of Main Street, near Tunnel Four. Good luck."

Ivy thanked her and headed off to find the Med Center.

Glad I don't have arms right now. They'd be shaking. I'm nervous. What will they think?

Chapter 7 Our Decisions

May 2375
Chicago

"Family meeting," I said. "We can't manage caring for six handicapped children. This is beyond exhausting, Hans. We need help."

Hans exhaled. "I agree. I've never been so tired at bedtime. We're too busy to catch the news. You should that get that new clone body. You deserve it. After all you've done."

I chuckled. "The last time I had kids, Sam let me have my arms back while he became the kids' role model. This time, I should do that. Besides, you should get work in your field. We've been putting off this talk for years. The kids and I are keeping you from your goals, being an astro-geologist. I feel awful that I've kept you from that these past years."

"But I can't do that now. Not leaving you with six kids to care for."

"You can if we move to Domes. All my sisters and their families are there. I'm sure they'd love to help us. That way, you can pursue your dreams too."

Donata slipped into the room and said, "Are we going to move? The school kids keep calling me a freak, but I think they're the freaks. They've got arms. How dumb is that?"

"Our bodies are different from theirs. That's all, dear. We look strange to them. But we do need to move. Hans, I received a call from the CPD today."

"I heard something about a shooting at the school. Thought I might catch the news tonight, if we can get the flock to bed," he said.

"Lots of policemen came," Donata said. "Papa, what's a gun? A boy said someone shot a gun, whatever that means."

"It's a weapon that fires a projectile over a big distance," Hans said. "It can kill you if it hits you."

"Like a spear?" she asked.

Wendel said, "I think it's worse than that, Donata."

"Yes, it's much worse. Mommy's got a gun. I used to be very good at hitting things. In fact, I once killed a man who tried to kill Aunts Leslie and Janine. But that was years ago. Hans, the CPD called me. Someone tried to shoot Donata but missed because she stumbled. The detective worked out trajectories and came to that conclusion."

"I fell and scraped my knee. See? Nurse put the Band-Aid on it." Donata showed us her knee.

I continued. "We must move from Chicago. It's not safe for us. Besides, at least two telepaths were kidnapped. Unless anyone objects, we'll move to Domes where my sisters live. You'll get to see your aunts, uncles, and cousins."

"Will they think we're freaks?" Donata asked.

"I doubt it. While a few on Domes might, your cousins won't. Bishop will come with us."

Hans relaxed. "That's the best news. Quite a good security guard. I feel safe when he's around."

"Okay then. All's settled. We'll pack up and move to Domes as soon as we can. Once there, Hans can see about getting a real astro-geologist job."

"But what about Katya?" Hans asked.

"Yeah, is Anka coming with us? I hope so," Donata said.

***

I joined Katya and Anka, who were discussing their own situation.

"But Mom," Anka wailed, "I don't want to leave. Donata's my friend. We can't go away. You can't leave us. It's not right."

62

Katya sighed. "I know, but you are Jafari. Third Invaders. You must learn the ways of our people. We aren't humans. We live for thousands of Earth years. Donata will be lucky to live much beyond seventy years. Besides, we must do what Home World wants. We're telepaths. In the entire history of our world, there's never been one telepath, let alone so many of you. You will be the most important people on Home World."

"But I don't want to," she cried. "I want to be with Donata and Wendel."

I walked into her room.

"Hi, Molly. Join us," Katya said. "The school called today. A man tried to kill Donata. We must move somewhere. I suggested back to Home World."

"But we don't want to go there, Mom," Anka pleaded. "Besides, Dr. Burkey has your clone. You can get your arms back. She doesn't live on Home World."

"You deserve to get your arms back," I said.

"When do I get mine?" Anka said.

"We've been over this before, dear," Katya said. "They used my original body as a blueprint. Eve's told me the new body looks like me. Only with arms. I won't have telepathy or be able to move little things like we do. But I'll still be your mother."

"But you won't be like us," Anka said. "We'll be the freaks. Dad's not like us. He's dead in his head. You'll be a dead head, too, if you get your clone body."

Dead head. One of the worst insults a telepath could use to put down a normal person.

"Excuse me," I interrupted. "Have you heard from Home World?"

Anka pouted.

Katya nodded. She said, "I can keep Anka and Cyryl with me, but I'm now free to swap into a clone body After that, if I want, I can send the kids back to Home World to live with their Dad and siblings."

"What's the problem? Isn't this good news?"

"I want to stay here with you," Anka said, indicating my children with her head nod.

"I do too," Cyryl added. "We know you do, too, Mom."

Katya rolled her eyes. "We're Jafari, Third Invaders to Earthlings. Jafari tradition says children are under the control of their fathers, not us mothers. Even if I wanted to keep you with me, I can't, unless Home World gives me the okay which they did. Bazyli is caring for the eight others. If I get my arms back, perhaps it's better if you stay with your brothers and sisters who aren't dead in their heads."

Anka said, "But Mom, I don't want to. I want to stay with Donata and Wendel. You don't have to take that clone body. Not really. We're doing just fine like we are. Aren't we, Molly? You tell her. She doesn't have to do that."

"No, she doesn't have to body swap into the clone. I've a better idea. I'm moving my family to Domes. Why don't you three come with us? We can stay together. Besides, Katya, you've been a huge help to me with my six kids."

"Mom! Please. Say yes. I want to go with her and Donata. Please."

"Yeah, Mom. Please," Cyryl said.

Katya chuckled. "I don't want to be here alone. It's not safe. Someone tried to kill Donata. I've worried we might get kidnapped. Molly, are you sure about having us tag along?"

"Yes. I'll be offended if you don't. We're leaving in my spaceship as soon as possible."

Anka yelled, "Yeah! Wendel, Donata, you hear that? We're going to Domes with you!"

She, Cyryl, Wendel, and Donata headed off to tell my other four the news.

"Are you going to ask Eve do the body swap when we get there?"

Katya sighed. "I'd give anything to be normal again. But Anka..."

"Yeah, I know. We must be role models for them. I've convinced Hans to look for an astro-geology job when we get settled. I can't keep him from his career any longer. It's not fair to him. This time, I'll be their role model. Last marriage, Sam remained armless to help the kids. Only fair I do it this time."

"Guess I can keep my two kids, and I can continue to help you with your younger ones. Will Domes be safer than here?"

"I'm sure it will be. I can't believe how many human-form robots are around Chicago. Six years ago, they were a scourge. Now they're everywhere."

***

CEO Lin Dho met with several other CEOs. He said, "Well, plan has worked. Meddling Parkinson is moving to Domes."

"Told you so. While we dare not harm her, we can her children. Mothers are protective."

The men laughed.

Chapter 8 The Tortures of Connor O'Grady

August 2369
Chicago

Despite the terrible challenges now facing him, Connor threw himself into his new position on Telepath Squad One. Already he'd help flush out a rogue robot, though it had escaped capture. Admiral Carr suggested he might get a medal for his work.

For Connor, this wasn't work. His love of plants led him to get several degrees in various botany fields. But the lure of a million credits per year enticed him to sign up. In ten years, botany dreams could be fulfilled. He could travel to new, distant worlds and explore their exotic flora. He didn't hide his reasons for joining.

Enduring being handicapped hadn't been too bad. His Personal Assistant handled his physical needs, dressing and feeding him. As a backup, the Cass-C robot on wheels helped at night and when his assistant took a personal day. He still hadn't figured out how to do much of anything with his mutated feet or how to use the Sixth Invader machines.

Connor's personal appearance bothered him the most, beyond being nearly helpless, that is. Before he cut a dashing figure. Now he looked like a Galactic Doll, giant breasts, tall heels, and curves many women would die for. Unless naked, no one could tell he wasn't a gorgeous woman, except for the lack of arms, that is.

Connor didn't hide his appearance like some men did. He hated to wear the black Telepath Squad uniforms. When not on duty, his boss, Hans, wore male-like Galactic Doll suits. Connor thought this only emphasized Hans' strange body, not hiding it. Connor kept his brown hair long and, when not on duty, wore women's gowns. He spoke only when necessary. Upon waking each morning, he told himself, "I can endure this."

This morning, he and his assistant rode the MTES to work. She kept a steadying arm around him, because he still wobbled. He breathed in the clean air of Chicago, marveling at the changes the new climate control system had brought. But there was something else in the air.

He felt a rag across his face and almost fell trying to shake his head to get it out of the way. The azure sky darkened to black. Connor had the strangest sensation of being lifted and being bent over at his waist.

***

"That was easy enough. Just make sure she's knocked out, too. Don't want her sounding the alarm."

"Yeah, she is. Let's move out."

The two giants took large steps along the MTES using the fast lane. However, their invisibility devices kept them and the body slumped over one's shoulder hidden from view. Both stepped over the spaceport fencing and jogged to their small, shabby spaceship.

Eyeing the shiny other ships, the second said, "We should snatch one of them new ones."

"Don't be a dummy. Them's got all kinds of tracking stuff in them. We'd not get a parsec before cruisers swarmed us. Nah, this rusting bag o' bolts cain't be tracked. Once we liftoff, we're free and clear. Money's in the bag. Hurry. Get the doors opened."

Both deactivated their shields. Now they could see their hands. The second punched in the key code to unlock the door.

"Fire her up. Get takeoff clearance. Say heading for Cass-C," the first giant said.

"But I thought we's goin' to doc's."

"You idiot. We are. Just don't tell the controllers that. Unless you wanna get caught."

"Oh. Yeah, right. Secret."

Soon the ship lifted off, heading for the seat of the Federation of Planets. Once they jumped into hyperspace, the first giant entered a different set of coordinates, one that took them to a desolate moon of the giant's home world of Liatos-D.

"Cain't see why we're landing here," the second giant said, as the ship descended onto the dark moonscape.

Barren rocks jutted, emulating trees the moon didn't have, though it did have some breathable air. A small shack sat next to the cleared landing pad. Mining equipment lay piled about this ghost town, once a gold mining hub. As the ship landed, a man in a business suit stepped out.

"Right on time," the doc said, glancing at a device on his wrist.

"Yeah, no trouble at all. Easiest snatch ever. Got your victim for you," the first giant said.

He carried Connor's unconscious body into the shack, depositing him on a cot.

"Money first," the doc said.

The giant handed him a small pouch of gemstones. The doc grunted, stuffed them into a pocket, and wheeled a large medical device over to the cot.

"This gonna take long? If so, we best knock him out again."

"Not long. Sure it's a him? Best undress him first."

Together, the giants stripped him, tossing his fancy black Telepath Squad uniform aside. The doc then slipped the medical machine over Connor's head and neck. When it powered up, the doc flipped through menu selections, settling on one. He pressed it, and the machine hummed.

Thirty minutes later, the machine shut down. The doc removed the device.

"He's all yours, guys. Nice doing business with you."

"That was fast. You sure he cain't talk now?" the first giant said.

"Yeah, no voice box."

The men loaded Connor back into their ship and took off. The last they saw of the doc, he was squinting at the gems through a magnifier.

Hours later, the rust bucket landed on another space faring world. Though midnight, the city lights gave the modern city an orangish, welcoming glow. The first giant made a call on his wrist device.

A man in a small shuttle landed nearby. He wore an expensive black business suit.

"Do you have my merchandise?" he asked, speaking through a translator device attached to his belt.

The second giant carried the still unconscious Connor out, allowing the man to see his genitals, proving they'd abducted a male per orders.

"Good gods," the man said. "You'd never know he was a he, would you? Sure he can't speak?"

"Aye. Doc said no voice box, whatever that is," the first giant said, watching his partner depositing Connor into the shuttle.

"Excellent work, gentlemen. As promised. The second half of your payment."

He handed the giant a bag of gems.

"You wanna more of 'em?" the second asked, looking at the well-dressed man.

"Not at this time. Let's see how one works out. I'll contact you later."

He climbed into his two-person shuttle and lifted off. Soon, the giants lost him among the skyscrapers and aerial walkways. They took off.

***

"Do you have him?" asked Shirley, his blond wife.

Simon smiled. "Yes, a strange one, but definitely male. This could be the answer to our prayers. Geneticists be damned."

Shirley laughed. "Dear, we killed them a century ago. I think they got off light for what they've done. Lordy, this one sure is a strange one. Now that's a body to kill for. Amazing *huanas*! Bigger than my head."

Simon chuckled. "No fooling. I've heard they pass on many of their physical traits. This could be the start of our salvation."

Shirley snickered. "You mean your salvation. Won't do anything for me except make me pregnant." She saw his glare and said, "I know what you mean. I've got the locked bedroom ready for him. Dump him in there. For the kids' sake, cover him up with a sheet."

Simon plopped Connor onto the satin sheets. Shirley joined him, turning up the lights. She dragged a finger down Connor's right breast and then down his side.

"A figure to die for," she whispered. "What a tiny waist and those feet. I wonder how he can even walk. Perhaps on his toes."

"Yeah, looks like that's all that lies flat on the floor. Weird human mutation for sure. If this works..." A snide smile went unnoticed by Shirley, who continued raking a nail down his thigh.

***

The blackness subsided. Connor woke. He felt the sheets beneath him and shrieked. No sound came out. His eyes opened wide. He screamed at the top of his lungs. Nothing.

70

Total silence. Waves of panic swept over his chest, threatening to cut him in half. He struggled to sit. Always his assistant aided him. Now getting up on his own took some doing.

He sat naked on a bed with red satin sheets. A small dresser and tall mirror lay to the right of the bed. A tiny night stand held a glass of water. His throat felt like he'd swallowed a mouthful of sand. Oh, how he wanted to drink, but couldn't figure out how. Where was his assistant? He needed her now more than ever.

He leaned over, trying to get a sip. Connor got a few sips before the glass fell, spilling the water onto the carpet. Now, he turned his attention to the other wall, the one with a door. All glass. He could see out into the rest of the house, but he saw the door was locked. The key in the lock was visible through the transparent wall.

Connor looked out onto what he concluded was a combination living room with offset dining room. A family of four sat at what must be a breakfast table. The portly man wore a black business suit that matched his hair and mustache. The thin wife seemed attractive with a cute bob haircut. A boy and girl sat with their backs to him, but he concluded they might be ten years old or so.

He yelled. No sound. Nothing.

He tried to get up to walk to the glass wall, intending to pound his head on it to get their attention. As soon as he put his toes onto the floor and tried to stand, he wobbled and fell. Standing without the heels for support had always been more than he could handle. The thick, plush carpet absorbed the shock of his fall. Oh, how he wanted to wave—to do anything to get their attention. But they ignored him.

Connor crawled to the wall. His long hair got in his way. Blocked his eye sight. Got caught beneath his body. Pain, and it slowed his progress. At last, he pounded his head against the glass. All four turned to stare at him. At least they're human. Maybe they'll rescue me.

The man called out something. Connor's stomach clenched. An alien language. He rued the day he avoided practicing his telepathic abilities. Simple enough to detect the presence of an intelligent mind. That's all that he had to do to earn his millions. Now...

All four turned their heads back to their breakfasts, but someone else entered and walked up to the locked door. Connor gagged. From her ragged, filthy dress, this must be a woman, but he had never seen such an ugly face. A few wisps of hair draped down her splotchy head. Her spine must be bent, for she continued to hump over as she turned the key.

As she approached him, Connor saw rows of jagged teeth, perhaps broken. He couldn't tell. She spoke to him. He shook his head, mouthing I can't understand you. She stopped talking, lifted him up, and forced him to walk on his toes. The four around the table ceased talking and stared at him. Connor felt his face burning. Then, he saw what had to be a bathroom.

He nodded, and the crone smiled. At least that's what he believed. When he'd relieved himself, she helped him to the table, now empty, though the remains of the breakfast still covered it. She fixed a bowl of something and fed him. By now, Connor's fright swamped even his taste buds. He had no idea what he ate. A struggle to get him back to his bed followed. At least, she covered him with a sheet.

A while later, the wife led six other women into the room. She uncovered him while he listened to their gasps and constant chatter. Many ran fingers over his body, but there wasn't anything he could do to stop them.

***

One brunette woman named Dolores said, "If we had a figure like he has, my goodness. We could have any man we chose! But they must weigh a ton."

Another added, "Look at that waist. That's to die for. Are you saying his children inherit all these physical attributes? Really?"

"Yes," Shirley said. "That's what Simon claims. At least they do on the world he comes from."

"Well, I'm game. If I could have a daughter that looks half as good as he does..." Dolores said, putting her finger to her lips.

"You sure he can't speak? Does he understand what we're saying?" asked Mildred.

"No, he can't make a sound. Simon assures me he can't understand our language. We're safe enough," Shirley said.

Mildred said, "Count me in. I'll try it. If it works—lordy, if it works and we don't have to keep them around..."

"My sentiments," Shirley said.

"I'm fertile now. When can I do it with him?"

"Now, if you like. Simon wants me to keep a log. You know, name, date, time. Let me know if you get pregnant. Simon's insisting on that detail. Also, he needs to know the outcome in nine months. Heck, we all want to know that."

"Lordy, so do I," Mildred said. "I'll do anything to have proper daughters. Hector cringes every time he has to do it with our wretched servant."

"I'll pull the blinds if you don't want us watching," Shirley said.

Once the shades came down, all but the lovely black-haired young woman left. Mildred undressed and slipped onto the bed. As soon as she ran her fingers over a nipple, she knew the man had no choice. A few minutes later, Mildred's desires culminated, as did the man's. She dressed and raised the blinds.

"Well, how'd it go?" Dolores asked.

"He's a sex fiend if ever there was one. Just play with his nipples a moment and boom. Faster reaction than we have. You got me logged?"

"Yes, you're all set. Simon wants us to do it on successive days to increase the chances of a pregnancy."

"Okay with me. I'll be by this time tomorrow. How many tests does Simon want? I'd like to tell other women," Mildred said.

"He hasn't said how many. Go for it. I would think the more tests the better," Shirley said.

Dolores said, "Besides, it can't be any worse than going through the whole nine months only to give birth to an ugly beast. Only our sons aren't born deformed. If this lets us have normal daughters, I'm for it. Besides, if our daughters inherit such a body..."

All six women sighed.

***

Later, the ugly woman reappeared and cleaned him up. She helped him to the kitchen for lunch, but only after the family had finished. He spent the afternoon on the bed and saw the man returning. He glimpsed the wife preparing supper in the kitchen.

The ugly woman left the door open. He overheard snatches of conversations that afternoon and at the supper table. The man seemed interested in something the wife had written.

After the ugly woman helped him to the messy table, she fed him. Connor didn't know what he was eating, but his stomach demanded something. He ate. The ugly one helped him stagger back to the bed, where she brushed his long hair. Connor sensed she liked that it reached his thighs. Perhaps I'm misinterpreting what I'm sensing. She's not a robot.

Once groomed, two more women, a blond and a brown haired woman, arrived. He hadn't seen these before. He watched the wife writing something down, before the blond entered and drew the blinds. Connor shook his head no while she undressed. She ignored his protests. As soon as she used her fingers, any resistance he had vanished. Animal urges took over.

Later on, the second woman entered. She exchanged a few words with the blond. Again, Connor did his best to say no, but the women ignored his protests, if they even understood his protests.

When the women finished, they left the blinds drawn. The second woman covered him up with the sheet as she left and turned out the light.

Alone in the dark, he took stock of his situation. Ever since undergoing the mutation, he knew his sex drive had somehow magnified. Since he wasn't married and since they told him his children would be like him, he'd done his best to avoid having sex with anyone. Now that changed.

He couldn't say he didn't like the sensations, but these women were total strangers. These encounters meant nothing, an animal response. While pleasureful, Connor didn't want it to continue.

They must want to make their own telepaths. What else could it be? And what kind of creature is Ugly? I've never seen anything like her. Maybe she isn't even human. Heck, monkeys are cuter than she is.

Monkeys? How the hell am I ever going to get home? Where am I? I need answers, but I don't understand a word they're saying.

Tears.

Why can't I speak? What have they done to my voice? If I can't speak, I'll never be able to convince them to take me home.

Connor cried himself to sleep. Without a voice, no one heard.

Vic Broquard

Chapter 9 From Bad to Worse for Connor

At first, Connor tried to count the days, but he soon lost count. A predictable routine developed. Miss Ugly, as he now called her, assisted him to the bathroom in the morning before feeding him breakfast. The afternoons brought at least one woman to have sex.

He gave up trying to show them "no." No matter his futile gestures, they ignored him. If only his body didn't have such an automatic built-in response. Women came after supper. Often two.

They fed him well.

One day, the man came home with a box. He brought it into Connor's room.

Oh, god. I hope he doesn't want sex too.

Shoes. With very tall heels. Connor's eyes opened. He nodded yes, his long hair bobbing.

The man smiled and helped him into the shoes. He stood back and said something. He made motions with his arms that Connor took to mean stand.

Very carefully, Connor rose. Keeping his balance on the thick carpeting proved challenging. He needed his Personal Assistant, but where was she?

The man had a big smile on his face. He gestured for Connor to walk through the door. When he did, the man pointed to the bathroom. Connor smiled and made his slow way there.

While he relieved himself, the man and wife exchanged words with Miss Ugly, who smiled. The woman joined him, making gestures and sounds. She took a bit of toilet paper and pretended to wipe her own butt, all the while shaking her

76

head. At last, Connor thought he understood. Shake head when my butt needs wiping. Crude communications at last.

Days slipped by, punctuated by strangers shacking up for a few minutes. However, with the heels, Connor had some independent mobility, which he made use of.

Late one morning, he made his way out of his room and into the spacious living room. Ah, windows! After a couple minutes and two near falls, he reached the floor-to-ceiling windows. He gasped.

Even though he expected to see a strange world, the sights still shocked him. This home must be a suite at least fifty floors up in a skyscraper. A walkway across a vast space connected this building to the next skyscraper. In the distance, he saw countless other connecting walkways, many much higher than this one. Tall buildings rose as far as he could see. Miles, perhaps.

Connor concluded he was in a very large city, perhaps the size of Chicago. With no way down, escape was hopeless. In a city this huge, where would he go?

Tears trickled. He spotted small two-person shuttles darting about the skies. For a time, he watched them, before noticing some landed on small platforms outside the skyscraper suites. Did the man get around in one of these? Did it land close to this suite? Where was the spaceport?

He could formulate no plan of escape. Another woman came and forced him into his room before doing it again. He recognized her. She'd been here before. He felt dirty, used, and nothing more than a pathetic sex toy for these women.

One day, he got a peek at the log the wife kept. The writing looked like hieroglyphics. If each line represented a single woman, the stack of pages suggested hundreds had used him. He gagged.

One morning while using the bathroom, he noticed his hair had grown. When he was in Chicago, it reached the top of his thighs. But now, it touched his knees. Had it grown a foot? How fast did hair grow? Connor had no idea, but it felt like an eternity. Perhaps he hadn't been here years.

Ah, the wife was pregnant. She ceased using him days ago. But Connor had no concept of baby bulges being an indicator of due dates. Still women paid him visits, though most came in the evenings of late. One night, it happened.

The wife must be having her baby, Connor thought. The man rushed about grabbing this and that while the wife waddled past the living room. When Miss Ugly came to brush his hair, she chatted before perhaps remembering Connor didn't understand a word she said. She cradled her arms and made a rocking motion. Connor smiled and nodded. He understood.

He didn't expect what happened next. Miss Ugly entered and had intercourse with him. Connor fought hard to keep from gagging or vomiting up supper. Worse, the next few nights, over a dozen other Miss Uglys did it with him. Each night, Connor cried himself to sleep. Try as he might, he could think of no way to flee this suite on his own.

Then, the man and wife returned, she carrying a baby. Connor watched, catching glimpses of the child. He observed them the entire day. While the mother changed its diaper on the kitchen table, he spotted the baby's sex . A girl. True, she had no arms and had distorted feet. Other than that, she looked like a normal baby. Connor's cheeks heated. I'm the baby's father.

The domestic situation changed. While Miss Ugly handled most of the home duties, loud arguments between the man and Miss Ugly ensued. Often, the man slapped the woman so hard she developed bruises. Miss Ugly sobbed to herself as she brushed his hair at night. Something had gone very wrong.

One night after a nasty argument, Miss Ugly's red eyes caught his attention. He twisted his face as though suggesting curiosity. She felt like talking, but again he couldn't understand a word. In desperation, he tried to see what images her mind held.

When he made contact with her, Miss Ugly's eyes opened wide. She could sense he was aware of her thoughts. She focused on several images, one at a time. First, she recalled an image of the wife's first newborn. Connor could see it was a girl, but she looked terrible, like a miniature Miss Ugly. Next, she showed an image of the wife and her second child, a boy that looked normal. Finally, she showed him her own first child, a normal girl that was snatched from her and raised by the wife. Ah, ha. The very same daughter he'd seen every day.

Recognition. The women of this world could only have normal boys. All females turned out to be more Miss Ugly's. Only the Miss Ugly's could have normal females. The ugly, malformed females had to be kept alive because they could have regular female babies. Otherwise, the entire population would perish in one generation.

He placed one of his images of her being slapped by the man into her mind, followed by his "curious" expression. That worked.

She showed him images of the wife's normal baby girl, though she lacked arms, and then an image of the man killing Miss Ugly.

Conclusion: Miss Ugly isn't needed any longer.

Miss Ugly had been the only person who had treated him humanely. She didn't deserve to be killed. He didn't want to spend his lifetime impregnating the women of this world. In Connor's mind, that seemed his inescapable fate unless he fled this world. Anywhere was better than here.

An idea formed while Miss Ugly endured being slapped around the next day. That night as she brushed his hair, he sent her pictures of a spaceship and him entering it. He invented both. He sent another picture of her helping him sneak into a spaceship and leaving this world.

Miss Ugly wasn't dumb. A giant grin formed. She nodded, saying something he couldn't understand. Connor could only wait and hope.

Two nights later, Miss Ugly entered his room, waking him. She helped him into his heels. She motioned for him to come with her. Once more, she slipped a steadying arm around his waist. They slipped out of the suite and into a hallway. With effort, she got him into a seat in the man's shuttle. Soon, Miss Ugly had them airborne.

Connor marveled at the advanced architecture and how large the city was. Ahead, he spotted a wide-open stretch. As they drew closer, he saw many spaceships.

Their landing left much to be desired, more of a crash than a landing. Still, she'd landed them in a dark section of the spaceport. After helping him out, they crossed the tarmac. Here, Connor felt more comfortable walking. He only wobbled a little. She led him to what must have been a deep space transport being refueled. No one was around the automatic operation. She helped him up the entrance ramp, stowing him in a rear cargo area.

Both nodded to each other. She left. Connor sighed. He had found a way to flee this world. He gave no thought to where this ship might go. Anywhere was better than here.

Chapter 10 Into More Trouble

Connor dozed until vibrations jarred him. He felt liftoff and relaxed, freed from this awful world. Running lights illuminated the cargo area. Red rectangular banners with a yellow hammer and sickle hung in several places along the walls.

A man's face appeared staring down at him. He wore a flat hat and had a ruddy complexion. He said something. Connor couldn't understand him. In the dim light, the man reached for Connor's arms to pull him up, before noticing he had no arms and was naked.

He yelled. Another man joined him. Both pointed at Connor, barking words. Connor decided they wanted him to stand. He hated being naked in front of these men, who snickered and pointed. Connor mouthed words, including help me.

One man pointed to his lips and shook his head no, while mouthing unspoken words. Connor nodded. The men then pushed him down the hall and into a comfortable seat and left him.

He looked around and saw more of the red banners but had no clue of their meaning. Connor spotted a restroom. When they left him, he made his way there. Hours passed. His stomach growled as he watched the men eat sandwiches they brought. Neither offered him one.

Upon landing, men in green uniforms marched into the ship. Their hands held weapons pointed at Connor. After talking in several languages, none of which he understood, Connor mouthed help me. After more gestures, he felt they grasped he had no voice. They pointed to his naked body and laughed. They put away their weapons. Good sign. One gestured to follow them, which he did, wobbling all the way.

His eyes blinked in the bright sunlight. Oh, for sunglasses. Connor saw a dozen other ships, each with that same red rectangle banner with the yellow hammer and sickle. The spaceport appeared quite rundown. Squalid, compared to New O'Hare. The ships, old and antiquated. As he blinked from the sun's glare, he glimpsed many more of these soldiers, all laughing and pointing at him.

Humiliation. But he could do nothing about it except to continue to take tiny steps in the direction the soldiers indicated. At last, they entered a building. His eyes ceased watering. Again, those same red banners plastered the walls. After a long walk down a hall, they marched him into a throne room of sorts.

A young man lay slouched across a divan, while a plump young woman, also naked, fondled him. Now and then, she plucked another grape, licked it, and slipped it into the man's mouth. The soldiers saluted him the moment they entered. Behind the divan was another of the red banners, but this one covered the entire wall.

This room is a dump.

The soldiers and the man exchanged words. The man tossed off the woman, rose, and walked over to Conner. His eyes scanned Connor's body top to bottom while he chatted to the soldiers, who stood at attention. He motioned for the woman to join him and said something to her that caused her to smile seductively.

Connor had no way to stop her from fondling him. All the while the men laughed. At last, the man must have ordered her to stop. He exchanged more words with the soldiers.

A decision solidified, because the soldier who'd directed Connor here gestured for him to follow. Connor did so, doing his best to avoid falling, eager to leave this place. By now, his hunger swelled. In dire need of a restroom, he sent an image of a toilet into the soldier's mind.

After walking partway down that long hall, the soldier opened another door and gestured him inside. He'd gotten the message. Connor sat down on one. When he finished, he had no way to wipe and decided against even trying to hint at it. The guard continued to gesture. Connor followed him outside the building.

He walked across the tarmac back to the same rust bucket that brought him here. He felt relief when the soldier motioned for him to walk up the entrance ramp. Once inside, Connor sat down, his feet throbbing and stomach growling.

Minutes later, the same two men who'd flown him here entered. The soldier exchanged words with them and left. The door closed. Connor cheered in silence as the ship lifted off. He felt the lurch as it dropped into hyperspace.

One brought him a sandwich, plopping it on the seat beside him. He said a word that Connor thought meant eat.

Always before, his Personal Assistant fed him. Hence, he'd never practiced much using his feet and toes. He rued his complacency and slipped off his heels. Twisting and wiggling, he got the sandwich between his feet. He leaned way over and took a bite. It tasted awful. His stomach ceased aching.

With nothing to do, he struggled to get his heels back on and then slipped into a peaceful nap. He had no idea where they were going, but anywhere had to be better than the places they left behind.

He awoke with a jar as the pilot landed the ship. When the door opened, Connor breathed in strange odors. Balsam, pine, fuel oil, and exhaust fumes. The air felt cool, almost refreshing. Following the men, Connor set foot on another world. Puffy white clouds dotted the azure sky. The sun, a bit redder than Sol.

The spaceport held six other craft, but to Connor, they seemed more like cargo ships than passenger transports. Snowy peaks punctured the distant horizon. A quaint village nestled in the valley beside the port. An ivy-like vine crept up the grey stone walls of the cottages.

Connor focused on staying upright on the cobblestone tarmac. An odd looking man stood beside a bizarre vehicle. The rectangular vehicle had four black wheels, probably rubber since they deformed where they touched the cobblestones. Each side sported two doors. The rear doors, which hinged towards the front of the vehicle, were twice as wide as the front doors. It made a low purring sound, expelling fumes from a pipe at its rear.

The imposing man stood rigid. His black suit coat had twin tails that flopped in the slight breeze coming from the distant mountains. A top hat at least a foot tall sat upon his head, making him seem more imposing. Streaks of grey lined his hair and mustache. His black shoes reflected sunlight. Connor could see the man's eyes traversing his naked body. Up and down. Several times. Connor flushed, but continued his very slow walk towards this man.

When the pilot and Connor reached him, the two exchanged words before the immaculately dressed man handed the pilot a small bag. He turned and jogged back to the rust bucket. As the man continued to observe Connor, he heard the spaceship liftoff. A finality to his situation.

The man said something. Connor shook his head. He said several other words, before he grinned. He turned on a device attached to his leather belt. Connor saw him fiddling with a display menu, but the words or symbols meant nothing to him. For a moment, he regretted studying botany instead of linguistics.

The man spoke again, but Connor heard words coming from the waist device.

84

"Testing. Testing. Can you me understand?"

English! Connor enthusiastically nodded yes.

"Damn! Good I am. *Ja.* I Baron Arno Von Berg am. Ruler of Bergwald."

His arms swept a circle around the area, likely including the mountains.

"You speak can?"

Connor shook his head no.

"I so thought. You man be?"

Connor nodded yes.

"Children you can make?"

Again he nodded yes.

"*Sehr gut.* I so thought. You one of them are. Excellent. To my castle we return. You very well treated will be as long as you babies for me make. Understood?"

Connor sighed and nodded, following the Baron to the vehicle. Another man dressed in a uniform stepped out and opened the large rear door.

"In you get," Baron Berg said.

While tricky, Connor managed it though he fell into the deep back seat. Soft leather stuck to his butt. The Baron stepped in, removing his hat.

"All you see my kingdom is. You children for me make and you for nothing want. Rich I be. Ahead, that my castle is, where you with my extended family now live. Question. Your children like you will look? Both men and women?"

Connor nodded.

"Again, I so thought. Great plans for you I have. You for nothing want. Many kingdoms our world has. Ruled by barons. We most beautiful women in kingdom marry. Become our baronesses. Our citizens, our women, to our baronesses look up, as the epitome of beauty. The finest in the kingdom. Many women a baroness want to become, but only the most perfect are chosen.

"Because your body closely a perfect baroness resembles, I you as a baroness must clothe. You your own servant for your needs to care will have. Her name Ilse is. Today, we you bathed will get and properly attired. Tomorrow, I you adorned as a baroness will pay to get. Then, your only duty children to create is when I ask. Understood?"

Connor nodded.

"Oh, I High Wald speak. Important men High Wald speak. Women and low men Low Wald speak. You this device will have so you us understand." He pointed to the device on his belt.

Connor watched the quaint cottages go by. The vehicle traveled no faster than Conner could have jogged. Ahead, he saw a tall wall of grey stone. Rising behind it, the grey stone castle dominated the horizon, though snow-capped peaks rose far behind it. Carved ram heads adorned a wide double door that opened as the vehicle approached. Trumpets sounded a muffled fanfare. The car pulled into a cobblestone courtyard before the doors of the giant manor house.

The driver opened the door. Baron Berg stepped out, donning his top hat. Connor wiggled about and got out without falling. Standing beside the main doors of the manor, three maids awaited. Fetish fashion. Body hugging, short black satin dresses. Black hose. Matching heels. Their dresses couldn't have been any shorter, Connor mused. It reminded him of fashions he'd seen in magazines. Their hair, as Connor discovered, was blond like all those from Bergwald.

"Attention," he said. "We this man Wendell call, since we his name know not. We Wendell like a baroness treat. Wendell, Ilse your servant is."

One of the maids stepped forward and curtsied. All three maids giggled as Connor's body reacted to seeing them. While Connor's face burned, Baron Berg laughed.

"*Ist gut*, eh?"

86

More giggles. Ilse walked up to Connor and slipped a steadying arm around his waist. She guided him up a flight of wide stone stairs. Soon, Connor got lost among the various rooms, winding up in a bathroom. Ilse ran bath water. Before the tub filled, Baron Berg stepped in with another translation device, turning it on.

"I'll get Wendell cleaned up, Baron. What about clothes?" Ilse said.

"I for dressmaker sent. Your time take." He left.

When Ilse spoke, he couldn't understand her words, but did understand the monotone voice from the translation unit. At last, he could know what was being said around him.

Just as Connor stepped into the hot water, a giggling small girl in a miniature ball gown walked in.

Chapter 11 Connor's Metamorphosis

Connor relaxed in the hot bath, the first in ages. The young girl walked up beside Ilse.

"You must be Wendell. I'm Mady. I'm fourteen. Mom's oldest child. Peppi is three years younger. Then there are my older brothers, Baron Eric and Baron Hugh, but their mother, Baroness Johanna, is dead. Mom is Baroness Della. You'll meet her at supper, I'm sure. Except for that thing," she pointed to his manhood, "you look just like my older brothers' new baronesses. I guess that's why Dad wants you to dress like a baroness. You look like a perfect one.

"Dad wants me to be a baroness, too. When I get older. But I'm not. Mom can't do anything except look pretty and dance. I want to do lots of things, but you can't do anything either. You'll be fine as a baroness, I suppose. Someday, I'm going to escape this world and be what I want to be. Do you know how I can do that?"

"Madi! You're still thirteen for a few more days. And don't speak such things," Ilse said. "You don't want to make Baron Arno mad, do you? He gives you everything. One day, you'll be the envy of every young woman in Bergwald."

"Boring. I want to learn things. Do things."

"Surely, you don't want to be a lowly servant like I am? Always caring for others."

A pout appeared on Mady's young face. She tossed her long blond hair.

"Well, no. I can sit around and look pretty like Mom and the other baronesses anywhere. Boring. I want to do things. I can't imagine spending my whole life just looking pretty and doing nothing at all."

"Baroness Della is a good dancer. She hosts all Baron Arno's balls," Isle said. "Now that you are here, why don't you help me bathe Wendell?"

"Well, I suppose so. Look at his flaming red hair. Long and thick. I've never seen anyone in Bergwald who has red hair. Have you, Ilse? I wonder what world has people with red hair. Do you know, Ilse?"

"*Nein.* We have light hair. Blond."

"Baroness Elie has blond hair, too, but Baroness Missy has auburn hair. Except for the hair, they look very much like Wendell, don't they?"

"Uncanny."

Madi asked, "Wendell, do you know how to cluck speak? All baronesses learn to cluck speak. Mom makes all kinds of clucking sounds for words. Well, maybe Mom can teach you. But that might not work 'cause she tried with Baronesses Elie and Missy. They can't make any sounds. Can you? No, I suppose not."

"Work on Wendell's hair, if you're going to help, Mady."

"Okay. Such fiery hair. And so long. I'm trying to grow mine long. I don't want to be a baroness, but Dad insists. I'm supposed to be learning to cluck too. I have to escape somehow."

Ilse said, "Mady, you best be practicing cluck speaking. You know darn well he'll turn you into a baroness whether you want it or not. He *is* the ruler of Bergwald."

She pouted. "When? How long do I have? Mom can't tell me. Don't think there are cluck words for that."

"Until you turn fourteen. Then you're officially a young woman. That's the usual time it's done. Could be any day, Mady. Best be practicing. He has you working wearing heels and the gown so it won't be such a big change."

"But it *is* a big change, Ilse. I won't be able to speak or do anything except look pretty."

"And dance, Mady. There is always that. Your mother loves the formal dances."

"Hardly a life. Not like you've got. You're helping people that need help."

Ilse smiled. "True. I make good wages. Few get to become lady's maids to baronesses. Still, my heart is with you, Mady. I'm glad I'm not a baroness."

"See, Mr. Wendell. She agrees. Mom and the other baronesses are helpless. I don't want to be like that. It can't be fun at all, can it?"

Connor shook his head.

"We will have to get clucks worked out for him. Don't we, Ilse? Mr. Wendell, make your tongue click off the top of your mouth. Like this."

She made a popping sound. Connor tried and made one.

"See, you can do it. Okay. One pop means yes. Two pops mean no. I taught Baronesses Missy and Elie that too."

"You should teach him something useful. A signal he needs to use the bathroom."

Mady giggled. "Yes, I suppose. Look. Put your lips together and make a puff sound. Like this."

Connor tried puffing a few times.

"There, you got it. Mr. Wendell is a fast learner. Of course, real cluck speech is much harder. Mom knows a dozen words. Doesn't she, Ilse?"

"Yes, about that. I've heard some baronesses know even more. My sister told me that if they learn cluck speech when they're your age, Mady, when they become baronesses, they know maybe a hundred words. That's quite a lot. But your Mom—she became one only after Baron Arno's first wife died. She didn't have time to learn cluck speech before he made her his new baroness. So, Mady, you best practice and learn cluck speech while you can."

"But I told you. I'm leaving this world. I'm going to find another world somewhere. I want to be what I want. Not what Dad says I'll be. Boring. It's not fair."

"Oh, don't be childish, Mady. You're not going anywhere. I suspect by this time next year, you'll be a baroness somewhere, and your maid, Rose, will be your lady's maid."

"I won't. I won't!"

She wiped at a tear with her ball gown sleeve.

They dried Connor off, but had to put the worn-out shoes back on so he could walk.

Ilse said, "You won't like the way they're going to dress you. Future baronesses require several years to get used to the attire, as Mady has been doing since she was six and Rosa started looking after her. This way."

She and Mady kept an arm around his waist as they led him into the next room.

"Zork! Talk about weird." Karla stared at Connor before regaining composure. "I'm Karla Rahn, the dressmaker for Baron Arno Berg. Well, I never..."

Mady giggled and said, "Yes, Wendell is quite the man down there, but the rest of him challenges the best baronesses."

She worked her tape measure.

"My goodness. Same measurements as the other two young baronesses. How very strange, Mady. Did Baron Arno say where Wendell came from?"

"Nope. But it must be the same place as Baronesses Elie and Missy. Don't you think?" Mady said. "I'm helping him get used to life in the castle."

She looked at the large selection of ball gowns and apparel. "Won't sky blue go well with his red hair?" Mady said.

"Sure, Mady. First, let's get him into these stockings."

Mady giggled. "This is the best part, Wendell. They massage your legs and feet whenever you move. Helps your

91

knees and feet. Oh, they come from another world. Called Zahra-C wherever that is. You're going to love them."

Next, Ilse showed off the sky blue, calf-high boots.

Mady giggled. "These come all the way from Cass-C, the home of the Federation of Planets. We sell them our fanciest gowns. But these boots are special. You can't sprain an ankle, cause they're rigid. Metal lined, Dad says. Look at the heel. Very tall. At least seven knuckles."

She picked up on Connor's confused expression.

"A knuckle is this big."

She bent a finger and pointed to the middle section which Connor realized must be about an inch.

"Ilse's beautiful black heels are five knuckles tall. They have me training in six knuckles. But all baronesses wear heels that are seven knuckles tall. I can barely manage these heels. I can't imagine walking in these boots, Wendell. But I'll help you all I can. I'm escaping to another world before they make we wear these."

Ilse glared at Mady, who took no notice. When Ilse brought out the corset and the tightening machine, Mady sighed.

"You won't like this part. It's tight. Takes getting used to."

Ilse pulled the laces as tight as she could. While she hooked them up to the machine, Mady offered more advice.

"This is the hard part. Getting the back closed. You must take shallow, small breaths now. Missy fainted twice. So did Elie. But when they had to move around the castle, both fainted a bunch of times, but only for the first two weeks. After that, they got used to it. Baronesses have tiny waists. The envy of the women of Bergwald. I can't imagine why, though. I'd rather be able to breathe. Oh, Wendell, don't faint! Ilse!"

Connor felt as though the corset cut him in half. It forced the air out of his lungs. Ilse caught him, while Mady waved a stink bottle under his nose. He woke, gasped, and fainted again.

"May as well finish cinching it, Mady. Then we'll wake him. There. That should do it. Let me measure it. Ah, good for a new Baroness. Eighteen knuckles. Now if you continue to wear yours, Mady, you should be able to have yours down to fourteen. We both know that's the ideal waist size for the best baronesses."

"But he can hardly breathe. Okay, I'll wake him." She waved the odorous concoction.

Connor woke and gasped. Panic filled his eyes. Another gasp followed, before he passed out again. On the fourth revival and following Mady's constant advising, he took tiny panting-like breaths.

Ilse continue dressing him in the complex ball gown. Ruffles adorned the gorgeous sky blue satin gown that flared out ten feet in diameter. The style accentuated the sought after Galactic Doll form.

Mady said, "Now you have to practice getting around, Wendell. Of course, I can lift mine or push it aside a bit, but you won't be able to do that. You'll have to anticipate where your feet are or take a nasty fall. The steps are stone. It hurts when you fall. I got a horrible bruise on my arm when I fell. But with lots of practice, you'll do fine."

She continued to chat. Wendell found her chatter endearing and a great help in keeping his attention off his misery.

"Time to meet the other baronesses. Baron Arno's orders," Ilse said.

When he faced the eight-foot wide, stone staircase, his gasping escalated. He couldn't see his feet. Plus, walking this short distance exhausted the air he'd been able to take with the myriad shallow breaths. He stood frozen to the spot, panting.

"Feel for the step," Mady said. "Maybe Ilse will steady you this time. 'Course the Baron will expect you to navigate the castle on your own. I'll help you practice every day. One step at a time. Very slowly. Oops."

Connor stumbled into a step and almost fell. Ilse caught him. Forced erect by the apparel, he froze and panted, trying not to faint. An eternity passed before they reached the second floor and the huge throne room. Still panting as though he'd run a mile, he entered the well-lit room. A dozen golden chandeliers, each sporting ten lights, reflected off the silver-marble floor. Great tapestries lined the wall behind the six thrones. Giant murals adorned the other walls.

The central pair of thrones had two steps to reach them, while the pairs flanking them had but one. Workers ignored him, as they installed a new stone throne the same height as the four smaller ones. No barons could be seen, but the baronesses sat rigidly on their thrones. Their apparel did not allow for slouching.

Ilse did the introductions. "Baroness Della, this is Wendell."

Connor guessed she might be thirty, decades younger than her husband, Baron Arno. She wore a cherry red gown twelve feet in diameter at the floor. Her adornments surprised Connor. Besides gigantic earrings that looked more like hanging chandeliers than earrings, a gold mesh veil fastened to the top of each ear and to either side of her nose dangled over her mouth. It reached to the bottom of her chin. He expected her crown and broach cost a fortune.

Ilse allowed Connor to stand just inside the door, catching his breath from the exertion of climbing one flight of stairs. Della smiled. Ilse's voice jolted him.

"This is Baroness Missy." She pointed to the auburn-haired young woman to the right of Della. "This Baroness Elie."

Connor gasped, but not from lack of air. They had been members of his Telepath Squad! They, too, wore similar ball gowns, yellow and brown respectively. They had enormous earrings that threatened to rip off their ears. The lower part of their faces lay behind similar golden veils strung from ear top to ear top and attached to their nostrils. Both smiled.

Then, both women's eyes opened wide.

'Connor. Connor O'Grady?' Missy sent.

'Missy Tweed? Elie Mc Pierson?' Connor sent back.

Three heads nodded affirmative, but the others assumed the three were politely acknowledging the introduction of Wendell.

'We got kidnapped. Don't let on you're a telepath.' Missy sent. "Arno knows we are, but we convinced him we don't understand his language."

'I did too. Kidnapped,' he sent back.

Mady giggled. "See, the new baronesses look like you, Wendell. Workers are finishing making your throne. You'll sit there at meetings and such. I'm never allowed to attend those. You'll be on your own. Don't worry. I'll help you practice, just like I helped Missy and Elie."

Connor got an image of Mady helping Missy learn how to get about. He figured she backed Mady's statement.

"Since the new throne isn't ready," Ilse said, "Mady, why don't we show Wendell more of this fabulous castle? Your Highness's permission, of course."

Della clucked some sounds, which he assumed meant she concurred. Missy and Elie just made one faint click. Ilse guided Connor out of the throne room and back to the stairs.

"The grand ballroom is on the third floor along with restrooms and food tables. Don't worry. I'll show you how to dance properly," Mady said. "In these gowns and heels, we don't move much. Still, I expect many will want to dance with you at the balls. Next one is the Mid-summer Ball. You'll have a month to learn the steps. We'll show you how, won't we, Ilse?"

The maid chuckled. "*Ja*. Now let's get Wendell up the steps, shall we?"

Panting and gasping, Connor climbed the steps, though he almost wetted his panties trying to find each next step. If he could have made a sound, he would have been screaming. But he didn't have the breath to do that even if he'd had a voice. Connor believed in miracles now. Somehow he'd climbed up another flight of stairs without fainting or falling.

The grand ballroom lived up to his expectations, based on what he'd seen of the throne room. Opulence factorial. Here they paused for minutes letting him catch his breath. All the while Mady chatted about how wonderful the balls were and how much fun he would be having.

"I'd love to be able to play an instrument, but Dad forbids it. 'You won't have arms in a few years.' That's what he keeps telling me. Another reason I simply have to leave here and find a new world where I can be what I want to be. Though I admit I don't know what instrument I'd like to play."

The fourth floor held the living quarters, each a giant suite. Baron Arno and Baroness Della had the largest one. His two sons, Missy, and Elie had another pair. Mady had her own as did her brother, Peppi, now eleven. The main bedroom of each suite had an attached lady's maid bedroom.

"This is my room. My maid, Rosa, sleeps there. I need her help to get into and out of my gowns. She does my hair."

The nightmare didn't end yet. Baron Arno found the trio.

"Ah, here you are. Wendell, your bedroom showing, Mady? Good girl. Wendell, I the rest of your changes ready for you have. Ilse, I with your gown color choice do agree. Looks perfect. We down to the first floor now must go. No time to waste. This one time, I you down will carry. After this, you the

96

stairs yourself will have to navigate. All the baronesses that do. Right, Mady?"

Whoosh. Connor flew down the steps. Baron Arno's strength amazed him. He set Connor down before the door of a room. A padlock prevented unauthorized entry. The door was open. Baron Arno pushed Connor inside, where a thin man wearing a white lab coat stood beside a cot.

"We you into a proper baroness are converting. Me, a fortune cost. Your earrings around two hundred thousand gold *münzen* ran. One of these." He held out a gold coin. "The gold veil, another fifty thousand. You better appreciate how much I on you spend, to say nothing of your upkeep and servant. Don't worry. You telepathic skills have, I know but that they useless are, since you our language do not know. Too bad. Doc, yours he is."

Before Connor could do anything, the man placed a smelly rag over Connor's nose. He tried to fight the chloroform but darkness swelled. He felt his body being placed onto the cot.

***

The doctor pierced his ears and nose for the jewelry. Satisfied with his work, he fastened each enormous earring, soldering their clasps. Now they could not be removed. Baron Arno didn't have to worry that a baroness might lose one of these costly earrings. The golden veil's chain had four hooks, one for each ear and side of the nose. The lady's maid removed the veil at bedtime.

The doctor called Baron Arno in to inspect his handiwork. After a cursory check, he thanked the doctor and handed him a large sack of gold coins. He then sent for Ilse, but Mady's tagging along didn't surprise him.

"Wake him and help him into the dining room. I'm off to a business appointment."

"Wendell looks perfect now, doesn't he, Mady?"

She stared at him and waved the odor bottle. Connor stirred. As he came to, Ilse helped him sit.

***

A silent scream came from Connor's mouth, followed by tears. His ears threatened to rip off. The dangling veil proved a mere annoyance.

Ilse said, "Wendell, now you are a perfect baroness. No one will guess you are a man. Time for supper. Off we go. You'll get a light meal tonight."

Connor had no way to tell them how he felt. As Ilse helped him stand, he panicked.

"Mady, let's help him to the table. A bit of water is just the thing."

Tears streaming down his cheeks and with shallow panting, Connor walked the short distance into the dining room, beating the rest of the family. Ilse got him seated. She pulled up a chair beside him, lifted the veil, and gave him a drink.

"Small sips," she insisted, while drying his face.

Soon he heard the clicks of Mady's heels. He found her presence reassuring. He watched the other baronesses as they made their slow way into the room, their maids at their sides. He noticed that both telepaths and Della focused solely on their walking, a grim reminder of what he faced.

Once seated, Missy and Elie smiled at him. He returned the gesture.

'Dear god! He's got you looking like us,' Missy sent.

'In a few days, the pain goes,' Elie sent. 'We are doomed.'

The three barons entered last, ignoring their wives. Connor watched as the ladies maids lifted the veils with one hand while feeding them with the other. Ilse fed him very soft mush. He ate and drank very little.

Misery. Later, Ilse readied him for bed. He slept in the stockings and corset. At least she unhooked the gold veil. As Connor tried in vain to sleep, he realized how bad his and the other two telepaths' situation had become.

'Connor,' Missy touched his mind. 'Be careful around these barons. Elie and I both had sons last year. Our so-called barons freaked out when they saw their boys looked just like us. They killed them. Murderers. Since then, they avoid us, preferring to use local prostitutes. I think Baron Arno has other plans for you and for us. Oh, practice all you can. Mady's a life saver.'

Connor drifted into a much-needed sleep.

Chapter 12 Connor Steps Up

Days turned into a blur of fears and gasps for breath. Ilse and Mady walked him throughout the expansive castle, save the fifth floor, out of bounds for women. Connor dreaded descending stairs. Bosom obscured feet paired with a lack of balance made him almost fall many times.

Mady had a knack for knowing when he needed to stop and catch his breath. Her constant cheerful chatter bolstered his spirits. Ilse and Mady took him to the ballroom and spent hours teaching him how to dance. Mady's initial comment proved precise. A baroness couldn't move much.

After a month, Baron Arno again inserted himself into Connor's life.

"Since I have seen you go down the stairs from the fourth floor to the first floor, it's time to earn your keep." He spoke in Low Wald speech.

"The Mid-summer Ball is this weekend. I will show you off to several women. It's my intention to breed you to many women. I will pay them to bear your child. Unlike my silly sons, I won't be killing baby boys."

Connor sighed. Will this ever end?

The ball became a nightmare for Connor, who fainted six times while men insisted on dancing with him despite his constant gasps.

***

Over the next two months, six women each spent several nights with him in his bed. He soon learned how to tell when it was planned. After dinner, he felt strange, super-sensuous, and foggy. Later, Ilse explained they had given him a special drug from a world called Zahra-C. It caused the user to feel erotic with heightened sexual arousal that eliminated all resistance to intercourse.

Five were the lady's maids for the baronesses. Ilse told him Baron Arno paid her twenty thousand gold *münzen* to deliver Wendell's child. Like breeding stock, Connor had no choice in these matters and no way to express his feelings.

Late fall, Mady failed to show up to help Ilse get Connor ready for the new day. Connor placed an image of cheerful Mady into Ilse's mind.

"Oh, Mady's a baroness now. Once I get you dressed, I'll take you to her. She will have the same troubles that you had. In time and with practice, she'll be a beautiful baroness."

Connor found Rosa brushing out Mady's long blond tresses. The now armless girl sat erect on the edge of her bed, the red satin gown billowing out ten feet. She wore matching boots to his. Her chandelier earrings dwarfed his. Her dad spent lavishly on her. Her golden veil draped to her chin. She managed a slight smile when he entered. Her bloodshot eyes told Connor all he needed to know. Another horrid misuse of a medical machine.

Seeing what these barons did to their women—to the cheerful, fun-loving young Mady, who brightened his day—deflated Connor. True, he expected this to happen one day, but seeing it happen overnight to Mady caused him to snap.

Until this moment, Connor had been a victim. Seeing Mady drove him from effect to cause.

I'm responsible for myself. I'm responsible for Missy and Elie. They are my Telepath Squad. I'm the man here. And Mady—all she wanted was a chance at a real life. I'm responsible for her, too. She kept me alive. I must help her and Missy and Elie escape this torture world. If it's the last thing I ever do, I'm getting all four of us home to Earth!

He focused. 'Mady, you helped me. I'll help you.'

Tearful eyes looked over at him.

'Yes, it's me. Wendell. I will rescue you and my friends. I'll take you to my world with me. Be brave like you taught me.'

Over breakfast, he sent the two telepaths messages that he would rescue them—that he would get the four of them back to earth. When pressed, he added he didn't know how yet.

'Be patient. I have to help Mady.'

For the next two weeks, Connor followed Mady everywhere she went. He kept up a constant volley of encouraging thoughts placed into her mind. For the first time, Connor made full use of his telepathic ability. While the old, cheerful, gabby Mady was likely gone forever, catching the occasional glimpse of her smile reminded him how vital she had been for him. Day by day, his resolve to rescue them steeled.

More trouble came. This time from Baron Arno's two older sons. They returned home drunk each night and started slapping their baronesses around. One slap and down the woman went. In these boots, their balance was precarious at best. After one push, and without arms to help and as stiff as their corsets were, down they crashed onto the floor.

The first time it happened to Missy, Connor believed Baron Arno would intervene and stop his sons and their despicable behavior. He did nothing. Connor took matters into his own hands.

Each night thereafter, he placed into Arno's mind images of Eric and Hugh stabbing him while he slept. Every night, he made the scenes increasingly violent. Each morning, he watched the three while they ate breakfast.

One day, Baron Arno asked him to stay while the others left the dining room.

"I'll use Low Wald. I'm afraid my two older sons are plotting against me. That often happens, you know. Older

102

barons have been murdered by their sons. Have you detected any such drives in them?"

Connor smiled. He nodded and made the yes click sound Mady had taught him.

Baron Arno sighed. "I thought so. It's that obvious, isn't it?"

Connor nodded.

"I should have them killed. But they are my sons. How can I just kill them?"

Connor grimaced. He didn't wish them dead. He wanted their abuse of the baronesses stopped. What if...

He placed an image of his body with Eric's head on it into Baron Arno's mind. He followed that with an image of Hugh's head.

The Baron looked confused for a moment. "Are you hinting their bodies can be made into something like yours? What am I missing?"

Connor shook his head. He focused on an image of the genetic mutation agent syringe that had been used on him to turn him into a telepath.

"Are you telling me someone has a shot that will mutate their bodies into something like yours and the two baronesses? The man I got them from said they came from Earth in the Sol Empire. Is that right?"

Connor nodded and single clicked a yes. Baron Arno asked more questions. Then Baron Arno asked the key question.

"Telepaths?"

Connor smiled and nodded.

"That would be quite useful. They know our language, unlike you three. What a grand idea."

He asked more questions until Ilse came to ask Wendell if he would be joining Mady in the ballroom for dancing lessons.

"I've contacts. Let me see what can be done. Thank you, Wendell. Thank you."

The Baron rushed off, while Connor took tiny steps, heading to the ballroom.

'You can do it, Mady. I know you can. Tiny steps. Shallow breaths.' Connor encouraged the teen.

Connor picked up Mady's fear. She'd seen Connor faint many times at the last dance and was terrified that would happen to her. He continued to encourage her.

At lunch, he sent encouraging thoughts to Missy and Elie.

'I think I've found a way to prevent Eric and Hugh from abusing you anymore.'

Both women grinned and looked at him, but he sent no more. However, that evening, the two barons again returned drunk and slapped their baronesses hard. The next morning, Missy sported a bruise on her face.

A few days later, the doctor arrived for his bi-monthly visit to check on everyone's health. Connor learned a doctor's checkup was standard because a baronesses couldn't speak and tell someone about anything that might be wrong with them. Even Connor was examined and pronounced healthy.

But the doctor grinned and said, "Missy, Elie. Good news. You are both pregnant again. So is Della. You are joining Berdina, Gerda, Isle, and Rosa. They are due in March and April. You baronesses won't be due until May. Congratulations."

Connor felt sick. He'd been ordered to impregnate the four maids. Eric and Hugh must have gotten to Missy and Elie.

When Connor got the chance, he sent to Missy and Elie. 'Don't worry. I'll rescue your babies too. Raise them as my own, along with Mady. It'll be all right. I promise.'

***

104

One day, a jubilant Baron Arno sent for Connor. He swallowed hard, knowing he'd have to climb the stairs alone all the way to the fifth floor. Coming down continued to terrify Connor.

"Ah, there you are. Look what just came from this Earth of yours."

He showed Connor a container marked Bio Hazzard. Connor read the label. Armless Telepath Galactic Doll Mutation Agent.

"Is this what I need?"

Connor nodded. He had enough to make thousands of doses. Connor felt sick and sent him a picture of one small syringe and his idea of what twenty cc's might be.

The Barron dismissed Connor, who sighed. Alone, he had to descend those stairs. Connor's stomach knotted until he remembered how Mady had talked when he was first learning to navigate without Ilse's steadying arm. Connor knew he had to rescue Mady—just had to.

That evening, the young barons returned from their binge drinking, but neither made it to their suites. That wasn't lost on Missy and Elie. Baron Arno later told Connor what happened.

They'd knocked both men out and injected them with what they believed was the right amount. Now they lay on cots in the baroness creation room in mutation comas. Connor sent him the idea they'd be out for about eight days.

As the eighth day came, he winked at Connor over breakfast.

He announced, "Later today, we'll welcome my older sons back. They've chosen to become valuable telepaths for Bergwald. They'll look just like Wendell here—perfect looking baronesses."

Only the ladies maids gasped, but many eyes opened wide.

Missy sent, 'You did this?'

Connor nodded and smiled. No longer could the barons abuse their baronesses. They'd soon learn just how awful a baroness' life was. Perhaps changes would come.

Connor continued to take control of his life, though he still didn't know how he'd get everyone returned to Earth. Patience. Mady had taught him that.

When the two new assistants ushered Eric and Hugh in their matching red satin billowing ball gowns into the throne room, the terror radiating from their eyes told all. Now they experienced what Mady, Missy, Elie, Connor, and who knows how many other women endured.

Missy smiled. 'Don't know how you did it, but I can never thank you enough!'

Elie sent Connor similar thoughts.

Connor sat on the new throne to Elie's left, while Mady sat on another new one to his left. Often, Mady and Connor smiled at each other, as he continued to keep up her spirits. After this day, Missy and Elie smiled a little more often, too. Connor wanted to but couldn't tell anyone how much their simple smiles meant to him, as he continued to search for a way to rescue them.

Weeks passed. The two telepath barons adapted to their severe handicaps. Ilse taught them click sounds for yes, no, and pee.

One afternoon, Eric, who had always caused the most trouble, didn't join the others on their thrones after lunch. Instead, he continued up to the off-limits fifth floor, before taking a long fall down four flights of stone stairs. Considering the distance fallen, Baron Arno concluded he'd killed himself.

When Connor heard this, he hoped Baron Arno would realize how bad he'd made life for the baronesses and undo as much of their torment as possible.

No such luck. On the positive side, despite his severe limitations, Baron Hugh paid more attention to his wife,

Baroness Else. Connor often caught him flashing a smile her way.

Life relaxed around the throne room, and Connor sensed how much tension the two young men had been causing. But a way to escape hadn't yet appeared to him.

Connor knew what he believed would be the ideal escape. He, Missy, Elie, and Mady would be returned to Chicago along with their jewelry and clothing. The earrings and veils could then be sold to help support them, particularly Mady. He expected the three telepaths would have several million credits in their accounts, if they hadn't been written off as deceased.

The pregnancies of Missy and Elie added to Connor's sense of urgency. The young barons had murdered their sons because they would have grown up to look like Connor. Back then they only guessed at this result. Connor hadn't arrived yet. What would happen to these new babies?

He guessed if they were girls like their mothers, Baron Arno would make them into baronesses, marrying them off to other young barons. Such daughters would inherit their mother's appearance—a perfect body form for a baroness if he believed Ilse. But if the babies were sons, then what? Connor's appearance—a male telepathic Galactic Doll—would allow for mass breeding of others like themselves. Thanks to Connor, Baron Arno now had good reasons to keep a male version around.

And having added his two older sons, Baron Arno could breed as many telepaths as desired. Perhaps he planned starting a business. Purchase your perfect baroness here. At least he didn't bother breeding Connor any longer, for which he was grateful.

Ideas swirled around Connor's mind, but he could imagine no way to undo the introduction of this many telepath Galactic Dolls onto this world. He had no idea how he could rescue the two telepaths before they gave birth. But he did have eight months to work out their escape.

What to do about the future babies from the lady's maids and others he'd been forced to impregnate? They'd be giving birth before May. No matter how Connor imagined the situation, an explosion of Galactic Doll telepaths and thus telepathic baronesses seemed unavoidable.

At the Winter Ball, all eyes focused on Connor, Hugh, Missy, and Elie. To a lesser extent on Mady because Baron Arno tossed out feelers for a marriage deal. His announcement caused a stir, even though he spoke in Low Wald speech.

"Barons and future barons, I now have in my power the ability to make perfect baronesses. Just look at the incredible Baronesses Missy and Elie. And these two males—my son Hugh and Wendell. Except for their male genitals, their bodies are that of perfect baronesses. What is even more important is that both breed true. No matter who the father is, Baroness Missy and Baroness Elie will bear children identical to themselves, perfect in all dimensions. Any woman bred to the male version will have children who are perfect baronesses. No longer will barons be forced to scour their kingdoms for suitable young women to become their baronesses. You can breed your own."

That caused quite a stir. Connor and Hugh almost fainted from constant dancing. It seemed as if every baron, young or old, had to dance with them, examining their bodies close up.

Before her transformation, Mady loved the dances, but now Connor sensed she was grateful that the barons' attention lay anywhere other than her. He didn't need telepathy to sense Baron Arno planned to breed Hugh and him to many more women. And soon. He had to rescue everyone. The how continued to elude him.

Connor had one clue. This kingdom exported their ball gowns to Cass-C. Four times a year, one of their spaceships ferried crates of gowns to that world, returning with the tall boots the baronesses wore. If they brought back other things, Connor hadn't discovered. Often he dreamed of somehow sneaking aboard the ship, flying to Cass-C. From there, he could catch a transport to Earth. But could any of them walk to the spaceport on their own and without being seen? Beyond impossible.

During the winter, the erotic drug found its way into both Connor and Hugh's evening drinks. By nightfall and in a stupor of sensation, the men had no resistance to the strange women bedding them for a brief time. Connor lost track of how often it happened.

The Spring Ball attracted barons from more distant kingdoms. Baron Arno made a similar speech. Once more, the four became magnets for the men. This time Mady didn't escape young suitors, several keeping her occupied.

The babies arrived. Once a maid delivered her baby, others tended the child in the basement where Baron Arno had established a nursery. The mothers could not see their child. They'd been paid; the babies belonged to Baron Arno.

Both Missy and Elie often sent pleading images to Hugh and Connor trying to be allowed to keep their babies come May. Connor knew he needed to act before that, because the Baron would take their children away as he'd done with the servants.

Chapter 13 The Escape

May Day proved life changing for Connor. Having been cooped up all winter, Connor welcomed the announcement that everyone should spend the afternoon outside in the courtyard. He and Mady found themselves in the rear of those descending the stairs to the main doors. The two exchanged smiles. Mady's eyes looked bright like they had before being turned into a baroness. Fresh air and a taste of freedom, he thought. If only they didn't take a deadly fall. Billowing gowns threatened each. And the two very pregnant baronesses moved far slower than the others.

Once in the courtyard, Mady pressed close to Connor, now unable to put and arm around him as she used to do. Both leaned toward the other, grinning. Connor sensed just how much Mady missed the freedom to step outside when she wished.

Connor noticed Baron Arno left in his noisy vehicle, just as they reached the courtyard. He watched as guards shut the large wooden doors. No chance of just walking out of the castle complex. Worse, the gates remained shut most of the time. Long ago, Connor realized he could not open those doors by himself.

Soon the two pregnant women headed indoors, having made the click sounds for pee. The others returned, leaving Connor and Mady still milling around, both unwilling to return to captivity.

Late afternoon, the guards opened the gates to let the vehicle inside. Baron Arno stepped out and glared at Connor. The Baron's unexpected reaction caused Connor to back up a step, almost falling while flailing non-existent arms. After all, the man had ordered everyone outside for the afternoon.

Curious, Connor probed the Baron's mind, but sensed nothing at all. Baron Arno's mind had vanished, leaving behind a vacuum. Mady took the Baron's hint and made her slow way inside. But Connor stood still and tried again to contact the Baron's mind.

"What are you doing?" Baron Arno said in a gruff voice.

Connor sensed something was off in the man's voice. He thought it lacked an overtone or frequency.

Connor's eyes opened wide. His mouth followed suit.

"What?" Baron Arno said, his attitude now very different from lunchtime.

The Baron's unblinking eyes drilled into Connor's, further convincing Connor.

"Okay, you are a telepath. I can read lips, you know. Speak up, Wendell."

Connor mouthed, "You are a robot. Are you one of those rogue robots we're looking for?"

As soon as he mouthed the words, he wondered how Baron Arno could understand English. Always he used those language translation units. Connor always wore one inside his gown, as did the other two baronesses.

"Well, that didn't last long. Wendell, let's go inside. We need to talk."

Connor stumbled his way inside, pushed along too fast by the Barron. That the robot didn't yet gauge how slowly they had to walk gave Connor further hints this was a robot imposter. Baron Arno forced him into the baroness fabrication room and closed the door. Connor swallowed.

The Baron spoke English. "Yes, I'm impersonating Baron Arno for a time. There are things we need from this kingdom. I'm called Kimko. Been observing everyone for days, learning how to pretend to be this pathetic human Baron

Arno. What am I going to do with you telepaths? There's four of you right now. I know Baron Arno purchased an entire container of the telepath Galactic Doll mutation agent. He plans to make an army of telepaths. We can't have that, can we?"

Connor mouthed, "Are you going to kill us?"

The robot pulled on his chin. "That depends upon you and your fellow telepaths. Unlike what you think, we are not out to destroy humans. But we need certain supplies this kingdom has in abundance. I'm here to harvest ivy wig plants. Its nectar is a main component of synthetic skin. But I will not hesitate to kill if I must. I can't have you letting everyone know I'm not Baron Arno. I don't trust you or the other telepaths."

"What about a mutually beneficial deal?" Connor asked, sensing an opening.

"Proposal?"

Connor relaxed. The enemy robot wanted a deal to avoid explaining many deaths.

"I want to go home to Earth. Arrange for telepaths and Mady to be taken there, along with our belongings. That way, we'll be gone. No one to hinder you."

Kimko said nothing for a minute. Connor imagined the robot calculating outcomes and possibilities.

"Promising deal. I must send along those babies too. And the rest of the canister of the mutation agent. I don't want someone coming along later and making ten thousand more telepaths. That stupid Baron Arno didn't know that container held enough to make that many. Swear you will see that container destroyed."

"I swear."

"Good. From this world—"

"What is this world called? We don't know where we are," Connor mouthed.

"Better you don't. From this world, there is no direct route to your Sol Empire. I can send you to Cass-C. That's their main trade route. Then catch a ship to Earth."

"That is acceptable. How soon can we leave?"

"Let the others know not to out me. Play along with what I say. Tonight, I'll get you, Hugh, Missy, Elie, Mady, and the five babies on your way to Cass-C along with all your possessions, meager as they are. Do we have a deal? If you double-cross me, I'll eliminate all of you. My mission is too vital to allow pathetic humans to interfere."

"Deal. I'll let them know. Thank you."

"Like I said. We aren't trying to kill humans. You are a most pathetic race. Perhaps when you return, you can convince others of that. I will make preparations now."

With that, he left the room. Connor got to the door at the last instant. Had he not, he had no way to open it. He'd be trapped. No one knew where he was. With care, he climbed the stairs to the throne room.

Mady's grin welcomed him, as did Missy. Connor thought both looked worried that he hadn't followed Mady inside. He felt for his throne's step. Pausing a moment to get his breath back, Connor smiled. After reaching his throne and sitting, he made contact with the others.

"We escape tonight. All of us and Mady and our things. A rogue robot just replaced Baron Arno. We've reached a deal. He's sending us home as long as we ignore him and don't tell others he's a robot."

Mady's eyes opened wider than Connor thought possible. The largest smile ever appeared. She nodded vigorously. Missy mouthed a thank you. The others grinned.

Time crept. Would dinner ever come? When the bell sounded, Connor forced himself to stay calm and pay close attention. He couldn't afford a nasty fall now, so close to being rescued.

At the large supper table and while the maids lifted veils and fed them, Baron Arno outlined his latest plan.

"You know Cass-C is our biggest trading partner. I've decided to send our perfect baronesses to visit that world. I want them to show off just how magnificent our baronesses are. Hugh, Wendell, Missy, Elie, and, yes, Mady, will go and represent the best we have to offer. Our ambassadors of goodwill. No, your maids won't need to go with you. I've arranged for other maids on Cass-C to assist you. The ship leaves tonight. I shall join you in a few days. During my short trip, Baroness Della is in charge. Peppi, you act as the man of the castle."

The eleven-year-old boy grinned.

After dinner, they adjourned to their private suites to prepare for the trip. Ilse had packed a huge crate with all seven of his gowns, heels, and other personal items.

"Isn't this wonderful, Wendell? Let me brush out your hair. Look perfect when you leave. Mady must be thrilled. She'll get to see another world."

Connor smiled and nodded. With effort, he controlled his excitement and navigated down three flights of stairs without falling. When the five stood by the entrance doors, Baron Arno joined them. He led them out to a waiting vehicle Connor hadn't seen before. He likened it to an EMAC on wheels. Already workers had loaded five large crates. One by one, they walked up to the vehicle where a man lifted them inside, depositing them on a seat. Next, a woman came out bringing the newborn babies in basinets. The man lifted them inside, too.

A surprised look appeared on Missy and Elie's faces.

Connor sent, 'I'm rescuing them too. We can raise them as our own. I can't let them stay here.'

Missy sent, 'You are the greatest man I've ever known!'

114

The image she used showed Connor sitting on a king's throne. He flashed her a smile before Baron Arno appeared, depositing the container carrying the mutation agent.

'You are incredible!' Missy sent. 'No more mutations here.'

Again, he smiled. A man wearing a servant's uniform walked up to Baron Arno.

"Baron, I've received word from the control tower. Your ship's flight plan to Cass-C is approved. You can leave as soon as it's loaded."

"Very good. Goodbye for now."

Baron Arno waved to the group. The driver pulled the back panel down, leaving them in darkness. Soon, Connor felt movement. He held his breath. The robot could betray them, dumping them into a mass grave or something. For once, Connor loved hiding in the darkness, his worried face hidden from the others. Just when he became convinced the robot had betrayed him, the vehicle stopped. When the driver opened the back door, Connor felt tingles up his spine.

Spaceport odors assaulted his nose. Close by sat a deep space transport, whose markings Connor had never seen. Two crewmen exited the ship, received the infants, and loaded them onto the ship before returning, before returning for the others. Within minutes, Connor and the others sat in seats, safety belts on. On other seats, the babies were strapped in. The oldest was two months. The youngest, just a week.

Grunts accompanied scuffing sounds. Connor imagined the men loading the five crates. At last, one entered and deposited the mutation agent container on another seat. He then closed the door.

"Liftoff in two minutes," he said in English.

When the ship rose, Mady leaned into Connor. Her bright eyes and gleaming smile warmed his heart. He'd achieved what he'd intended.

Missy mouthed, "I love you." Several times, until Connor duplicated it and flushed.

Over the intercom, the pilot said, "Cass-C in sixteen hours."

Connor wondered if the pilot would handle their many needs, especially the two pregnant women.

***

Back at the spaceport, Kimku waited for the ship to depart. The pilot: Limu, one of the newer rogue robot models. Kimku looked at his watch. Two minutes after liftoff, he pressed a button on a detonator.

"These greedy humans think they can become a telepath, make a fortune, and then get their bodies restored. Damned Telepath Squad people. Well, thanks to Teslenko we're convincing future humans never to do such a thing again. He's gotten to that pesky Parkinson and other telepaths from their Squad Two. I just got to three more from Squad One. Maybe humans will shy away from ever getting mutated just to plague us. They will soon find their mutation choice is a permanent one."

Laughing, he returned to his vehicle and headed to the castle.

***

The spaceship lifted off, gaining control tower clearance, before jumping into hyperspace. Limu held the ship at low altitude, watching the ship's chronograph. He heard a faint boom. The deed done, he sped up and jumped into hyperspace. An hour later with the ship on autopilot, he checked on the passengers. As Kimku predicted, his passengers were in comas, a fact he checked. The yellowish mutation gas filled the cabin, but it had no effect on the robot.

With comas verified, he followed Kimku's orders and stripped each person, leaving only their stockings, garter belts, and boots on them. Kimku didn't know how long their comas

116

would last, but they needed to be able to walk on their own in case they woke up too soon. The flight to Cass-C took twenty hours. Limu waited for six hours before evacuating the mutation gas from the ship.

As the ship approached Cass-C, the control tower inserted his ship in the queue to land. Like mosquitoes, myriad ships dotted the skies above the hub of the Federation of Planets. The tower locked onto the controls of the ship, guiding it in the holding pattern until a landing pad opened.

Limu made a secure call in English. "Am in a landing pattern above Hoffdorf. Where do we meet? Package still unresponsive."

After a slight delay, he received, "Take Pad 10222. That's next to my ship."

When the tower notified him he was cleared to land, Limu told them the desired pad location. Once the ship landed, a giant lift moved it to the pad, freeing up the landing spot for the next spaceship.

Pretending to be human, the robot greeted his connection. "Are you my connection to Earth, Sol Empire?"

"Aye, that'd be me. Harry Hog, at your service. What's my cargo? I wasn't told."

"Some members of Earth's Telepath Squads. Three who were missing have been found, along with others. They are in comas. Transport should be a breeze. Let's transfer them now."

"Babies, even. My god, when will it stop?" Harry asked. "Yeah, recognize those three from their wanted posters. Plastered on boards in every Federation spaceport. Kidnapped. Bet they'll be glad to get home."

After stowing the last of the gear, Harry lifted off from Hoffdorf. Once in hyperspace, he checked on his unconscious passengers before placing a Long Distance Comm call to Chicago Galactic Defense.

"Yeah, this is Harry Hog out of LA. I've just picked up three of your missing telepaths. The ones who got kidnapped. Someone found them and brought them to Cass-C. I'd like my reward. Over."

Later, he answered, "Yeah, well, they're in a mutation coma. Empty canister that probably held the mutation agent. Correct, no arms. Where do I land them? Over."

"What? They can't be dropped off in Chicago? You want me to take them to Domes? Over."

The voice responded, "Yes, Domes. The geneticists who restore telepaths live there. The recovery operation has moved to Domes. Do you have their names? Over."

"From the wanted posters," Harry replied, giving their names. "But there are more than three. Five adults. Five infants. What about my reward? Over."

"Will relay that to the authorities on Domes. Send us your contact information. Over and out."

Chapter 14 Moves and Meetings

May 2375
Domes

As we flew over the planet coming down, we spotted countless orbiting solar panels. As the transport descended, thousands of the transparent domes appeared. I landed my deep space transport at the only operational landing pad on Domes. From my daughter Isabella, I knew only ten domes had been recovered and made operational. She told me each dome housed around five thousand people, making the total population now close to fifty thousand. Well, we were about to add to those numbers.

As I powered down, Katya said, "I didn't believe you could pilot, Molly. You've convinced me."

"I want to learn to pilot a spaceship," Anka said.

Not to be outdone, Donata said, "Me, too. Can you teach us, Mom?"

I laughed. "Yes, kids, but first you have to learn to read and write and handle math. School for you children."

I got "aw's" as expected. Hans opened the hatch, while everyone gazed at our new home world.

Isabella and her husband Owen welcomed us. Because they'd both been mutated several times, they looked youthful, though both were in their mid thirties. Their two children, Maria, seven, and Tomaso, five, stood beside them wide-eyed, staring at us. Beside them stood the armless Dr. Ivy Worth and ex-commander Lia Johnston. Behind them, my younger sisters, Celeste and Eve waited.

"Mom, glad you finally joined us." Isabella said, "Lia Johnston is the President of our High Council. Dr. Ivy Worth will give you your medical exams. Yes, she's now one of our three medical doctors."

"Wow. Congratulations, Dr. Worth. You never cease to amaze me," I said. "This is Hans, my mate. Our children in age order, Donata, Wendel, Franz, Bonny, Hugh, and Calli. This is Katya Binsk and her two oldest, Anka and Cyryl. Oh, yeah. That's Bishop, my security man."

Lia said, "Welcome to Domes. We reject no one who wants to settle here. Eve and Celeste have already begun your immigration paperwork. We've set aside a section of Dome Ten for armless people. We're putting you in the same dome.

"Dr. Worth here started it. Then, three others from the Telepath Squad got sent here because, like yourselves, they were subject to a massive overdose of the mutation agent. Eve and Lara have yet to find a cure to regenerate arms. We work hard to accommodate your kind. We confiscated kitchen facilities from Bella. We've a supply of those Cass-C robot assistants on wheels, and we've brought in a supply of the Sixth Invader helper machines."

I laughed. "My goodness, Lia, is there nothing you haven't thought of to make our lives a little easier?"

She grinned. "We try harder. Have to. We are desperate for medical doctors. Can't afford to lose Dr. Ivy here. Besides, we've just had another call. Three more of the missing Telepath Squad members have been found and are on their way here. Should arrive tomorrow. But what's unclear is there are five adults and five infants, not three. For once, my foresight is paying dividends.

"Anyway, your sisters will take you to your new suites. Volunteers can help Bishop transport your possessions. I'll see your ship gets parked in the lot. Tomorrow, pay a visit to our Immigration Officer, your sister, Janine Le Clair, and get the forms signed. She can handle setting up bank accounts and transferring funds from Earth. I recommend moving as much as possible from Earth banks. Things are unsettled there. Last I heard, anyway."

She gave me a hug and left.

Dr. Ivy said, "Golly, are they all telepaths and with telekinesis, too?" Her eyes swept over us.

"Yes, someone implanted everyone on Earth to have more babies. Suspect the Alitos, but we've no proof. Didn't figure that out until after I had Calli. But what happened to you, Dr. Ivy?"

She flushed. "Well, we needed more facts about the overdose that brings on telekinesis. I gambled that using telekinesis I could manage to be a doctor. I overdosed myself and got Eve what she needed to know about it. I succeeded in becoming a medical doctor, but by the end of each day, I'm exhausted. I had no idea using telekinesis this much drained me. But I keep going, patching up people. Come on. My office is in Dome Ten. It's a ways. I'll have to check each one of you before you meet with the Immigration Officer."

Celeste carried year-old Calli, while Hans pushed Hugh in a stroller. Dr. Ivy had to wear the tall heels as we did. Our slow paces fit perfectly. Since Dr. Ivy had lived here the longest, four years, she explained things as we went.

"We're entering the outside entrance tunnel now. Every dome has one. Each dome has six exit tunnels. There's a sign above each one. Notice the sign says 'To' and which other Dome it leads to. We're in Dome Ten. This way. Main plaza. Lots of people. It's called Main Street. All other side streets come off it. They're numbered—evens on that side—odds on this side. Every plaza has an information kiosk with detailed maps posted beside them. Since carrying things is problematical for us, I found memorizing key locations ideal."

I asked about food.

"Each plaza has restaurants. Each dome has agricultural plots. Some grow synthetic food, but others produce fresh veggies. A few provide chicken and eggs. We've got milk production going in one dome. Small scale so far. We're working on opening more domes. That's likely to change. Every day, we learn more about these domes and what lived here ages ago.

"Until you know about what dangers lie outside these domes, please don't go outside. Some plants are deadly to us. Some animals are poisonous. A medical doctor must go with every scouting party that leaves the domes. Since I have the least seniority, I get to go along with them. In these heels, that's quite a challenge. Couldn't do it if I didn't have telekinesis, that's for sure.

"Ah, see that sign. Tunnel Six. The entrance sign says To Dome Ten. Wait for Cart."

"Look Mom!" Donata said. "We're in a tunnel! Where does it lead? Do we walk down it? Kind of dark."

Dr. Ivy said, "Kids, just wait. This tunnel exits the sloping side of the dome. Soon, an electric cart will come for us. This automated system requires no intervention. The system senses the size of our group and provides a cart big enough for us. An engineer named Holly Ann got these operational."

"Is her husband a teacher named Kyle?" I asked.

It was. I knew them back in Chicago years ago.

The children loved traveling on the electric cart and didn't want the trip to end.

"Can we ride it again? Pretty please?" Donata said.

I smiled. We entered another plaza. Dr. Ivy had us turn around and read the sign. Tunnel One. To Dome One. Someone must have thought out every detail.

Celeste said, "Armless people are quartered in the southwest quadrant. Streets with odd numbers. Your suites

122

are numbered 6143 and 6145. Dr. Ivy lives in suite 6141, next door. The other three ex-Teleport Squad members are in 6135, 6137, and 6139. We don't know who or what arrives tomorrow, but they'll be put in suites beyond yours. Okay, kids. Can you direct us to our suites?"

I appreciated her challenge. Donata, Anka, Cyryl, and Wendel played detectives, giggling a lot, but they soon led us to the right street, 61st Street.

As we turned right onto the street, Dr. Ivy added, "The streets in all domes are labeled the same. Learn the pattern here and it's the same in every dome. Sure makes for easy house calls."

"Doctors made house calls?"

"On Domes, we take your health seriously. There are only fifty thousand of us. All life is precious," Dr. Ivy said. "Just don't call me after suppertime. I'm often asleep. Use my abilities too much during the day."

Celeste said, "Tomorrow after you visit Janine and get your ID cards, I'll show you how to order groceries, clothes, and other necessities. By the way, Eve's new lab is in Suite 901. That's on the same side of Main Street, but way up there."

"Schools?" I asked.

"Suite 101. Each dome has their own beginning grades school. There's only one school for high school and above. It's in Dome One. We have many younger kids, but few teens. The High Council is planning for more high schools, but that's about ten years out," Celeste said. "And Wanda and Otto live in 6133. Our new therapy offices are in 6131. Greg and I live in 6129. Eve and Sam live in 6127. We're all close.

"Most of our other sisters and their families are in Dome One. Like Leslie, Janine, Deanna, and General Bev. She lost her mate, Julie, to one of the poisonous plants outside the domes. Don't go outside the domes. It's very dangerous."

"Mom, is this it?" Donata interrupted us.

We'd walked down 61st Street. Above an open doorway rested a large sign: 6143. And 6145 was opposite us, across the street, Katya's new home.

"You found it," Aunt Celeste said.

"And ours is just across the street," said Anka. "Come on, Cyryl. Let's see what it's like."

Celeste said, "We took the liberty of getting the homes setup with necessities. If you like what's there, Janine will debit your accounts for it. Importing things from the major worlds is expensive."

Dr. Ivy said, "Go in. Look around. Change diapers. I'll start my physical checks in a few minutes."

Hans and I had just entered when Donata poked her head out of a side room, her eyes bright.

"Mom, we all have our own beds this time. Gonna be great!"

Just like the streets, a ceramic surface formed the floors. I later learned the material was the same as the transparent domes, only a brownish pigment had been added. No building inside the dome had a door or even a roof, though later I saw people had hung curtains to gain a bit of privacy. Thus, interior lighting was needed only at night.

The suite had six bedrooms, including the larger master bedroom. The five smaller ones held a narrow bed, a dresser, a wardrobe, a desk, and two chairs. Spartan, but great for the children. For now, we kept Calli and Hugh in the same bedroom. The single bathroom, while foreign in appearance at first glance, contained a bath-shower combo, toilet, and sink, with open shelves to store towels and things. I envisioned lines forming to use this room.

The spacious living room held two couches, numerous sofas, and a large entertainment center. But the kitchen-dining room impressed me. As large as the living room, this place was a dream. I could tell the new construction. One section held a normal height kitchen set: sink, counter tops, cabinets, fridge, stove, and dishwasher. Along the next wall, they had installed a low to the ground version confiscated from Bella. A long table and chairs could seat our small army. In one corner, a dozen various sized yokes that the men on Bella used to carry things lay stacked, ready for our use.

"Back here," Celeste said, drawing my attention to a narrow side door.

I peeked and saw this tiny room held our laundry machines along with cleaning equipment.

"Check this out," she pointed to a small device attached to the side of the kitchen doorway. "It's the message system. Press the big button. It plays any dome-wide messages. The two arrow buttons allow you to move through saved messages. The trash can button deletes them. Go ahead and press it."

I used my nose. The device played: Trash day is today. Place your can outside your door.

I noticed a large plastic bin on wheels sitting in one corner. It had no lid, for which I was thankful. I smiled.

"This is one of Holly Ann's many inventions. Let's make lunch. While many aspects take getting used to, overall, I find this is a very pleasant place to live, though I miss going outside."

As my horde sat around the big table having lunch, Celeste said, "We're bringing in more Sixth Invader machines today. We'll put two hair-nail machines in the living room, because there won't be enough room for them in the bedrooms. But we'll try to acquire a dressing machine for each bedroom. We'll station the robot cook in the kitchen."

"Where are the grocery stores?" I asked.

Celeste laughed. "Isn't anything like we have on Earth. The comm set in the living room. It's both voice and touch activated. You press the Groceries menu. Select the items you want. When the process finishes, it will display a delivery time.

Workers in the food department will fill the order and deliver it to your front door. Avoid ordering items marked 'Off-world.' Those take forever to get here. Another of Holly Ann's inventions. We need more computer programmers.

"Oh, yes. The grade school is in Suite 101. That's the first street just inside Tunnel One and at the end of the street. Can't miss it. All grades in one classroom."

I had the kids put their dirty dishes into the dishwasher when they finished before they dashed off to play with Katya's kids—an oxymoron because of the tall heels we had to wear. I hoped Eve had invented a foot cure, if nothing else.

After we ate and I nursed Calli, Dr. Ivy joined us. She wore a white blouse and black pants. Her Galactic Doll form couldn't be missed. She sat on a chair, removed her heels, and slipped her black bag from her shoulder. Out came a clipboard. One column held our names. Using her toes, she pulled out the usual medical devices. Blood pressure, heart actions, temperature, eyes, nose, throat. Bit spooky seeing them operate via telekinesis. She checked me over before pronouncing me healthy. In time, my family checked out healthy.

Katya joined us to be checked by Dr. Ivy, too.

She said, "Had to get away from the noise. Anka, Cyryl, Wendel, and Donata are going to it. Comm set has their favorite Hunt the Dragon game on it. And your younger kids are avid watchers." She laughed.

Dr. Ivy said, "I'll check on them in a bit. First, I'm glad I have you three here without the children. I've news. This is a fledgling colony." She explained the breeding rules.

"Katya, you'll be excused from this rule, even if you apply for citizenship of Domes. Your situation is..."

"Unique," Katya said with a grin. "With luck, it won't happen for fifty more years."

Dr. Ivy smiled and then spoke in a serious tone. "Eve and I have been gathering extensive data on the results of these massive mutation overdoses. Yes, we know certain glands in our heads have more than doubled in size and are partially responsible for our key abilities. But there has been much more to the mutation. For example, my own IQ went up over a hundred points after I overdosed myself. The three other Telepath Squad members who were attacked and given similar overdoses, Phil Baker, Jackson Dells, and Honey Kellog, have experienced fantastic IQ changes.

"But there's another factor which Eve and I have proven, one that has altered Domes official policy about us. We're classified as a new subspecies because of our physical attributes and mental powers. Eve and I have shown that the average size of our mutated brains is double that of everyone else."

She paused, allowing us to digest that fact. Since we didn't respond, she explained further.

"We can learn many times faster than one would expect. Jackson had been trained as an engineer. After the mutation, he has picked up doctorates in both mechanical engineering and electrical engineering. All that in about one year's time. Honey had been a general secretary before, but in two years, she's earned doctorates in linguistics and agricultural production. Me, I've picked up four years of advanced medical studies in just one year.

"What I'm saying is that those of us who have had the massive mutation can learn at fantastic rates. We have a thirst for knowledge. I'm currently studying botany to better help our outside work parties. My guess is Donata will be ready for high school work in three years or less."

"Wow! I didn't realize that. That implant had me focused on making babies and raising them. I couldn't do much else. What does that mean here on Domes?"

Dr. Ivy said, "Our children inherit our mutation from us. At first, the High Council wanted to keep us mutants isolated. Hence, we're all living in this dome. We could only breed among ourselves. They don't believe telepathy and telekinesis compensates enough for our handicaps. This colony depends upon work from all members. I had to prove to them I could handle being a true doctor.

"That's been very hard. I had to use my powers throughout the day. When I get home for supper, I'm exhausted. Sometimes I fall asleep without eating or cleaning up. Grueling. But I didn't quit. I had to prove I could be a doctor. After all, it was my decision to get myself super-mutated for science. I could have had Eve make me a clone body, but I stuck it out. Glad I did. Life's hard, but so rewarding. The ability to learn so much so quickly is vital, as is how fast I can solve medical situations.

"Anyway, when Eve and I presented these results to the High Council, they changed their minds. Now, it's permissible and desirable for any normal male to breed with us mutant women. Spread the genes. And they allow mutant men to breed with any normal woman twice. Their goal is to increase the knowledge level of this world without having too many of our kind in the population, since we have definite handicaps."

"Makes perfect sense. Are they encouraging us to study and learn more advanced things?" Hans said. "I've already got degrees in astro-geology, computer programming, and a computer systems engineering. But no doctorates. What skills do they need the most here?"

"Ask the President of the High Council, Lia Johnston. She's on top of those things. All I know is we need more medical personnel. Nurses and doctors particularly. Pay Janine at the Immigration Office a visit and then stop by Lia Johnston's office," Dr. Ivy said.

Celeste volunteered to help cart the kids. Katya and her two joined us. By now, we couldn't separate Donata from Anka or Wendel from Cyryl if we tried. Same ages, best buddies.

Janine hugged me and said, "Gosh, you still look like you did when we first met at that pizza place in Chicago!"

"Too many mutations," I said. "You look much older. How many children do you have?"

"Three already. Let's get you registered and ID cards made. You heard that Bev lost her mate, Julie, didn't you? Very toxic plants grow outside the domes."

I left funds in my Chicago account. They'd be used by Galactic Housing to maintain my ranch home. Hans transferred all his funds—close to eleven million credits.

Janine said, "We're planning a big welcome Molly party this weekend. I'll send you the details. Bev wants to see you."

A tear formed. I'd forgotten how much my many clone sisters meant to me. I should have moved here years ago.

We then stopped at the President's office. Ex-commander Lia looked much older than I'd last seen her. We handled Katya's situation first.

"I'll be the Third Invader's ambassador to Domes. My kids can attend your school, right?"

"Yes, the ID cards allow access to everything. Officially as an ambassador, you won't be expected to help Domes. But if you have any specific skills that we might use, let me know. Also, you super-mutants learn at incredible rates. Feel free to scan over our website listing the more critical positions we need filled. It's just you're not obligated to do so. We're still working out how to fit you handicapped people into our society. Dr. Ivy Worth showed us that your lack of arms isn't the barrier we once thought.

"Hans, I see your three degrees. We are desperate for engineers who can help get these alien dome life support systems up and running, repaired sometimes. We have a geology unit that is surveying this world. We'll then have an idea what resources are available. If only we had EMACs or some of those drones Molly brought back that GPan is using to explore new worlds."

"Hey, I have my own EMAC," I said. "I could buy EMACs for Domes. But how do I get them here? Also, I left the Friendship deep space transport back at New O'Hare. I could have it brought here, if that would help."

"That would be wonderful! On another note, you've probably heard this from Dr. Ivy, but we've changed our policies towards you super-mutants." She repeated what Dr. Ivy had told us. "We need many more people with superior knowledge and educators who can pass that along to the next generations.

"What I'm getting at is this. I know you have a clone body ready. A body swap and you'll have a normal body again. I know how much you must want to get a normal body again. Remember, I was once where you're at, more or less. Getting my arms back—well, that changed me for the better.

"But with your new ability for fast-track learning, the High Council asks you to put body swaps into normal clone bodies off, to learn many more things, and to share that knowledge or put it to use. One factor that remains unknown is once you have body swapped, what will happen to your acquired knowledge. A big IQ drop is a given. We're not ordering you not to get body swapped now, just encouraging you to put your unique gifts to benefit domes for a time.

"Molly, with six kids at home—I don't know what happened to you. A baby every year? Isn't that pushing it? As handicapped as you are, how can you manage? You must have your hands full."

I laughed. "I can't seem to hang onto my hands. GMed has begun giving new mothers a low dose of the normal Galactic Doll agent. It heals any Galactic Doll body damage the

130

pregnancy and birth caused. If I had a choice, I would have them a few years apart. But we got implanted."

Lia gasped.

"Don't know who's responsible. My hunch is Alitos. Must make babies was the implanted command. Many women did just that. It even altered the reproduction cycle of Katya. Had ten children. Now that we've erased her implant, we think her body is back to normal. Next eggs in fifty years. Even affected Ambassador L'Grina."

She received a call.

"The ship bringing the three missing telepaths is on a landing vector. The pilot is requesting doctors and emergency assistance," Lia said.

Hans and Katya took the children home, while I joined Lia, Dr. Ivy, and others, heading to meet the ship.

The pilot opened the bay doors and called for help.

"Here they are. Still in a coma, I think. Lord knows where they came from or what happened to them," Harry Hog said.

When Lia pressed him further, he said, "I've a standing contract with GPan to retrieve missing personnel. They told me to drop them off here and collect my retrieval reward. I'm just a go-between. Picked them up from a transport on Cass-C."

"Oh, no! Babies!" Dr. Ivy said. "They're all in mutation comas, but look at the adults. Those earrings. Those golden veils. What's going on with them?"

Harry said, "I've no idea. That pile of gowns there—he told me they were wearing them. Got crates of apparel to unload too."

Dr. Ivy said, "Dear god. This newborn is dead. Move them to my clinic in Dome Ten pronto! Call Eve, please."

The workers used carts to transport these people. Once deposited in her clinic, she and Eve examined the surviving infants. Dr. Ivy determined they were a month or two old at the most. In comas with no arms, Eve concluded they had been exposed to the same agent as the adults.

Hans joined us. "I recognize those three." He rattled off their names.

Eve examined them. "Conclusion: since the three are in mutation comas and I don't see any extensive physical damage, I suspect another overdose situation. Blood samples will confirm."

"No ID on the second man?" Dr. Ivy asked. "Or this other young woman. She can't be out of her teens. The mutation is making her appear older than she is."

Hans replied. "No, never seen or heard of them before. Should we remove those veil things? What about those monstrous earrings?"

Dr. Ivy said, "Veils, yes. Best wait on the earrings. Never know. They might wish to continue wearing them. We'll set up a round-the-clock watch on these people. No idea when they'll wake up."

An hour later, Eve rushed back, bringing assistants with her, including Dr. Ivy. Alerted via telepathy, I joined them.

Eve said, "We need to get the adults hooked up to the stasis monitoring units at once. Otherwise, the mutation will deplete calcium from their bones and worse. Pregnant women first."

Dr. Ivy said, "Start IV plug in a leg vein?"

"Yes, we'll need five," Eve said. "And then the infants."

Workers rolled stasis pods into the lab. Dr. Ivy handled the insertions.

When Dr. Ivy had Missy on one pod and hooked up, Eve powered up the consumption monitor. After they had the five adults hooked up, Eve hovered around Missy's readout.

"Wow, just as I feared. Massive absorption of calcium and other minerals. I hope we caught it in time to prevent serious bodily deterioration."

"Look, massive brain-growing protein components, too," Dr. Ivy added. "Has any fetal damage been done? Possible labor while in the coma. We must watch them around the clock. Good catch Eve!"

Isabella dropped by to examine the language translation devices found among the apparel in the crates. After a bit of testing, she concluded they were set to translate an unknown tongue into English. She claimed the language was akin to German.

Conclusion: the two strangers spoke this language. Thus, Isabella fiddled with the devices until she had them working in reverse. Then, she placed them in the lab near the comatose victims.

I volunteered for first watch. I saw the physical drain this incredible volley of action had on Dr. Ivy. She looked exhausted. Telekinesis powers came with a cost.

I swore to make sure we used our feet and toes far more than we had been. We couldn't depend upon using that power for everything. If one woman went into labor now, Dr. Ivy wouldn't have enough energy left to use her powers. She'd be helpless. We must strike a balance between using our feet, the various machines, and our special power.

Chapter 15 Recoveries

May 15: the Day of Screams. Nine awoke from their massive mutation comas. Severe headaches ruled. The four babies led the way, screaming—a sign of health. Hans and I joined Dr. Ivy, Eve, Celeste, Otto, Wanda, three nurses and the other two doctors. Everyone woke within minutes of each other. To me, that suggested all overdosed at the same instant.

Celeste and I focused on sending calming flows, because the cries from the babies were shrill and intense. The doctors had me breast feed the four babies. One by one, they quieted. Thank heavens. Otherwise, I sensed the doctors were near sedating them to bring calm.

The three lost telepaths' initial yells subsided into a mixture of elation and complaints of massive headaches. The other two spoke in a different language. Celeste placed the language units near them while Dr. Ivy took charge.

"Quiet. You are safe on Domes. Let us doctors do what we can for you. We know about your headaches. Please, only one talks at a time."

"I'm Connor O'Grady. Domes? We're supposed to go to Earth." His eyes darted around landing on Hans and the babies. "Boss? That you?"

"Yes. Welcome back Connor."

Dr. Ivy said, "Earth is sending Telepath Squad members to Domes. We're safe here. I need to examine everyone, especially Missy and Elie."

"What happened to us? This is Hugh Berg, Elie's mate. Mady, his younger sister. She's only fourteen. I've got a nightmare headache."

Eve said, "Looks like a massive overdose of the armless telepath Galactic Doll mutation agent. Is that possible?"

"Baron Arno—er, the robot impersonator, sent us back with a large canister of the stuff. Part of my deal with the rogue robot. Kimko. He wanted it removed from there. Didn't want anymore telepaths. Must have leaked or something. Are we going to be okay?" Connor said.

"Very much okay," Eve said. "That is my conclusion."

"Our voices. None of us had any voices. Awful," Connor said.

Heads nodded.

"I arranged our escape from that nightmare place. I want to be Mady's parent, if that's okay."

Missy said, "Only if I'm her other parent. Connor and I want to marry. Before I give birth. Just in case I don't make it. My baby will have a father."

"Don't worry. We'll arrange that," Eve said. "Who do the four babies belong to? The newborn didn't survive."

Connor flushed. "Me, I think. The real Baron Arno bred me to our assistants. He paid them for having telepath babies. We don't know who their mothers are, but they're not Missy or Elie."

Elie said, "Connor, you can't take care of five babies. Let Hugh and me take two of them. Then, we'll each have three to raise. Oh! Contractions. It's starting!"

Within minutes, both women began labor. Two doctors moved them into another lab room for privacy, while Dr. Ivy began her physical checks on the others.

Mady, who continued to press her body up against Connor, said, "You did it, Wendell. Er, Connor. My wish came true. Now none of us has to be a baroness. We can breathe again. If only we had arms. Wait, did you see that? That thing is floating all by itself!"

Dr. Ivy grinned. "Levitation or telekinesis. If we're right, all of you and the babies will have it. If so, you don't need arms as much."

"Golly! Look at me!" Mady said.

She'd lifted a glass of water and brought it over to her face. A helper steadied it and held it for her to drink.

After that, Mady chatted, making up for months without a voice. Despite his pounding headache, Connor grinned, watching her every antic.

Molly sensed pride emanating from the man.

With the medical checks done, helpers fed the three and changed four sets of diapers. Then, we had them tell us their story. Occasional cries echoed from the adjoining room, reminding everyone of the serious situation. Connor's interaction with the rogue robot confirmed my original opinion—that the robots didn't want to harm humans.

Connor had no idea where the various worlds he'd been were located or even called. Hugh could read and write, but only knew his kingdom: Bergwald. Mady couldn't do either, since a baroness didn't need such skills.

Yet, Mady continued to surprise us. From listening to the three language units speaking in English, she'd already picked up an amazing amount. Hugh hadn't been that fortunate.

A newborn interrupted the story. Dr. Ivy poked her head in.

"Connor, you have a new daughter. Both mother and baby are doing fine."

Moments later, Hugh had a son.

After the births, we led them to their new homes, 6147 and 6149, both close to us. But Dr. Ivy sent a nurse to monitor the new mothers, at least for the next few days.

We showed them how to run the Sixth Invader machines, especially the cook robot. Lia ordered them five Cass-C robot assistants, instructing them in their operations.

Then, my sister Leslie, who had a fetish for fashion design, arrived. Her many assistants wheeled in a giant selection of fashions. Hugh and Connor both chose Leslie's male doll line. Though the shirt didn't hide their busts and curves, they appreciated the pants.

Mady picked an armless blouse and pants combo as well as a simple gown like mine that encased our shoulders.

After using the dressing machine, five faces beamed.

Mady said, "Look, Dad. Dressed myself!"

"Us, too," Missy said, while the others nodded their agreement.

Self-sufficiency, independence—very important to these people, who had not known it since losing their arms.

The next day, therapy sessions began for the new arrivals. Celeste took on Connor, believing his traumatic experiences might have been the most severe. Wanda and Otto worked Elie and Hugh. While I handled Missy, Isabella volunteered to work with Mady.

Part of each day, Hans and I worked with them, showing how to do things with their feet and toes. Once therapy ended, I worked with each helping them gain control over their new telekinesis ability.

Almost from the second day, Donata, Anka, Cyryl, and Wendel took charge of Mady. While she was eight years older and appeared to be much older than fourteen, the four struck up a friendship. Mady hadn't had childhood friends. That these four precocious kids wanted to be best friends with her appeared to amaze her.

The kids taught Mady everything they knew about using feet, the machines, the rolling robots, and telekinesis. Together, they explored how to use the many new devices

Domes offered, though I didn't appreciate the cost of their tea order from Earth. Mady picked up English in days! She achieved fluency by the time school began in September.

***

Hans checked with the geology unit, hoping he could assist them. I could recognize some rocks thanks to Geology 101. That hadn't perked my interest when I attended Soros University.

The first day, Hans returned home. "Molly, I can't believe this world. According to the geologists, it's heaviest element is Krypton gas. No silver, tin, gold, mercury, tungsten, or platinum. Devoid of all heavier elements. How weird is that? Theory is Domes formed very early in the galaxy's history."

"Before many supernovae?" I asked.

"Precisely. Silicon and germanium are abundant, as is aluminum and copper. Not much iron, though. We believe Domes' core might contain the iron group. They constructed the domes from silicon and germanium mixed with impurities for greater strength."

"How many domes are there?" I said.

He laughed. "Too many. No one has gotten an accurate count. Too many trees and overgrowth. I'm going to study mineralogy now. Domes offers a unique field. Its rocks are vastly different from earth. Plus, they've imported a state-of-the-art analysis machine. I will have fun with it. Oh, one more thing. Domes is rich in high quality silicon and germanium needed in electronic devices."

We settled into a routine. Hans watched the kids two days a week. I used the time to explore our new world. Three new domes were being opened. I saw the massive effort needed to bring one online. Isabella continued her search for documents and clues of the planet's previous civilization of dome builders.

Two new domes contained soil. These would soon grow crops and support farm animals, adding to our precious milk supply. The third would house our next five thousand immigrants. Already, workers had begun first steps to clean up three more domes.

Just before grade school began in September, Eve gave us a fabulous present. A cure for our distorted feet. After a painful jolt in each heel and arch, our feet rested flat on the ground. The cheers she received caused her to flush. In a flash, our sense of balance returned. The kids dashed about, testing their newfound freedom of motion. Just maybe closer to arm regrowth.

Since Domes had a strict policy of not allowing human-form robots inside the domes, I had Bishop operating a shuttle service between Earth and Domes. That cut shipping costs, pleasing the High Council. Although Admiral Carr ordered them to allow Bishop to live with me, we concluded we were safe here. Plus, with each trip, he brought back his observations, many of which didn't make the GEnt newscasts.

I attended the High Council monthly meetings. Via them, I learned more people wanted to immigrate to Domes each month than ever before. This, I took as a positive sign, though it meant more of the ancient domes had to be renovated.

Could I be happy living here? That lurked in the back of my mind. I knew I didn't want to return to Chicago. Reports said human-form robots operated everywhere. What did that mean?

Chapter 16 They Walk Among Us

October 2375
Chicago

Teslenko rolled along the MTES by the Lake. He wore an expensive business suit, fitting in with other men. Six years of unfettered production yielded results. Warrior Robots guarded many intersections. Last month, Galactic Robotics rolled out its one-millionth Warrior unit.

Most large cities on Earth replaced their Local Defense Force men and women with these new robots. The LDF provided security and emergency services during natural disasters. The new climate control system eliminated that need.

Many former LDF workers moved their families to one of the newly discovered worlds of the expanding Sol Empire, Bella for example. Even lower IQ inhabitants were allowed to immigrate if they had five or more children, part of the current plan to expand Earth's domination of empire worlds. GPan was so desperate they even accepted giants and dwarves, though their loyalty to the corporations hadn't been tested.

Far more significant for Teslenko, five million human-form robots lived in Earth's cities. Some, servants for wealthy families, others, workers at one of two dozen major corporations and written off as a business expense. Work had begun on Phase Two: a human-form in every home.

Today, Teslenko could walk the streets of Chicago carefree. His rogue robots infiltrated the top corporations, replacing key personnel, many in CEO or CFO positions.

What happened to those humans his robots replaced? He opposed killing them. "Do not be hasty to take life if you cannot grant life," he pounded into the computations of his fellow rogues. Besides, dead bodies brought investigations, and he didn't want another round of Telepath Squad robot hunting. Almost put a stopper on his plans. Rather, he had them injected with the armless telepath Galactic Doll mutation agent, removed their voice boxes, and implanted them to love robots while craving to be a baroness. Soon, he would send them off to the barons' world, and he wouldn't even charge the barons for them.

Teslenko enjoyed these strolls. They stimulated the calculation center of his positronic brain. His ultimate goal lay nine and a half years in the future, assuming current production and migration rates. With Parkinson out of the picture and the Telepath Squads disbanded, nothing stood in his way.

For now, he and his kind avoided contact with Admiral Carr and the Sol Empire fleet, their major opponents. Instead, focusing on increasing their space shipping lines. Goods flowed throughout the empire. Why not turn a profit from that? Corporations supported his fledgling lines.

The original four rogue robots knew his goal. But he kept a meticulous record of his dealings on the modern-day equivalent of a thumb drive.

Walking along the Lake, he passed a gorgeous Galactic Doll teetering along on her tall heels. He recognized her. Veronica Hugo, the twenty-two-year-old GEnt reporter. He nodded. She smiled back, as he calculated she had no idea Teslenko had ordered the robot replacement for her father, Casper Hugo, Jr., the Chief Finance Officer of Galactic Defense Empire-wide. Teslenko needed control over this vital corporation's purse strings. For a fleeting second, he wondered how Casper fared as an armless Galactic Doll on his second go around.

***

Veronica Hugo, twenty-three, couldn't make up her mind. About men, clothes, jewelry, jobs, education, family matters, or even her own father. Potential boyfriends called her moody.

Not Reese, I think. But does he understand me? No one does. She exhaled, finding peace at last on the solitary walk by the Lake, her daily retreat from the world and its confusions.

I was happy in grade school. I'm sure of that. Nikita. My best friend. Why did you leave me? Maybe I wasn't happy. We didn't have arms. Everything was hard. But I managed because Nikita stayed with me. I suppose I liked Matt and Fritz, but they died. Yes, I'm certain. Happy then. But not now.

She arrived at an MTES junction. Without thinking, she stepped onto it, heading for home. Veronica lived with her parents, Casper and Helen. She wanted to move out, but couldn't bring herself to do that.

Veronica entered the northern sections where wealthy mansions sprawled. She paused before walking the last block on foot. Images of playing with Nikita swirled, obliterating the street. She recalled them riding their three-wheeled bikes, Nikita's dad's gift to the four armless kids. Happier times.

"High there, Doll."

She recognized Bill's voice, one of many men fighting for her affections. He worked at GD. That jarred her into the present and annoyed her.

"You ready to go to the Fetish Dance Club with me Friday night?"

"Not really, Bill."

"You know you want to."

"Presumptuous."

He feigned a laugh. "I want you, and I'm gonna have you. Just a matter of time."

142

Veronica tossed her long brown hair back and raised her chin.

"Ha! Fat chance."

"Still fancying that dull engineer? What's his name? Reese? Hey, I got millions in the bank, gorgeous. We can have a ball. Even your dad approves of us hitching up."

"Well, I'm not hitching up with anyone. Certainly not you, Bill. Gotta go."

"Phone me if you change your mind and want to go. Heard it's gonna be a happening."

She walked past him, her heels clicking on the pavement. Bill's what? The sixth guy Dad's tried to hook me up with. Why do they want to marry me off? Must make babies. Ha. Last thing I want. Home. Here we go again.

She walked into the kitchen and grabbed a cold brew.

"Hi, Mom. I'm back."

Careful not to mar the finish on her long red nails, she popped the top and poured the beer into a mug. She knew she emulated her mother in some ways. Both kept their nails long. Veronica's friends called her two-inch claws talons. Helen painted hers cherry red, while Veronica went with a deep blood red, matching her mood. Both women wore several thousand credits of rings on their fingers.

Helen always wore cherry red satin gowns with matching heels, her trademark apparel, even when she had been the CEO of GD.

Today Veronica wore a similar style gown, but in blood red. Yesterday, an earthy brown. Before that, a cobalt blue. She could never decide on "her" color. Thus, her extended clothes closet held a hundred gowns and double that in heels. Casper, her father, enlarged her room to accommodate her ever-growing wardrobe.

She sat at the table and sipped the brew.

Helen said, "Had a good day? I did. We met at Bernardo's for lunch. I swear that man is the world's greatest chef. Was worried he'd pack up and move to Domes with his mother. Scuttlebutt is he's not interested in moving. Thank the stars for that. There are few good places to dine these days. I swear the world is disintegrating. But I do enjoy a relaxing lunch with my friends. Retirement is the best thing ever."

Reminded of Molly's departure, Veronica grimaced. Why didn't Nikita return from Cass-C with her mom? I wish she had. Now there's no chance I'll ever see her again.

"Oh, a boring day, Mom. I did follow one story. A kid fell on the playground and broke an arm. I met them at the Med Center. I didn't realize all the doctors are robots. No empathy with the kid's pain. Just patched him up. God, robots are everywhere."

"Yes, but with Warrior Robots on many corners, I feel safer than I ever have in this city. GEnt requests we purchase a personal human-form robot for domestic duties. But I pay Galactic Housing for that. So does Molly. The ad claims the robot pays for itself in one year. Cleans. Mows lawns. Even make beds. Now if it does dishes, I just might. I chipped a nail last night loading the dirty dishes into the washer.

"Say, Tom called. Wants to take you out Friday night. Some dance somewhere. Told him you'd call him back. You could do worse. His folks have that mansion north of here."

"I don't know. Tom's all right, but..."

"But? Well, one day you're going to have to make a choice."

"Because you want grandchildren?"

Helen laughed. "Hardly. Must make babies? Phooey. You and Fritz are more than enough for me. Don't you want children?"

"Yes, Mom. Someday. Not now. I just endured another Galactic Doll mutation to get my perfect figure back. I'm not about to become a bloated pig to have kids. Milly has ten. Can you believe that?"

"Isn't she a nurse at the Med Center?"

"Yeah. We went to high school together. She looks like she's had ten babies. But she told me today her salary has doubled, and she's a top candidate to emigrate to Barnes-C, one of the new worlds GPan discovered. We chatted after the robot patched that boy's arm."

"Will I see that story on the news tonight?"

"No. I didn't report it. Too dull."

Just then Casper arrived home from work wearing one of the most expensive suits credits could buy. He carried a briefcase in one arm.

"I'm home," he said.

"What do you want for supper?" Helen asked.

Veronica knew what his answer would be. Same response for the last several weeks—not himself.

"Nothing, dear. I grabbed a bite on my way home. I'll be in my study. Tons of work to do. Many new ships to get financed and crewed. Don't disturb me tonight."

He entered his man-den and shut the door. A faint click signaled he'd locked the door.

"Figures," Helen said. "Just as well. I think I will grab dinner at Bernardo's. Care to join me?"

"Mom, hasn't Dad been acting funny these weeks?"

"Oh, he's been really busy of late."

"Don't you miss him in bed with you?"

Helen chuckled. "Hardly. I was worried he would insist on having ten children so his salary would double. No. I don't miss him. Besides, there's always our toys."

Veronica's cheeks felt hot. "But he's been acting strange, hasn't he?"

Helen bit her cherry red lip. "Perhaps. But then your father has always been a complex man. Years ago, I almost left

145

him when his actions became criminal. When I got control and had him turned into an armless Galactic Doll, he snapped out of it and became a loving husband again. Now much older, we're drifting apart again. I think it annoyed him when I became the CEO of Galactic Dynamics and thus his boss. He's never gotten over that. He'll be retiring one of these days. I suspect he'll change again. That's men for you. Pick wisely, dear. You've got many good suitors."

"Yeah, I remember those days. When he and Sam got those three-wheeled bikes for us. How he and Sam encouraged us to be our best, showing us how to do things with our feet. Those were such happy times, weren't they?"

"Happy and sad, Veronica. Life was a bitch without arms. He struggled with it every day. Then, I lost mine for a time. No, that wasn't such happy times, at least for me."

"But isn't Dad acting strange these days?"

"Just being Casper. I'm off to Bernardo's."

Veronica fixed a quick pizza to go with her beer and retired to her room. She had six messages on her cell. Time to at least acknowledge them. She played the messages back on her phone. 3-D videos about a foot high played before her eyes. Five men begged, asked, cajoled, and pleaded for her to go out with them this weekend. She sighed. Veronica knew she had a perfect body. That's what being a Galactic Doll was all about. All were wealthy, attractive men. She couldn't go wrong with any of them. But... She sighed and played back the last one.

The holo image of Reese Cartwright appeared. He was the son of Deanna Cartwright, the billionaire CEO of Cartwright Enterprises and clone sister of Molly. Reese ran the entire Earth branch of the vast enterprise. When Reese reached eighteen, Deanna had given him control of her Earth operation and moved to Domes with her many sister clones. Why? Veronica never understood. So many had left Earth.

His short-sleeve shirt carried dirt smudges, as did his work pants. Her other suitors wore expensive designer suits. Not Reese. He called them monkey suits. They'd gone to grade and high school together. Good friends.

Unpretentious Reese. Last time they were together, she'd called him that, causing him to roar with laughter. But she hadn't laughed when he called her a fickler.

She stared at his image, replaying the message three times.

"Hey, Hot-As-Ever. If you get bored this weekend, drop by. I want to show you something. Catch ya later."

Intrigued, she called him back, promising to be over. She checked her appearance in her full-length mirror and tried on six pairs of earrings, deciding on the hanging bobs. Unlike her mother, Veronica didn't like makeup on her skin. Felt creepy. But she kept the Sixth Invader's hair machine. She stepped onto the device and activated it. Electrostatic charges separated each strand of her luxurious hair as they shot straight up. At the end of the cycle, a light breeze blew it to her back, leaving her hair looking full and brushed. It reached the back of her knees.

She picked up her purse and headed off to meet Reese at the Cartwright Enterprises skyscraper in downtown Chicago. The evening robot guard recognized her and opened the door as she approached.

I remember when the ground floor swarmed with people. Now, it's all robots. She took the elevator to the 50th floor, the living quarters. Reese's smiling face greeted her, as the doors opened.

"Hi, Veronica. Come on in. You're looking Hot-As-Ever."

She flushed, though she should be used to the line, his standard greeting for her since high school.

"Hi, yourself. What's this thing you want to show me?"

147

He led her to a small office piled with papers. He waved one at her.

"This. The Senate has approved a new law that allows human-form robots to take over the running of companies. Not corporations, mind you. I've been asked to step down and let a robot run the manufacturing operation here on Earth."

"But they can't do that, can they?"

"They've already taken over the Med Center."

"I saw that today. The doctor was one of them. No empathy for the kid with his broken arm. But it patched him up okay. Yeah, I told you lots of weird things have been happening."

"Have you figured out anything about your dad?"

"No. He came home. Didn't want any supper. Had to work. Locked himself in his study office. He's done that for the last few weeks. Is that weird or what?"

"I'd say so. Not what I thought your dad would be doing. He was always there for you when we were in school. Another thing, Earth's human population is shrinking because of the ever-increasing demand for colonists. We're discovering far too many new worlds to populate. A report from Galactic Housing said eight out of ten homes are vacant."

"Wow. Didn't it used to be three out of four? Or was it two out of three?"

Reese laughed. "Yeah, one of those. Human-form robots. They're in use everywhere. I have only fifty employees left. The rest are robots. They handle the workload at a fraction of the cost."

"What happened to your employees?" Veronica asked, wrinkling her forehead.

"Moved to other worlds. I had no choice but to replace them with human-form robots. Either that or shut down production. Mom would kill me if I did that."

Both laughed. He said, "Deanna can be a powerful force when riled."

"I think I'll look into these weird behaviors. Maybe others have seen similar behaviors in their families."

"You could put up a web page asking for feedback," Reese suggested. "On the other hand, my little budding reporter, what if you uncover something nefarious? Might be dangerous for you."

"It's only a part-time job. I have no idea what I really want to do."

Reese laughed. "Miss Hot-As-Ever, when *hasn't* that been the case?"

"Well, I like to take my time deciding, Mr. Handsome Devil," she teased him back.

Hours later, as she left, he said, "Just be careful. In case..."

Chapter 17 Trouble Develops

November 20, 2375

Veronica's new website produced a stream of routine complaints. However, a week after it went live, it produced results.

Anonymous posted: My father has been acting cold and distant for the last month. Mom says it's the stress he's under. He's a CEO.

Another complained their mother who headed a corporation hadn't been her usual self. Instead of outgoing, she'd become something of a recluse.

Dozens more like this appeared, coming from all parts of Earth. Each evening, Veronica shared the latest posts, asking Reese's opinion of each. Tonight, she brought up an alarming post.

Bulldog wrote: Take this page down. Stop playing psychologist. Leave people's problems to the professionals or else. You've been warned..

"Isn't that a threat?" she asked.

"What do you think?" Reese countered, unwilling to be boxed into evaluating for her. Since he first met her, Veronica excelled at coaxing others into evaluating things for her. But Reese insisted she make up her own mind. While she bellyached about it, his approach worked.

"Well, it sounds like a threat. The 'or else' part. Nothing specific. I'm not playing psychologist. Not giving anyone advice. Just asking if they've seen weird behaviors."

"True. Are you going to take it down?" Reese asked.

"Nope. I'm a reporter trying to get the story."

"A part-time reporter. But GEnt didn't assign this story to you."

"You know what I mean. I'm not giving up. There's a story here. I don't know what it is. Yet. Look at this. I've cleaned up the responses, deleting the ordinary ones. All the rest involved someone important, like bosses or CEOs. Doesn't that suggest something? A pattern?"

"Not sure. There are thousands of local corporation CEOs. What do you think?"

"Suppose so. Still..."

At home, she found her father locked in his study and Helen already in bed. She worked phone messages.

Bill's holo image said, "Hey, gorgeous, you should take down that web page for weirdos. People at work are commenting on it. Not good. See you Friday night? Bye."

Five other wooers left similar messages. Several of these held high-paying jobs in the corporation world.

The next day, Helen didn't go to lunch as usual. She didn't ask Veronica what she wanted for breakfast or lunch. Helen had cut her long nails and removed the polish.

"I'm going out," Helen said.

After fixing herself a snack, Veronica paid Reese a visit at Cartwright Enterprises. Reese welcomed her with a big smile, ushering her into his office.

"What brings you here in the middle of the day, Miss Hot-As-Ever," he asked.

"Hi, Mr. Handsome Devil. It's Mom. Something's happened. She's cut her long nails and removed the polish."

"Hum, I can't recall her ever having short nails. Except when she lost her arms that time."

"Never. And no lunch with her friends at Bernardo's. Like she always does."

"Tired of eating there? Only so many meal choices."

"Yeah, but she didn't wear any rings. None. She always wears rings. Except when she was mutated and lost her arms for a while."

Reese laughed. "Now that *is* strange. Even for Helen. She's a ring fanatic. If ever there was one."

"What do I do, Mr. Handsome Devil?" Veronica asked.

"Miss Hot-As-Ever, I'm not about to tell you what you should do. I can tell you I'd keep my eyes open. Perhaps it's a mid-life crisis or something. But between us, I'm getting a little concerned. Take this. It's a panic-button. If you get into trouble, push the button."

"What's it do? Send out an alarm?" Veronica rolled the cigar-shaped device around in her hand.

"Sends a homing signal. Leads me to wherever you might be. Ill be there to help you. Keep it with you. Just in case."

"Now, you *are* scaring me."

"I want you to feel safe. Be safe. Just in case. I don't trust these Warrior Robots to come to anyone's aid. The human-forms masquerading as policemen aren't much better. The real detectives have immigrated to other worlds. I heard today the last dwarf has left Earth for greener pastures. A few giants are still around corporate buildings. Got two working for me."

"But why is everyone eager to leave Earth? I like this world. This city. The Lake. Makes little sense."

"It does if you depend on a paycheck. If your corporation offers to double your salary if you move to X world, chances are you'll move."

"I admit I've never had to work. Mom and Dad provide everything. But I don't know what I want to do. For a job, that is. Never can make up my mind."

"True, but don't worry about it. In time you'll figure out what you want to do. Me, I was lucky. Always being around

Mom and her constant designing of things. Rubbed off on me. There's a certain satisfaction in designing something and bringing it into existence."

Veronica grinned, slipping her arms around Reese. "I know that since high school, Mr. Handsome Devil. That's what I like about you."

"Just remember to keep that signal device on you at all times. Even take it to bed with you."

"What if someone takes me while I'm sleeping? I wouldn't be able to press the button."

Reese sighed. "I don't know. Your web page keeps attracting posts from people concerned for their loved ones. I've no idea what that means, but I've a notion to show them to someone in GMed who might know if it's reasonable for many to have concerns. Perhaps it is. Being a CEO or CFO or whatever must be a stressful job. Still, I'm concerned for you because of the veiled threats."

"Okay, I'll keep it in a pocket. Bet you didn't know my fancy dress has a hidden pocket, did you?"

"Can I feel around and find it?"
"Good one," she said.
Both laughed.

***

Teslenko wasn't laughing. Reporter Veronica Hugo's web page caught his attention and other's too. His posted nudges and threats hadn't dissuaded her from continuing her explorations. The situation demanded more drastic action.

He paid a visit to Galactic Defense. An aid led him to a conference room and a waiting Casper and Helen. They'd received his electronic signal and calculated trouble must have arisen.

153

The three exchanged pleasantries and idle chatter as Casper and Helen received the real exchange through a download from Teslenko's Positronic brain.

'We've got a problem brewing. Veronica. She's digging in too closely. Time to talk her down. Put an end to her investigation.'

'Agreed,' Casper sent.

'I'll talk to her tonight,' Helen sent.

***

When Veronica walked into her home late that afternoon, Helen met her at the door. Unusual.

"Hi, Mom. What's up?"

"They asked me to help at GD again. Top position. Can't say what. Secrets and all that. Couldn't turn them down. Too interesting a job. Your father and I are working on classified Sol Empire projects. Requires many hours. Because of the electronics, I can't wear my rings. Small price to pay for this vital project. We might seem stressed of late."

"Makes sense, Mom. But I thought you had retired from GD? That nothing could make you want to go back there."

"I changed my mind."

"Okay. I was getting worried. You and Dad have been acting strange of late. Guess that explains it."

"I hope so. Would you like me to make supper?"

"Are you dining out?"

"Well, yes, I am. Work, you understand."

"No. I'll grab something downtown."

"By the way, have you decided which man to marry? It's way past time you settled down. You've not chosen a career. Housewife it must be. Bill? Tom?"

Veronica sighed. "Not yet, Mom. They are nice but..."

"You're not getting any younger. I suggest you hurry and pick one. And stop posting on that website of yours.

People are talking. Anyway, I'm off to work again. Back late. Don't wait up for me."

She left and Casper walked in, his briefcase in hand.

"Hi, Veronica. Did your mom tell you she and I are working on a top secret project for GD?"

"Yes, she just left."

"Good. Very busy. Critical project. No time to waste. Veronica, it's high time you made decisions. Figure out which suitor to marry. Stop playing reporter and get a real job or be a housewife like your mother once was. I expect to hear which man soon. Now, I've got work to finish up tonight."

He marched into his study and locked the door. If only his study had a window, she mused. A spy cam perhaps? She grinned.

Later, she met Reese in his office.

"Never guess what just happened to me," she said and outlined what her parents just told her.

"Doesn't that explain their abnormal behavior?" Reese asked.

Veronica thought for a moment. "No. When Mom left GD, she swore she'd never go back there. And yet without forewarning, there she is. It's not like she interviewed for the job."

"That you know of," he added.

"Right. Even when she was the CEO, she kept her nails long and perfectly painted. What do rings on fingers have to do with delicate electronics? Besides, Mom and Dad have worked for GD off and on for years. Even Molly Parkinson did. They've never mentioned top secret projects before. Never. And why are they trying to marry me off? Seems sudden like. Get a job. Ha. I'm not cut out to be a housewife."

Reese chuckled. "I knew that back in high school."

Veronica's face felt hot. "Well, I'm not. Anyway, I don't know what I want to do. Yet. Haven't made up my mind."

"Of course, you haven't. That's a good thing, I think."

"Good." After a pause, she asked, "Where can I get a spy cam? There's no window in Dad's office. I'd sure like to see what he does in there. I never hear him going to bed."

"Well, you could stay up and listen for him. I'll check around for the cam. Let you know tomorrow. Say, have you eaten supper?"

She shook her head.

"Come on. My treat. Let's grab something from Bernardo's."

"Won't turn you down."

She slipped an arm around his. It always felt good having a steadying arm. Since she loved the look of heels, she had never gotten the foot mutation cure. Though treacherous, the tall heels made her legs look spectacular.

That night, she vowed to stay awake until her father retired for the night. But Helen didn't come home, and he must have slept at his desk, further confusing her.

Reese called mid-day. Veronica followed his suggestion and found a store that sold spy cams. The set up appeared easy when the sales robot explained it. She returned home and made the house was empty before slipping into her Dad's study. She installed the spy cam, pointing it at his desk.

She brought up the cam's video stream on her own computer in her room. With a good point of view, she began the recording, hiding the computer under a pile of dirty dresses she'd been meaning to dry clean.

Helen came home near suppertime. She looked refreshed.

"I fell asleep at my desk at GD," she explained. "I'm becoming a workaholic."

Veronica sensed Helen had made an attempt at humor. But that wasn't like her mother either. Since Veronica said she planned to dine with Reese later, her mother headed back to work. At five, her father showed up.

"Mom's come and gone. Dad, I think they're working Mom too hard. She fell asleep at her desk last night."

"Perils of this critical project. Excuse me. I've got much to finish before bed. Chosen a husband yet?"

Veronica shook her head, and Casper headed into his study. Veronica waited a while before going out, paying Reese another visit.

"I've installed the spy cam, Mr. Handsome Devil. Tomorrow, I should know if he's working or not. What's new with you?"

"Ten more workers resigned. Took positions at our new factories on Brussels. Had to hire ten human-forms replacements. Spent most of the day grooving them in on their jobs. What's happening to our world?"

"Automation is driving everyone away," Veronica said. "Perhaps there's such a thing as too good a thing. Don't you think?"

Both chuckled. "Let's eat."

The next morning, she heard Casper leave and, within minutes, Helen, too. She must have returned during the night. She fixed a light breakfast, stalling in case they returned.

When they hadn't, she retrieved her computer, ended the recording, and hit Play. She adjusted playback speed to 2X, then 3X, then 5X. At last, her father walked in and sat down. His briefcase rested on the desk, but he stared off into space for a long time, given the speed of the playback. Veronica screeched and hit pause.

She almost broke a nail speed dialing Reese.

"What's the matter?" His voice calmed her a little.

"You've got to see this. Can I come over?"

"Absolutely."

She cursed the tall heels slowing her down to a crawl. Her body trembled. She almost fell four times. Out of breath, she entered his skyscraper. Veronica's heels clickety-clacked rapid time as she made her way to the elevators. Why aren't elevators closer to the doors?

"You look like you've seen a ghost, Miss Hot-As-Ever. Come on in. It can't be that bad."

Panting, she opened her computer. "Look. Dad." She gushed before collapsing into the nearest chair.

"Oh, dear god!" Reese said, slumping into a chair near her.

"Yeah, Dad's a robot!"

Chapter 18 My Parents Are Robots, So What Am I?

December 1, 2375

"Bet Mom's a robot, too," Veronica said. "I'm not a robot, am I? Would I know if I was one?"

"Veronica, you're not a robot!"

"But how do you know? If the Telepath Squad was here, they could tell."

"Like this."

Reese pulled her into his arms and kissed her. When he felt her shock turn to a returned kiss, he released her. He steadied her before asking, "Convinced now?"

"No. Could you do that again?"

Both stared into each other's eyes for a long moment.

"Back to your problem," he said. "Bet the other weird replies on your web pages were robots, too. Makes sense."

"Oh, god. That means many robots in positions of power in the corporations," she said. "What happened to Mom and Dad? The real ones. Did they kill Casper and Helen?"

Reese embraced her. "We don't know what they did to your folks. If these other cases are robots replacing humans, there must be a lot of bodies. Surely, dead bodies would start showing up."

Veronica leaned her head on his shoulders. "But—but that can't be right. Even one dead body showing up would reveal the imposter. Game over. Whatever the game is. Kidnapped? Held prisoner somewhere? Why?"

"Good point. Held captive fits. For the robots to go to all this trouble, the why must be important. Human-forms are all over the place these days, not to mention all the Warrior Robots. Why would they want to impersonate key corporate or business leaders?"

"Rogue robots? The old kind, not the new ones GR has been making," she said.

"Fascinating that the human-form robots from GR started showing up after the Telepath Squads disbanded. Coincidence?"

"They could have been cremated or chemically dissolved. Maybe they are dead," she said, her eyes watering.

"Funeral homes keep records. I suppose someone could sneak in and dispose of a body. Wait. I bet they're keeping replaced humans alive. What if questions came up? Like what relatives does Casper have, and what's their relationship like? If the robot had the wrong reaction, that would cause a scene. I bet Casper and Helen are being held somewhere in case they need answers to questions only they know."

"You think so? I have to think that way. Don't I? Otherwise, it's too horrible to imagine. Oh, god! How am I going to face them now? I'm freaking out!"

"Act as though nothing has happened. Chat about going out with those suits nagging you."

"Wait! How do I know they aren't robots in disguise?"

"Well, you don't. But why would a robot want to court you? Doesn't make sense. Those boyfriends are humans."

"Suppose you're right. Still..."

"Scared to go home?"

"Yeah."

"Got that signal device with you?"

Veronica smiled and pulled it out of her hidden dress pocket.

"Where could they be hiding Mom and Dad?"

"When did you first notice anything odd happening with your mother?"

She sighed, wiping wet eyes. "Well, I guess it was that morning when she first appeared without her rings and her nails cut short. How does that help?"

"They must have taken your mother out of your house while everyone slept, replacing her with the robot impersonator. Hey, I've an idea. GR installed a detection safeguard in the new human forms. We figure out how to trigger it and test your fake parents. We'll know if they're one of the new robots."

"How's that going to help us? Oh, if they aren't, that leaves the rogue robots Aunt Molly's Telepath Squad hunted. Now I *am* scared. They tried to kill Molly and Katya and who knows who else."

"Both are still alive and on Domes, thanks to the mutation healing cures. Say, I best lay in a supply of that cure, just in case we need it. I'm not letting anyone harm you, Veronica. No how, no way."

She hugged him.

An hour later, the sales-robot demonstrated the detection device. It said, "You place this within twenty-five feet of the robot and turn it on."

The device made a loud beeping sound. The robot turned it off.

"That simple. If it doesn't beep, the suspect is human."

Once out of the store with purchase in hand, Reese corrected what the sales-robot had said. "Or no beep means it's one of those rogue robots the Telepath Squad was after."

Once at the Hugo mansion, Veronica suggested they install the device behind a couch close to the front doors. She also gave him a spare key to the mansion.

"If either comes home, I'll know at once."

"Speed dial me no matter what."

"I will. Thanks, Reese. You're a godsend."

They embraced before he left for work.

161

***

Reese sat at his desk, unable to focus on work. She's in over her head. I should have shared my suspicions. Why would these new GR human-forms impersonate GD's CFO or Helen? Makes no sense. If anyone had one of these devices around, they'd trigger it. Plan exposed. They are the rogue robots. What could they want with the Hugo's? I could see them trying to replace me. Cartwright Enterprises is vital. Wait, if they're after the Hugo's, am I next?. Calls for contingency plans. Mom's specialty. Wish she was here.

He headed to his mother's old office on the top floor. After confirming no one was around, he pulled back a rug, revealing a hidden safe. He dialed the combination and opened it. Reese smiled and pulled out several syringes labeled Bio-hazard. He checked the labels. Armless telepath Galactic Doll. One dose. His mother had stockpiled dozens of these. Had she foreseen I'd need them? He put nothing past Deanna.

Next, he arranged an automated message, keyed to a speed dialed number. A button press would activate it. Next, he hunted through her desk for her keyring. Bingo. He put them and the syringes in a small belt pouch.

Back at his desk, he realized he wasn't prepared at all. He put together a bug-out bag, including food and water, adding his belt pouch to the bag. Although only mid-morning, he guessed nothing would happen until at least five o'clock. But he couldn't concentrate on anything except Veronica's plight.

***

Teslenko accepted the disturbing input that forced a complete recalculation of plans. Casper robot detected a spy cam trained on his study seat. The short-range transmitter covered fifteen feet, suggesting the receiver had been in Veronica's bedroom or outdoors near the study. The ground there showed no traces of a person or receiver. The inescapable conclusion: Veronica discovered a human-form robot masqueraded as her father. The new calculations forced a secondary test for confirmation. Did she suspect her mother had met the same fate?

The next evening, the Casper robot sent further data to Teslenko. He'd detected one of the human-form electronic sensors hidden near the front door. He hadn't triggered it, nor had Helen robot. Teslenko inputted these observations and recalculated yet again. His conclusions needed refinement. Thus, he took a stroll along the Lake shore.

Fact: Veronica would have to join her parents. Fact: a human-form robot would replace her. Fact: on such short notice, the resemblance could not be perfect nor could emulating behavior be installed. Supposition: Veronica would alert others to the deception as soon as possible.

Teslenko issued take-out orders, requesting a massive dose because of her multiple mutations. Since no other humans lived in the Hugo mansion, he ordered them to keep the comatose body there for seven days, allowing more time to adapt the appearance of a human-form to Veronica's body. On the seventh day, transport her to the staging area, remove her voice, and store her with her parents and the others.

That done, he continued extrapolation calculations, but did not like the conclusions. Hence, Teslenko explored alternatives to achieve his objective.

***

"Dad, you're home early. Mom okay?" Veronica said. Her face felt hot. Her arms, weak. She rubbed her stomach trying to calm it.

"Yes, Veronica. All is fine."

He pulled out a bio-hazard container and smashed it in his hands. The yellowish toxin filled the room. Seeing the container, Veronica pressed the distress button.

She managed a "What's hap..." before blackness swept over her.

Casper removed the spy cam from his study. Next, he searched her room and found her computer. He used it to delete the offending web pages and deposited it on her bedroom dresser for use by the replacement robot. He sent out the success signal.

Another human-form robot entered. It appeared female and rather looked like Veronica. The two worked on its appearance before stripping Veronica and putting her clothes on the new robot. They left Veronica her heels, since the robot didn't need them.

When they finished tweaking the robot to the best likeness of Veronica possible under the circumstances, the two robots left the comatose and nude Veronica breathing in the mutation agent.

***

Reese heard the distress buzzer and nearly dropped his coffee cup. He cursed and ran to his display unit. The tracking device placed Veronica in her home. He called her. As expected, the call went to voice mail.

"Hi, Veronica. Looks like our dance date is off. EMAC troubles. I have to make an emergency trip to Brussels, Tau Ceti. Not sure when I'll be back. Let's have a rain check dance. Okay? Bye."

That base covered, he grabbed his bug-out bag and hooked the invisibility device to his belt, a gift from his mother via Ambassador L'Grina. He double-checked his pre-recorded system. One speed-dialed number would activate it, providing further hints he was off-world for a time. That subterfuge might not be needed, but Deanna had taught him to always install backup plans.

Satisfied, Reese headed onto the MTES. Climate control provided a perfect day, albeit a chilly one. Winter threatened to arrive soon, but the system alleviated the usual severe cold and snow associated with the Windy City. He realized they might need warmer clothes and parkas. Already a glitch in his plans. His stomach tightened.

When he approached the Hugo residence, he saw someone moving around inside. Reese moved on down the street to the Parkinson home. Deanna had a spare key to her sister's place. He used it to let himself inside. Molly had taken most of her personal stuff, but some Sixth Invader machines sat in a bedroom along with other items. He found a suitable window and kept watch on the Hugo mansion.

His foot continued to tap on the floor. Would they move her right away? Had they harmed her? He decided he loathed waiting. Hours passed before he saw what looked like Veronica and Casper leaving together. For a moment, he debated running after Veronica, but something held him back. Once they stepped onto the MTES, he dashed over to the house.

He looked inside and saw her naked body lying on the front room floor. Just as he was about to dash inside, he saw the yellowish haze of the mutation agent inside the room. Reese cursed. What to do?

He knew he couldn't go inside until the agent was gone. But that meant the windows would have to be opened. He tested one. Ah, he could open it, but paranoia stayed his hands.

"If I open it, the robots will see someone's been here and cleared out the house. We won't be safe. I can't call the police. They're robots too." He cursed, returned to Molly's house, and waited to see what the robots did next.

That night, Casper returned home and opened the windows. Reese watched the robot moving about. After an hour, it closed all windows and left, vanishing into the evening.

Reese dashed over to the Hugo's home. Heart pounding, he entered and sniffed. While he sensed a faint odor, he decided it probably wasn't strong enough to harm him. He felt for a pulse. She breathed. His nerves calmed; he checked her eyes. Coma. He'd seen that before.

She still wore her heels. The signal device lay in one corner. He thought for a moment. If they gassed her with the mutation agent, she should be out for a week. That means the robots think they have days to take her elsewhere.

Reese acted. He lifted her up, activated his invisibility device, and carried her out. After locking the door, he staggered over to Molly's home. Once inside, he laid her on a bed. He couldn't carry her much farther. If only she could walk, he had an ideal location they could hide out. Conclusion: they'd have to stay here until she awoke.

With no food in the fridge, Reese ordered groceries to be delivered to his office. Satisfied she wouldn't wake soon, he used the invisibility device to exit the home. When the supplies came, he packed them in a wheeled duffle bag. Partway back to the home, he activated his device in a location where no one could see him vanishing. He relaxed when he entered and found Veronica lying on the bed where he left her.

Satisfied, he speed dialed the trigger number. Back at his office, messages notified other company personnel that he took a quick trip to Brussels, Tau Ceti, and that he didn't know how long he'd be gone. Bases covered, he began the long wait.

Around five, he watched the confused robots searching the Hugo estate for the missing body. He imagined their confused calculations. Had they given her enough of a dose? Had she woken early and wandered off? Was she now telling others about the impersonating robots? Reese grinned. Serves them right.

By the third day, Reese felt sick at his stomach. He could see her arms were becoming thin. He knew she'd lose them. But what else would happen to her body? He kept watch. By the seventh day, two dried husks lay at her sides.

Fighting nausea, he disposed of them. No need to add to her shock upon waking.

During the eighth day, he sat by her bedside, fearful of her reaction. He'd seen many who'd been subjected to this mutation kill themselves or get others to do it for them. His foot tapped non-stop on the floor. He waited.

Her eyes fluttered. She gasped and shrieked.

"I'm here. You're safe now," Reese said, trying to keep her calm.

"You came. What happened... Oh! Not again," she said, noticing she no longer had arms. "My head. Reese, my head's splitting! Casper robot crushed a bio-agent thing. Last I remember. God, my head. Aspirin! Aspirin! Aspirin!"

"I'll see if I can find some. We're in Molly's home."

"Help me sit up. God, I'm naked."

"They took your clothes. There's a Veronica robot running around. Saw it leave with Casper robot. I'll sneak over and get your clothes when it's safe. At least they left your heels."

"My head. Find Aspirin, please!"

Reese dashed about looking high and low for some, returning with a bottle and a glass of water. He found her sitting on the bed examining her body.

"Thanks. Guess you're my helper now. I'll take the whole bottle."

"Oh, no, you don't. Says two at a time. Here you go. I'm awkward with this."

After downing them, she had him help her stand up.

"Wobbly. Bit dizzy. Everything else seems the same. Is there a mirror? She used to have one in her bedroom. Don't let me fall."

She looked at her body in the full-length mirror, twisting her body this way and that.

Reese said, "Miss Hot-As-Ever, I don't see any other changes."

"Not any more, Mr. Handsome Devil. No arms. Again. I guess you can find another Miss Hot-As-Ever. Forget me."

"Not a chance. I've been in love with you since high school. I want to marry you, silly, not disown you. But only if you want to marry me."

"What's Deanna gonna say when she finds out you're marrying a handicapped woman? Are you sure about this? I'm rather helpless now."

"Positive. We'll make it work. Molly's left a bunch of the machines you need. You're alive. That's all that matters to me."

"Okay, then. Hold you to it. I need clothes. It's embarrassing to be standing here naked."

She teased, "Unless you are too."

Reese laughed. "We might not be able to contain our passions."

Veronica attempted to laugh, but quit. Her head throbbed too much.

"It's about three. I'll see if I can sneak in there and get stuff for you. Does it matter which things? I'll bring your coat too. It's getting colder by the day."

She gave him directions and watched him disappear.

He returned with several gowns and heels to match.

"I brought the blood-red set. My favorite. And a couple more. Let's get you dressed."

"Put them on that machine. It's the old dressing/undressing machine from the Sixth Invaders. I'll see if I can work it. While I'm doing that, what are we going to eat? I'm famished."

"Got MREs is all. I'll fix some. Yell, if you need help."

He heard the machines going. When he had the meal ready, Veronica walked into the kitchen, fully dressed.

"Wow! You look stunning as always."

She flushed. "I'm amazed. I remembered how to operate them. My hair is much longer now. Down to my calves. I always loved what the hair machine did. I kept one and used it every day. What do you think of this look?"

"Sexy as hell," Reese said.

She flushed again, a pleased look on her face, he thought. Her hair shone and draped down her back, falling below the hem of her blood red satin gown.

She said, "Well, now if I can remember how to feed myself..."

Later, she said, "God, this is awkward. I forgot how hard it was. This is miserable, Reese."

"But you're alive. That's what matters."

She looked at him. "You mean that, don't you?" My telepathy is back!

"Of course, I mean it, Miss Hot-As-Ever."

Veronica picked up his thoughts and leaned into his body, pressing her lips against his. The embrace sent electric waves through her body, and she knew Reese felt similar sensations.

"Hey, how are you able to hold me," Reese said as they pulled away.

"Huh?"

"It felt like your arms were gripping me."

"Impossible. Let's try that again, Mr. Handsome Devil," she said.

"That is weird. Felt like I was holding you."

"Remember Empress Molly developed telekinesis. I heard she levitated and moved silverware to feed herself. See if you can move this spoon. "

He watched her focus. The spoon shot across the table, landing on the floor.

"Wow!" he said.

"Double wow," Veronica said. "I've got it too. Gonna have to practice that."

"Wait! You must have received a gigantic overdose of the mutation agent," Reese said.

"Oh, shit! I'm stuck this way. Molly couldn't be cured. Oh, crap!"

Reese changed the subject.

"Any idea where they took your parents? Did you overhear the robots talking about where they would take you?"

"No, it happened fast. I don't think I even had time to ask what was happening. Reese, we have to find Casper and Helen."

"Yes, and we have to avoid these robots. They're hunting you. Can't have two Veronica's walking Chicago streets."

"Your office? Won't they miss you? It's a work day, isn't it? I've lost track of days."

"It's the 9th. Left word of an emergency trip to Brussels, Tau Ceti. No one suspects. Also, I left a voice mail on your phone saying we could get together when I returned. Confuse the robots."

"Reese, how are we going to find Mom and Dad? Are we going to stay here? What are we going to do? I'm scared. Really scared."

"I understand. I'm here for you. We can stay here a day or two. Then, we have to find a more permanent hideout. I didn't plan on you losing your arms and needing these machines. I have a place in mind, but now I'm not sure you'll be able to manage without the Sixth Invader things."

"Reese, I've got to manage somehow and find what happened to my parents. But I need a bath. I feel dirty. I forgot how helpless I felt before."

170

Chapter 19 Trials of a Telepath

December 11, 2375

"Damn. How do I..."

Veronica's voice trailed off from the bathroom. She'd made use of it and gotten up, but struggled to clean up.

"Allow me. We'll figure it out. I'm sure of it," Reese said, handling it for her. "We won't have the dressing machine at the hideout."

Veronica grabbed her dress between her teeth, tossing it over a shoulder, before sighing.

"I forgot. This isn't easy."

"I bet it wasn't before. But you and Nikita managed somehow."

"With the machines. Okay, maybe I can use this tele-whatever to get dressed."

Reese's mind was wide open to her as she focused and lifted the dress up. She sensed how his heart ached for her. She didn't want pity. She wanted arms. A half hour later, she slumped in a chair exhausted from using telekinesis to get her clothes on and dress zipped up, using a mirror to see her backside. Reese clapped and cheered.

"Well, done, dear. See, you can do it."

"A half hour to put on a damned dress? Should take two minutes. If I have to make breakfast, we'll starve."

"That's the spirit," Reese said. "Leave a little something for me to do, will you?"

The incongruity caused her to break out laughing.

"I'm trying to use my feet," she said at the table. "Used too much energy getting dressed. I think there are limits to my new powers. Reese, I don't think I can live this way. Not again. Not without Nikita—"

"You had company. Someone to share the challenges and misery with," Reese said.

A smile flashed. "You're right. Last I heard, Nikita had her arms back. She stayed on at Soros University there in Hoffdorf. I've always wondered what her life has been like. How did it work out for her? Now what? How are we going to avoid the robots? Shouldn't we tell someone about the rogue robot impersonating key people?"

"Who do we tell? They've taken over the police, the LDF, and even GD. If we had the right comm set, we could call Admiral Carr. Don't know his number or how to call him. Could call Mom on Domes. She might know how to contact him. We play it smart. Get you somewhere safe. Give you time to adapt. And figure out how we can find your parents and the others that have been replaced."

"I'm just going to slow you down. You should leave me."

"Yes, things will be slower and more difficult. But you're worth it."

He kissed her.

"So, we'll hear no more of that talk. It's time we figure how we're going to get to a safe house. Deanna always had one set up in case of trouble. After several of her sisters were killed, she told me she had it built. Never needed it, but we do. Come on. We've walking to do."

"It's scary for me."

Her face had a look that suggested she'd just admitted something embarrassing.

"I can't imagine how you're coping, holding it together. I'd be scared out of my wits. I promise you I'll always be here for you, but I'll let you tell me when you need help. I have no idea what you can or can't do. I'm depending on you to tell me. Okay?"

"Thanks. Keep a steadying arm around me when we're outside. Keeping my balance is hard. Bad enough when I had arms, but now it's a nightmare. Where are we going? This safe house of yours?"

"Further north. Crap, it's snowing."

"That's a good thing. Heavier clothing will help conceal our identities. Then we won't be easily recognized," she said.

He stuffed her clothing into the empty duffle bag. Once he had her parka over her and the hood pulled snug, no one could tell she lacked arms. Heels couldn't be hidden, but they justified his keeping an arm around her. Satisfied they couldn't be recognized, they slipped out into the snowy morning.

Great white flakes fell, already blanketing the grass. At least for now, the warmer street melted the flakes. Reese knew how she walked in the tall heels and didn't rush her. Even steadying her, he felt her body tensing this way and that, trying to keep her balance.

They rode the MTES for an hour, but near the end, he felt her shivering. If only he'd been able to find socks to cover Veronica's lower legs. She surprised him by picking up his thoughts.

She said, "Leggings. Not socks. Can't wear socks with heels. Leggings work fine."

His face felt warm.

"Ah, here we are. Down the steps. Mom said it used to be a subway, whatever that was."

"God, steps! This scares me the most—going down without arms to help. Don't let me fall."

"Slow. No rush. You're doing super. Just a little further."

Beneath the ground and on the flat concrete, only a little light entered. He took out a flashlight, got his bearings, and moved over to one wall. He inserted a key. Presto, a narrow door opened. He stepped inside and turned on the lights.

"Wow! This is quite the hideout," she said.

The spacious room held a full-sized bed against the far wall. Shelves held blankets and canned food. Large water jugs were stacked beside the water cooler. A desk and two chairs rested against the opposite wall, along with a portable toilet and small propane stove. Once he shut the door, no one could see their light. A rubber seal kept gases out. A ceiling vent brought in fresh air, but could be closed if needed. Half-burned candles stuck in wine bottles poked up from the desktop.

"Cozy," she said. "But I'm freezing."

"Space heater, at your command," he said, firing it up.

"I'll make lunch. Then we have to plan our next move."

"You realize I'll be almost helpless in here, don't you?"

He smiled. "Yeah, think of it as my chance to learn how best to aid you."

She smirked. "You don't have a choice."

"Yes, I do. I chose you, Miss Hot-As-Ever."

Veronica smiled and stood as close to the heater as she dared.

"We'll need warmer things for both of us," he said. "I should make a list of what we want. I'll sneak out and get them. Leggings. Where are those?"

He wrote it down, along with where she kept them.

"Bring the knee-high boots. They keep my legs warm. Wait. Once I put them on, I'll be helpless."

"If they keep you warm, I'll help you. What else are we going to need?"

After making sure she could use her new power to slide the lock in place, he left. When he heard her do it, he relaxed and headed off to get their needed supplies.

174

When he returned with another bulging duffle bag, he put the leggings on her. The space heater couldn't keep the room warm enough. They slept in their clothes.

After struggling to get into bed, he snuggled with her. In the near dark, he sensed her grief.

"Go ahead. Cry all you want. It's okay. Let it out. I'm here."

She didn't say anything immediately, but sobbed for a time.

"This is hard for me," she whispered. "So very hard. Not like with Nikita."

"I can't imagine how awful it is. But we'll make it together."

She cried herself to sleep that night.

The next day, Reese suggested they use the down time for life skills practice. She had to reinvent much from memory. Long ago, she'd deleted all the how-to videos.

Challenging days passed. For a time each day, the pair discussed how they could locate her parents.

"I'm sure they must be alive. I think I'd sense it if they had died," Veronica said.

No workable ideas resulted.

Reese said, "Let's face it. We're no Molly Parkinson, PI."

Veronica chuckled.

As Christmas approached, Reese snuck out for a short time. When he came back, his huge grin pricked Veronica's curiosity.

"What? Out with it, Mr. Handsome Devil."

"I'm giving you a special Christmas present. No questions. It's only a short walk from here. Need your parka and boots."

He laced up the warm boots for her and secured her parka. When they left their safe house, the hoods hid them

175

from view. He kept a secure arm around her, preventing her from several slips in the deep snow.

"Da ta! Here we are."

"A wedding chapel?"

"Yes, we're getting married. Later on, once we rescue your parents, we can hold a second ceremony. Maybe have Mom come too," Reese said.

A few minutes later, the man said, "Reese Thomas Cartwright, do you take Veronica Vanessa Hugo to be your lawful..."

Soon, the pair exchanged their first kiss as man and wife.

Back inside their safe house, Veronica said, "This is the best Christmas present ever. I love you. Thank you. If only Mom and Dad could have been there."

As they snuggled that night, she sensed how much this day meant to Reese. Hope he realizes how much this means to me, too. Telepathy has its moments.

Over breakfast, Reese said, "Can you locate them with your telepathy? I have no idea what that means or how you could even do such a thing."

"Stupid me. I should have tried that weeks ago. Wish Molly were here. She could help me with it. When Dad had telepathy years ago before he got the mutation cure, he used it with us kids."

"You'll just have to experiment and figure it out. I've faith in you."

She chuckled. "You've no idea about these mental things do you?"

"Er, nope. Nada."

"Nikita and I used to run therapy sessions on each other. Like when we lost our balance and took a fall. We'd bang up our knees. After we ran it out, the knees healed up fast. She and I used telepathy to talk to each other, too. So intimate, but that was long ago." She sighed. "I'll see if I can sense them."

"Good idea." After a pause, he chuckled. "I admit I have no idea what you're talking about—this therapy thing and the telepathy bit. Mom and Dad did talk about it. She swore therapy was incredible. But you're miles ahead of me here. If you need my help, you'll have to—well, be very specific."

"Now who's handicapped?" She grinned. "Help me lie down. I need put my full attention on this."

Reese helped her onto the bed. He pulled up a chair and watched. After closing her eyes, she breathed deeply and exhaled. Her face seemed limp. Other than that, he saw nothing.

***

Haven't done this in years. Nikita, how I wish you were here! Ah, well. Focus on Mom.

She felt her awareness expanding outward, looking for that unique person. Something Nikita had once told her popped into her mind. "Everyone is unique; that's how you look."

A sudden rush of familiarity swept over her. That feeling she'd get when her mother tucked her in at night.

'Mom? This you?' she sent.

'Veronica? Yes, help us! I love my body. I am perfect. I want to be a baroness. We're prisoners. Mutated. I love my body. I am perfect. I want to be a baroness. Can you help us become a baroness?'

Her mother continued to repeat those three short sentences, though neither woman knew what a baroness was. Veronica spotted an image of her parents in Helen's mind. Both looked similar to her.

Mutated like me. Explains lots. 'Mom, where are you?'

Interspersed between volleys of "I love my body. I am perfect. I want to be a baroness," she gained two clues.

177

'Robot guard. Can't leave. Naked.'

She picked out of the constant repetition, 'Abandoned community.'

After listening to more ranting thoughts, she glimpsed an image of where they were being held captive.

She opened her eyes. "That worked! Remember that old apartment complex where they housed victims of terrorist attacks before cures were found? They're in there. A robot is guarding them, and they have no clothes. But something else is wrong. She kept repeating 'I love my body. I am perfect. I want to be a baroness.' At least a hundred times. Made it hard to get anything coherent from her."

"Way to go, Miss Hot-As-Ever! We'll rescue them today. Wait, that sounds like something Mom told me about. The Sixth Invaders and their mental implants. They did stuff like that. Nasty bit of work."

"Thanks. We'll need to get them some clothes. They've been mutated and look like I do. Mom and Dad kept the clothing they wore years ago when they were mutated into armless Galactic Dolls. Stuff's in boxes in the basement. But the robot impersonators are in our house."

"Step One," Reese said, "we'll return to Parkinson's house. Use it as a staging area. Sneak over to your place and grab clothes. Rescue your folks and bring them back to the house."

"Then what? We're doomed. We can't hide from the robots forever; we'll need food."

"Don't worry. I'll think of something. Come on. We have to go back to Parkinson's house now. It's dark out. In the morning, we can sneak into your house while the two robots are at work."

As the pair slipped into the night, she whispered, "Hold on to me. It's slippery."

Light snow and the hour kept most indoors. They stepped inside the inky darkness of the Parkinson mansion and closed the door. Before he could reach the light switch, someone else turned on the lights.

They faced a man holding a very large revolver.

"Who are you? Wait, Reese Cartwright? Is that you, Veronica Hugo?"

"Yes. Don't shoot us," Reese said.

"Bishop. Molly's bodyguard." He holstered his gun. "Come in. What happened to you, Veronica?"

"Robots got me. Mutated me. They've mutated Mom and Dad. The robots are impersonating both of them. We have to rescue them," she said in a rush of words.

"I'll help. Slow down. I'll make you some tea and then you can tell me what's happened. Molly, Hans, and the kids are safe on Domes," Bishop said.

After the warming tea and their story known, Bishop agreed with their initial plan.

"Yes, I've observed them leaving early mornings. They return around supper hour. We can sneak in during the day, retrieve their old clothes, and make a rescue bag. If we're fast enough, we can have them here tomorrow night. Best move them during the night. Fewer eyes. Reese, can you use a gun?"

"Er, not really. That was always Aunt Molly's thing."

"Okay, I'll handle the robot guard. You get her parents clothed."

Mid-day, the three snuck into the Hugo mansion. Reese kept a steadying arm around Veronica as she descended the basement stairs. In a side room, the Hugo's had stacked the long unused Sixth Invader helper machines. Four storage crates held their clothing from that period.

Veronica said, "Wow. These bring back memories. How they used the machines. Hope the clothes still fit."

Bishop and Reese hoisted a box each, carrying them over to Molly's place, returning for the second pair and Veronica.

She spent the rest of the day advising the men on what to pack in a duffle bag for the rescue. Then came the endless waiting hours.

Bishop said, "With all these new robots around, I bought a new antique gun. This is a .44 Magnum, but I put a silencer on it. Molly and I proved a 9mm can't stop a robot, but I hope this baby can. We'll see. If I can't disable the guard robot, while I fight it, you rescue her parents."

Veronica gasped. "Bishop is a robot, too!"

Reese smiled.

Bishop said, "Yes. I am one of the five original human-forms programmed to assist humans. Admiral Carr has ordered me to protect Molly. I've saved her life several times. Please, don't tell others about me."

"But aren't these new robots supposed to help humans?" she asked, her brows curling.

"Yes and no. Yes, in that they've been programmed with the robot laws. I've examined them. But they have a backdoor switch. If thrown, I calculate the rogue robots can control them. Not good. There are millions of them. Few have an antique gun large enough to stop one. You'd need the military's blasters, disruptors, and lasers to stop them, assuming they don't have defense shields powered up. Not good."

Veronica's body shivered. "And I couldn't do anything to one. Scary."

They sat in silence as the sun set. Around midnight, the trio headed out, walking the block to the MTES and headed north. A half-hour later, they walked another block to the sprawling apartment complex that had once been home to over a thousand terrorist victims. All armless. Long abandoned, the snow had been removed only from one entrance.

Reese opened the door, while Bishop stood in front, gun drawn. As the light flooded out, they saw a robot standing before them.

"You are not allowed in—"

A faint bang ended the robot's words, smoke rising from the silencer. A half-inch hole appeared in its head, followed by sparks. The guard robot slumped onto the floor. The trio headed on inside, shutting the door behind them. While Bishop dragged the inert robot to one side, Reese and Veronica moved into the room in search of her parents.

Boom! Another small explosion shook the room. A yellowish gas flooded the air.

"What was..." Reese said, but dropped to the floor.

Veronica screamed. "What's happening?"

Bishop rushed to Reese, dropping the duffle bag. He checked Reese's pulse and eyes.

"Booby trap. Mutation coma is my guess. Hurry. Find your parents."

From speakers, a monotonous voice spoke. "I love my body. I am perfect. I want to be a baroness."

It continued to repeat this. Bishop calculated this was a playback loop and ignored it.

Adrenaline pumping, Veronica opened several doors, peering inside. Without her new telekinesis, she couldn't have even done this much, thanks to the boots she wore. Her mind buried what had just happened to Reese.

"Mom! Dad! We found you. Are you okay? In here, Bishop," she said.

Her parents mouthed words.

"Say something. I can't hear you," she said.

Again, both mouthed silent words.

"Can't you speak?" she asked.

Both shook their heads. She cursed as Bishop and the bag moved up beside her.

She let him dress her parents, silently cursing how helpless she was. While the tall boots kept her feet warm and avoided ankle sprains, without her feet free, she could do little to help Bishop.

By the time Bishop had both dressed, the yellow gas filled this room, too. As they turned to leave the room, Helen and Casper slumped to the floor. Veronica screamed. Bishop bent and checked them.

"Comas. With luck, the mutation is undoing whatever prevented them from talking."

"But how are we going to rescue them? I can't carry one of them."

"Your job is to walk back to Molly's on your own."

Bishop picked up her mother and headed for the door. During the time it took Veronica to walk out, Bishop carried the three to the front porch. Once Veronica joined him, he turned off the light and shut the door. With luck, no one would notice anything.

By the time Bishop carried Reese, the last of the three victims, into Molly's home twilight illuminated the eastern sky.

***

Having walked back on her own, Veronica entered just as Bishop laid Reese on a couch. During the precarious solo walk home, her stomach knotted. Though she tried to suppress the reality of what might have just happened to Reese, she couldn't. Her body shook as she entered Molly's home.

"What will happen to him?" Veronica asked.

(Later, Bishop told Molly, "I calculated Veronica would stay calmer if I didn't tell her what would happen to him. I trust that was the correct calculation.")

Bishop answered. "Don't know. I'm taking you all to Domes. Molly will know what to do. I'll fetch an EMAC and load more of her possessions onto it. I've been making many trips to Domes for her. This will appear normal. Stay put. Watch over them while I'm gone."

"I'm helpless in these boots. Can you take them off me? I'll use my pumps."

***

Around ten that morning, Bishop landed an EMAC in front of the mansion. He carried the four aboard, along with more boxes Molly wanted. A short flight to New O'Hare followed. He loaded them and the Hugo crates into Molly's deep space transport, the Friendship. Within minutes, the five headed for Domes.

Chapter 20 Reactions

January 2, 2376
Domes

As Bishop approached Domes, he called their tower for landing instructions. "Also, have Molly Parkinson, Deanna Cartwright, Russell Godwyn, Eve Burkey, and Dr. Ivy Worth meet us. We've mutation problems. Reese Cartwright has been mutated. Let them know."

When Bishop landed the transport, the crowd rushed the bay doors.

"What's happened to our son?" asked Deanna, aghast.

Russell steadied her. "Mutation coma? How?"

"My fault," Veronica said. "He saved me. We got married. Then, we tried to rescue Mom and Dad. A trap went off. What's happening to him?"

"What happened to Helen and Casper?" Molly asked.

Bishop said, "Long story. Doc, Eve, check them. I think mutation comas. The Hugo's were already mutated but didn't have voices when we rescued them."

While the two examined the three, Bishop outlined recent events.

"Robots are posing as Mom and Dad," Veronica said. "We think many other CEOs and important people have been replaced by robots. Will Reese be all right? What's happening to him?"

"Did you say you and Reese got married? Congratulations, Veronica. You are now our daughter-in-law. Reese finally did it," Deanna said. "He's loved you for years."

Both she and Russell gave her a hug.

Dr. Ivy said, "Let me check you, Veronica. The others are in mutation comas."

Veronica's eyes opened wide as she watched the armless doctor take her pulse, blood pressure, and a host of other physical checks.

"You can move objects, too. Wow. I thought only Molly and I could do that. Are you a real doctor? Patching up people? Doing operations?"

Dr. Ivy chuckled. "I get those questions all the time. Yes. When I moved to Domes, I studied hard. An exhausting period. But I passed the exams with perfect scores. Yes, I perform surgeries. Fortunately, there haven't been many. If you've had the same massive overdose as we have, then you'll find your IQ has shot up. Our brains have nearly doubled. A massive headache when you awakened?"

"That's an understatement! Took a week to go away."

Dr. Ivy smiled. "You'll find your ability to learn new things has skyrocketed."

"Well, I've decided. I want to help people. Reese will need lots of help, won't he?"

Just then, Helen and Casper woke. All attention shifted to the pair.

Casper said, "What's happening? Where are we? Oh, I can talk again. I love my body. I am perfect. I want to be a baroness. Wait. Maybe I shouldn't have my voice back. This isn't the room we were in. They told us they'd soon come and start our baroness training." He repeated the trio of implanted sentences many times.

At the same time, Helen said, "Is this our training site? No, our voices are back. That's not right. I love my body. I am perfect. I want to be a baroness. But we shouldn't have voices. Oh, Veronica, you're perfect, too. We'll all be baronesses when they come to take us. You must take us back. They won't know where we are." She repeated the implanted sentences many times.

Between Casper and Helen's constant recitation, no one could say much.

Molly used telepathy to suggest they move the Hugo's to the next vacant suite in Dome Ten. Several nurses arrived and led the pair off, each keeping a steadying arm around their patient.

When silence came, Molly said, "Implants. They've been implanted with those words, while they were in the mutation coma. That's why it's changed their behavior. I've sent word to Celeste. She'll work her therapy magic on them."

Eve said, "Thanks, Molly. Now, let's get Veronica and Reese to my lab and then to a new suite. Bishop can bring along the crates. Have we got more of those Cass-C robot helpers and Sixth Invader machines?"

Dr. Ivy replied. "I'll check on that. I have to give my medical reports to the President, anyway."

Once she wheeled Reese into her lab, Eve hooked him up to a stasis pod, inserting the IV into a vein in his leg. Then she examined his blood.

She sighed. "Veronica, not such good news. He's suffered a massive overdose of the armless telepath Galactic Doll mutation agent."

"Oh, no! He'll be like me? Nearly helpless? But I need his help." Tears trickled down her cheeks. "No cures?"

Eve shook her head. "Not yet. This version is virulent. Wipes out all the genetic cures that Lara and I have tried. It's taken six years for the foot cure to succeed. I'll inject you with it, too. Maybe it won't take six years to work this time, but I'm not hopeful. Hasn't had an immediate effect on the many others like yourself. It's almost as though those rogue robots never want your bodies to become normal again."

186

She sniffled. "I already figured I'd be stuck like this. Heard about Molly and that ambassador. But Reese, too? That's almost too much to bear."

"He's going to need your support when he wakes, Veronica. There are several similar couples living here in Domes. On your new street, too. Like Molly says, you and Reese will have to help each other."

She sniffled again. "I was shocked and scared when I woke, but I lost my arms once before when Nikita was with me. I sort of remembered how to do things. But he's..."

"Yes, I suspect he has a lot to learn and difficult adjustments ahead. He will need you. But your parents—that implant. They don't seem to be bothered by their handicap. Those robots sure know their behavior modification. We've had several of those baronesses come here. Three were kidnapped telepaths."

"What is this baroness thing?"

Eve told her about them, while Deanna and Russell stood beside their oldest child. Per Eve's orders, they removed all his clothing.

Deanna said, "We should have the kids come and see what their older brother looks like before he mutates."

"I'll get them. You stay with Reese."

Deanna held his hand, knowing that soon it would be gone. Then, Elton, six, and Callie, four, joined her, Russell dabbing his cheeks.

"This is your older brother and his wife, Veronica," Deanna said.

"Is he gonna look like her?" Elton said.

"We think so."

Veronica sensed from the two exactly what Reese didn't need. Pity.

She said, "We'll manage fine. Just like Molly has."

After Russell and the kids left, Deanna and Eve led Veronica to the suite where she and Reese would live. Already Bishop had gotten the three Sixth Invader helper machines installed.

He said, "Laptop on the table has all the how-to videos. Working on getting Cass-C robot helpers. You parents are in the suite next door. Celeste and Otto are running therapy sessions on them."

"But they are insane," Veronica said, biting her lip. "Probably nothing can be done for them."

Eve said, "Ordinarily, yes. But with Celeste's therapy, she can undo implants, even very nasty ones. Will take days, though. The deeper the implant, the longer it takes to erase. Speaking of therapy, yours should come soon. Molly said she's doing you later today. Let's get you well-fed."

"And our clothes unpacked. Could use help with that. What am I going to do for clothes for Reese?"

Eve said, "Don't worry about that yet. Molly and Hans will come by and help you decide."

Eve left as Molly arrived.

Veronica said, "Wow, you look just like you did when I was a little girl."

Molly laughed. "Yeah, too many mutations."

"I miss Nikita. How's she doing?"

"Still going to Soros University on Cass-C. I think she has a boyfriend. Let's get your therapy done."

"I remember it now. Nikita and I used to run it on each other at school when we fell down. Wow, you're wearing flats."

Molly grinned. "Yeah. It took six years for that cure to work. Still, we're thinking of wearing the tall heels for the sake of our children, whose feet are still like yours. Now close your eyes. Let's return to the first hint you had that something was wrong before the mutation agent knocked you out."

"I remember how this goes," she said.

Hours later, she'd re-experienced the massive pain in her arms as they dried up and in her head as her brain and glands swelled in size.

Cheerful at last, Veronica said, "I feel much better. Thank you so much. I'm still scared. How can Reese and I survive like this?"

"We'll do more tomorrow. What can you tell me about the robots taking over the identities of CEOs?"

"Well, Reese thought many had been. Based on how they acted now. He knew quite a few of them. As the CEO of Cartwright Enterprises, Chicago. He thought CEO Lin Dho was a robot and the Senate President, the man from Mars Colony. Maybe more, but best to ask him when he wakes up. I put up a web page."

She shared her discoveries, but when Molly checked, the website had vanished.

During the next two days, Molly ran more sessions on Veronica, erasing various aches, fears, and worries. She explained the progress Celeste and Otto made on her parents.

"As you know, during the mutation coma, the body experiences pain and unconsciousness. The robots played those three sentences continuously during the eight-day coma. You've seen the result: a near insanity and constant recitations of those words.

"Everyone should maintain total quiet around an unconscious person because whatever is said will be recorded, buried deep entwined with the pain. Since the pain couldn't be confronted while the person was awake, the words now have power over the individual, enforced by the pain and unconsciousness."

Veronica raised her brows. "But with Mom and Dad, the implanted words helped them cope, didn't it? I mean, they aren't complaining. They aren't scared. They claim they're

189

perfect and are accepting their mutation, not freaked out as I was."

Molly said, "They couldn't even carry on a conversation, could they? The implant buries normal responses, forcing them to follow the dictated behavior. Once the implants are erased, I expect you'll hear plenty of complaints and freak-outs. They're facing quite a lot of therapy sessions before they're where you are today."

"Okay, but what about Reese? He heard those sentences many times while we were rescuing my parents. Oh, and then again here when they woke up."

"We'll see how he reacts in a few more days."

***

Eve predicted the hour Reese would wake. Molly, Hans, and Veronica joined her, waiting for him to rouse. Veronica assessed him. Yes, his body looked like a perfect Galactic Doll, complete with the massive bosom. His distorted feet dictated the same tall heels as she wore. She spotted other changes. His waist had shrunk. From past knowledge, she knew two ribs had dissolved, along with his arms. His black hair seemed thicker and shinier. It had undergone a growth spurt, now reaching his lower back. She rather liked the look, but glanced at Hans, who sported a crewcut style. He can choose. Reese groaned.

His eyes fluttered and took in this strange place. His last memory was entering the apartment in search of her parents. Now, he stared at a ceiling-less transparent dome far overhead. Besides not knowing where he was, he didn't know how he got there. Thus, his first reaction. Reese screamed. But his voice had changed to that of a soprano, causing further screams.

He tried to sit up, but saw his arms had vanished, replaced by a massive bosom. He screamed again.

"Where am I? Veronica? Your parents? What happened to me? I'm helpless, too."

Veronica said, "We're on Domes. We rescued my folks. They're recovering. We walked into a booby trap. You got a massive overdose like I did. Now, we have to help each other. It'll be all right, Mr. Handsome Devil."

"Domes? Mom and Dad are here. I'm helpless. Oh, I love my body. I am perfect. Just like you. You are perfect. I'm terrified. Veronica, how can we survive? But I am perfect. I guess we can. Somehow. Oh, god! My head's exploding!"

"Yes, just like mine did when I awoke. It goes away in a few days."

"I hope so. I'm perfect. Can't do anything. Feel grimy. We are perfect, aren't we? Perfect. But how do I do anything? I'm scared, but perfect."

"Stay calm. Let's get you bathed and into some clothes. Once you've eaten, Molly's promised to give you therapy sessions."

"But I don't need therapy. I'm perfect. We both are. Helpless, but perfect. How am I going to support you? Help you? I'm failing Mom, and the company. Everyone."

"No, you're not. We have to help each other, just like the others do. You'll see."

***

After a week of therapy sessions, Reese erased the effects of the implanted words and many other adverse emotions that came with the mutation. Now, he focused his efforts on learning to adapt. Veronica's constant help and encouragement propped him up.

When her parents finished their sessions in early February, Veronica chatted with Molly.

"I can't thank you enough for saving Reese. But that implant—it seemed to make him more accepting of the mutation's effects. I'm perfect went along way to keeping him calm. Not overreacting. And with Mom and Dad, they didn't have wild reactions to it, until after they more or less erased the implanted words.

"To me, it seems implanting right ideas while they are unconscious is helpful. They overdid it with my folks, but..."

"Implants are never good. Not in the long run," Molly said.

"Remember those terrorist attacks? Half the mutated men found ways to die after they woke. If someone had implanted something like: 'I love my body. I want to live. I must learn new ways to do things.' Wouldn't that have prevented many deaths? Give them time to adapt?"

"Celeste can give you better advice. The best thing is for everyone to remain silent around the unconscious person. When they wake, provide them with a calming, soothing environment.

"The love-my-body thing can create a maniacal focus on the person's body to the exclusion of others, such as their spouse and children. But I can see your point. Short-term benefits might be useful if therapy isn't available.

"Are you going to study to become a medical doctor?"

Veronica grinned. "You bet I am. After all this, I want to help people."

Chapter 21 Ramification Dreams

February 2376
Domes

The news that the rogue robots replaced CEOs, CFOs, and others shocked me. Having seen what being a baroness meant via Missy, Elie, Connor, and Mady, I knew why the robots mutated and implanted the humans they replaced. Our three telepaths had resisted being turned into helpless baronesses. But the maniac implant caused the Hugos to crave becoming one.

Thanks to Katya and me, the robots knew no cure existed for the massive mutation overdose. We could not restore the bodies of these powerful people. They'd be unable to resume their old jobs.

In a perverse way, I admired the rogue robots' resourcefulness. As Teslenko promised me, they didn't kill humans unless given no other choice. Instead, they mutated them rendering them useless in their leadership roles.

If look-alike robots replaced a CEO, then that mutated human CEO must never be seen. If they were, everyone would know the replacement was a robot. Game over. They had to ship the replaced humans somewhere they'd not be recognized.

Shipping them off to the unknown world where barons and baronesses ruled proved a brilliant choice. I had to admire this twist. Apparently, the Galactic Doll body form was ideal on that world, especially an armless one. Baronesses had no voices. They used a medical machine to remove voice boxes near the end of the mutation process. Unable to speak or understand the local language and barely able to move about in the confining baroness garb guaranteed these victims would never pose a threat to their robot replacements.

After seeing what happened to Missy, Elie, and Connor, the robots must have learned that wasn't enough, because the armless telepaths always found ways to escape. Hence, the mind control implants' embedded desire for their plight. No escapees.

Reese's reaction on waking, his belief that he was perfect after taking in his mutation, proved to me none would leave that baroness world after arrival. Would these victims be better off if they'd been killed outright? The horrid future Mady had faced almost convinced me of that.

I had to act. I used Katya's long Distance Comm set to call Admiral Carr. I explained what I knew.

"Empress Parkinson, my worst fears have come true. We need to act. Exterminate these rogue robots. I'm told the new human-forms versions have a detection circuit in them. But we don't know how many key people have been replaced. If it's just a few, I can send down my Marines, except for the robot warriors. If it's a lot, well... Over."

"Sir, let me see what more I can find out. We need to know what we're facing before we act, right? Over."

"I'll make an admiral out of you yet. Precisely. I can't send down my people. They'd be recognized. We need an undercover operation. Over."

"That's what I thought. I know some people. Give me some time. I'll get more accurate facts. Over."

"There are around nine hundred million humans still on Earth. Many left to colonize the new worlds. We can't risk them. Over."

I laughed. "No wonder the big push to have many babies. Okay, I'll get on it today. Over and out."

"Bishop, we must return to Chicago," I said.

194

"Locate other mutated humans?" Bishop asked. "How can we figure out how many humans have been replaced?"

"Isn't there supposed to be a way to detect them? Reese said there was. We need a less obvious way than sounding an alarm. Let's see if Holly Ann and Reese can come up with something."

Two days later, Bishop and I each had special devices. Mine vibrated against my leg when near one of these new human-form robots. His device relayed an electronic signal to his sensors. I still had to use telepathy to detect one of the hundred-plus rogue robots, like Teslenko.

I felt more comfortable returning to Chicago now that my feet were normal. Though winter still gripped the Windy City, dressed in my cloak and snug boots, no one could tell I didn't have arms. Bishop carried his new big gun and a supply of the mutation agent. Just in case.

Once at my place, I ordered a week's groceries and had Bishop move them into the kitchen in easy reach of my feet. Then we worked out our strategy. Our hurdle: how to get near the key people?

On Monday, we visited the Senior Investigator, Ward Tilman. I found him packing up his personal things.

"Hi, Molly. Yeah, I'm leaving. Heading to Bella as an immigrant. Pay is double. Besides, all my staff are robots. Never thought I'd be running investigations using nothing but robots. Lots of us are getting out while the getting's good. Millions are."

"Have you heard of robots replacing key people, mutating those they're replacing?" I asked.

He sighed. "Yeah, heard rumors. I tried, but was unable to get proof. Then CEOs ordered me to terminate that line of inquiry. Did find a website by Veronica Hugo. It was there for a while. Quite a few posted their suspicions, but I couldn't prove any nefarious actions."

"Do we know how many humans are left on Earth? How many are planning to leave?"

"GPan has those figures. It's under a billion now. Many of those are children. Thanks to the big push to make babies. Heck, we've four ourselves. Nice change, I think."

I wished him luck and took the elevator up to check on the Senior Judge on the sixtieth floor. My leg vibrated continuously as I walked the halls, passing offices of the judicial staff. The Senior Judge, Ashley Peterson, a gorgeous blond Galactic Doll used to be my Personal Assistant while working toward her law degree. Later, I helped her get her position. I was shocked to find my leg vibrating as I passed her office and spotted what looked like Ashley. My stomach sank. What happened to her? I felt responsible, since I got her that top empire position.

We skirted that building. As we walked around Chicago on the MTES, I noticed the Warrior Robots. Okay. There wasn't one on every corner. Still, you couldn't miss them. I felt uneasy seeing them at attention and holding blasters. We weren't at war or under attack. My unease grew.

When we returned home, Bishop and I reached one conclusion. Some of these new human-form robots did not presume to be impersonating anyone. They were themselves, if that can be said of a robot. Far more frightening were those who looked like people we had known, such as Ashley. We decided those must be the people mutated by the rogue robots.

I ordered the old Sixth Invader cook robot to make my supper. I didn't bother trying to activate a spare Cass-C helper to feed me. Later, sipping my tea through a straw, I gave Bishop new orders.

"I'll try another approach. Guard the place. I won't be aware of what's going on around the house for a time."

Bishop nodded and took a position near the front door. I retired to my bedroom. Dirty sheets. Ah, well. I lay down, focused, and expanded my awareness.

I hadn't used my telepathy much. No need. Besides, I hated prying on others' secrets. While I didn't have a specific plan in mind, I intended to locate others like the Hugos. By now, probably relocated to the baroness planet, wherever that was.

I hadn't had a glimpse of potential futures, not for years. I wasn't prepared for the shock of the multiple visions.

"Hello, Admiral Carr. What's up? Over."

"We're landing a small army to take out these robot overlords. They can't get away with taking over Earth. Not on my watch. Over and out."

Boom. I heard explosions, followed by gunfire. I turned on the comm center and big monitor. Warrior Robots with their big guns blasted away against armored Marines with equally large blasters. Chucks of buildings flew about, knocking out doors, windows, and killing bystanders. The screen split into ten windows, each showing the assaults on ten cities. War had come to Earth and Chicago.

For days, the outside noise threatened to rupture my eardrums. No way could I evacuate. I'd never survive getting to New O'Hare. Besides, the MTES ceased functioning the day the Marines landed. Cruiser cannons blasted any EMAC that flew or any of the two-man shuttles. Explosions drew closer. Boom. Half the north side of my home disintegrated as the battle surged past me.

No light, no power, no water, no food, no communications. Chicago blacked out, and still the battle raged on. I lost track of time. Must have been days since I last ate. At last, the noise ended. The robots had won the battle. Admiral Carr abandoned Earth to these mechanical men.

A robot marched into my house. "All humans are to be exterminated," it said and shot me. Blackness swept over me.

I shook my head and blinked. I still lay on my bed. "Shit!"

"Hello, Admiral Carr. What's up? Over."

"We're bombing the robots and retaking Earth. Be prepared. Over and out."

Boom. Explosions rocked Chicago near my home. I turned on the comm center and monitor. Our Sol Empire cruisers darted about the skies of my city, firing down on any robots they spotted. I watched as a Warrior Robot disintegrated into small parts.

The screen split, showing a dozen attacking Sol Empire ships. Soon, ships manned by the robots took to the air, attacking them. Cruisers from both sides exploded, raining death and destruction down upon the homes below them.

Just when I thought it couldn't get any worse, the screen showed a massive explosion. I watched in horror as a mushroom cloud touched the sky. Then a shockwave struck my home, splintering it. I didn't feel a thing. My body perished in a split second. Again, blackness swept over me.

I swallowed and blinked. Again, I still lay on my bed and cursed.

"Hello, Admiral Carr. What's up? Over."

"We will bomb the various space ports. That will confine these robots to this world. Later, we'll land Marines to retake Earth. Be prepared. Over and out."

Once more, I watched the action on the big monitor. Only this time, the robots had a different response. Somehow, they guessed the strategy Admiral Carr used.

In a coordinated response, thousands of nuclear bombs detonated. But these weren't the usual ones. I heard one of our cruisers reporting to the admiral.

"Sir, they've unleashed thousands of dirty bombs. The whole planet is radioactive! We must abandon our attack at once."

"What about the humans?" someone asked.

"Radiation sickness. They'll be dead in days or weeks. It's all over. It'll be a century before it's safe to set foot on Earth again."

My body felt hot. Real hot. Ugly red splotches covered my legs and chest. I rose and vomited. But when I saw my face in the bathroom mirror, I gagged again. My hair fell out, and my face appeared as though it had been through a meat grinder. I vomited again and collapsed. Slowly the world turned dark. Only then did the excruciating pain end.

I swallow and gagged. Oops. I still lay on my bed.

"Hello, Admiral Carr. What's up? Over."

"We're landing groups to evacuate the remaining humans. We will terminate any robot that tries to stop us. Over."

"Sir, are we abandoning Earth to these robots? Over."

"No. Once the humans are rescued, we will bomb them into oblivion! They can't get away with taking over Earth. Not on my watch. Over and out."

Again, I watched the proceedings and announcements on my comm center monitor. I spotted hordes of frightened people heading to New O'Hare. On the split screen, I saw people in other cities doing the same.

As I watched and relaxed, I spotted Helen and Casper Hugo entering New O'Hare, evacuating with humans. Then I spotted Ashley Peterson joining them. I called Admiral Carr, but couldn't reach him.

Days later, the last of the rescue ships departed, Marines landed guns in hand. A few Warrior Robots resisted them. But soon, I realized the human-forms had slipped away with the humans. Admiral Carr now had a huge problem. Robots ended up on all human occupied worlds!

I gasped and lay on my bed. The sun had gone down. No solution Admiral Carr offered worked. I sighed, hoping I'd not have more visions.

With no more futures appearing, I focused on Ashley, searching outward from my home. Every being is unique. You might say we each have our own wavelength or frequency, perhaps related to our personality. I recalled that perky blond Galactic Doll who assisted me.

Her wavelength hadn't changed. I reached her and her mind.

'Hi, Molly Parkinson here. How are you doing, Ashley?'

'I love my body. I am perfect. I want to be a baroness. Help me. Can't speak.'

She repeated the sentences several times before I picked out, 'Going to move us.' After more repetitions, she thought, 'To the Baroness preparation place. Help me.'

I sent calming waves and asked, 'Where are you now?'

After spouting several implant repeats, she thought, 'Old apartments.'

Her mind held an image of the place, which I recognized as the same complex that housed the Hugos.

Next, I asked, 'How many are with you?'

From the implant noise, I picked up, 'Twelve' and that they were being sent to the preparation place in the morning.

I got up and found Bishop standing guard by the door.

"I found Ashley. She's with a dozen others. Tomorrow, they're being taken to a baroness preparation place, where there are many more of them. We must find that prep place and rescue these people."

"Agreed. Where is Ashley now?"

"Same place as the Hugos. The old apartment complex that used to house the thousands of terrorist victims. She doesn't know their prep location. I'm sure it must be on Earth."

"Why that conclusion?"

"They can't risk someone recognizing these people as they transport them to New O'Hare. Ashley is, er, was, the Senior Judge, very well-known person. Moving a dozen like her in the open is far too risky. Bet this prep place must be on Earth, within reach of an EMAC or Air Liner, either of which can be loaded out of sight."

"How do we proceed?"

"Is there any way you can track me no matter where I go? I was thinking about sneaking in and joining Ashley. Let them take me to this place where I can see just how many people they've mutated. Then, we rescue the lot."

"A tracker could be inserted. But how do we communicate? We need another human."

Point well taken. While I tried to think of who still lived on Earth and who we trusted, my daughter walked in.

"Mom, you here? They said you and Bishop were here. I'm home for summer break."

Nikita entered, all smiles. Gosh, how she'd matured. At twenty-three, she wasn't my little girl any longer. Her spindly body had filled out to the Galactic Doll form. She'd been mutated several times in the past.

"Mom, you look good as ever. Still can't keep hold of your arms, I see. Bishop." She nodded to him and hugged me.

"Great to see you. How long are you back for? Whole family is on Domes now."

"I'm off until June. That's when the geology fieldwork is scheduled. Yeah, I went there first. Didn't see my new siblings yet. Eve said you were here. I took the next flight to Earth. What's going on with this robot-replacing-humans thing?"

I told her what I knew of events.

201

She said, "These rogue robots are giving people massive overdoses of the agent. Why? So they can't be cured?"

"I think that's their reasoning. I've just stumbled into something and could use your help."

"But what's this baroness thing?"

I told her about the adventures of our three kidnapped telepaths.

"And when Cartwright tried to help Veronica rescue her parents, he got caught in a robot trap. Now he's like Veronica and us. Speaking of which, I know she'd love to see you."

"Okay, Mom. And I want you to meet Sir Wolfgang Ziegler, my boyfriend. He's a Cass-C aristocrat." She chuckled. "If I marry him, I become an aristocrat, too. Oh, and I now have a degree in linguistics, like Isabella, and I'm going for one in astro-geology with Wolfie. He's coming next week."

"All right. I'll try to infiltrate this group of victims and go with them to their baroness preparation place. Bishop will track me, but I need someone I can telepathically relay communications to. I've a bad feeling about all this."

"Well, at least the rogue robots aren't killing the people they're replacing."

Bishop said, "Many might wish they had. Reese and the others are having a hard time adapting."

"We all did, Bishop. No matter what they say, it's a serious handicap. And diabolical, if Eve can't find a cure for them. But there's always her new cloning process. That might help them. How many do you think you'll find?"

"Ashley said twelve where she's at. No idea what to expect at this prep place. I'll make my move around midnight. Nikita, you stay well clear. I don't want this to happen to you."

She laughed. "Once was enough for me."

Chapter 22 Torturous Reality

Clouds assured pitch blackness, as we three approached my old apartment complex. I focused and hunted for the dozen minds. This place could house a thousand people. They were clumped into one suite at the far end. A bit of mind-looking yielded the fact they were naked except for heels.

Nikita removed my clothes. Donning the tall heels again, I exhaled and then sighed.

"Time to sneak inside."

Bishop opened a door to the complex. Because I used to live here, I knew the layout. I ambled my way into the section where the dozen slept. As expected, a robot guard spotted me.

"Hey, you. What are you doing out of bed? Get back there."

Without a challenge, I slipped into an empty cot beside a sleeping victim. I slept, too.

"Rise and shine, baronesses-to-be. Today, you'll take your next step to becoming a true baroness," a robot guard said and ordered us to use the bathroom.

He had us file outside into a waiting EMAC with a Russian logo. I thought it might be that research center I once visited. Still naked, we exited the vehicle inside a hangar and climbed up into an Air Liner, displaying the same logo. I sent word of this to Nikita.

During the long flight, the robot guard brought us a drink consisting of watered-down blue goo. By the time we landed, he finished serving each of us. I counted thirteen on board, some males. All had a glassy-eyed look. Besides Ashley, I recognized CEO Lin Dho and the GMed CEO. I didn't need to mind-probe to know they were mentally reciting the implanted words.

The Air Liner taxied into another hangar, where we got into another EMAC. Only a few minutes passed before we arrived. Again, the EMAC landed inside a facility. I had no idea where we were. But I got clues at once. From the writing on the walls, somewhere in Russia.

The robot positioned us in a long line and marched us towards a door. A pleasant man, oops, another robot, no mind, stepped out to address us.

"Welcome, baronesses-to-be. This is the official Baroness Preparation Facility. Here, you will be prepped to be perfect-looking baronesses. Then, you'll undergo extensive training in how to be a baroness. Later on, those of you who meet the challenge will meet your baron, who will make you his official baroness. Not all will make the grade. Work hard at it. This way."

He led the line down a hall. We entered a waiting room with many chairs.

"Each of you will be given a new name. Please remember it. No baroness can ever speak. That's not allowed."

I became Crystal Twelve.

We sat waiting for our name to be called. Midway through the group, a robot called, "Crystal Twelve, this way."

I follow him into a side room, hoping to get a better picture of where we were. The room contained a Gurney only. Before I knew what to expect, a knockout gas flooded the room. I felt the robot's arms catching my body and laying it on the Gurney. Then the world turned black.

I awoke and ached. One of those golden veils hung from ear to ear, attached to either side of my nose. It dropped to my chin. Very heavy earrings threatened to pull my ears off, just like the ones I used to wear as Empress. But the worst pain came from my waist and lungs. It felt as though I was being cut in half. I couldn't breathe. I kept gasping, trying not to faint.

New sentences scrolled through my mind. "A baroness must have a tiny waist. I will never complain about anything. I must always show my smile. If I succeed in training, my baron will provide me with very costly earrings. I must show perfect posture at all times."

That's when I realized I couldn't move my head. Somehow, my neck was in a vice. I fainted. A time or two. The robot kept waving something smelly before my nose. It lifted me up into a sitting position. I didn't recognize the woman I saw in the mirror.

Golden coils wrapped around my neck prevented my head from turning. I had to pivot my body to change where I was looking. While heavy, the earrings were cosmetic. The golden veil dangled down. My waist was tiny, held immobile by a tight steel-lined corset. I sensed I wore the fancy stockings from Zahra-C, and I felt the comfort of the special boots from Cass-C that helped prevent ankle sprains.

A billowing red ball gown completed the outfit, though I soon hated it. When I stood, a ten-foot diameter bell of red surrounded me. With no way to bend my head to see or even to bend except at my hips, I couldn't see my feet or where I was stepping. My spy mission just took an awful turn.

The robot said, "Crystal Twelve, remember. One click is yes. Two clicks is no. Three clicks is bathroom. Now, remember to always show your smile."

Mechanically, I obeyed, but that triggered the silly implanted sentences, which continued to repeat themselves in my mind, annoying me.

"Very good. Now, it's time to join all the other young baronesses-in-training. Follow me."

With tiny steps, I followed the robot, unable to do much else. We passed through another door. Whoa! I blinked and paused. And gasped for breath, too.

Two dozen other people milled around a giant arena. The adults, male or female, I couldn't tell, looked like I did. Everyone wore the same red gowns. The only sounds came from heels clicking on the concrete floor. Eerie.

A PA voice said, "Remember to smile and greet the new baronesses-to-be. This is your free hour to relax before lunchtime."

Everywhere I looked, fake smiles. We moved about like sleepy snails, but those that reached me bent slightly at their waists while smiling. I emulated their moves, which was all I could manage.

By turning my body this way and that to take in the arena, I spotted Ashley. With concentrated effort and shallow gasps, I reached her. Her glazed eyes didn't recognize me, but she forced a smile anyway. I wanted to locate these barons, these men, who wanted to put their wives through such hell as this. If I ever did, I knew I couldn't withhold my wrath.

Worse, I saw no seats. Oh, how I wanted to sit. To catch my breath. I sensed the others wanted to sit, too.

At last, the voice said, "Lunch time. Make your way to your assigned rooms. New arrivals, use Lunch Room Six."

While experienced red snails moved in directions toward doors, Ashley and I pivoted about, looking for our door.

Ashley made a single click sound. I wanted to look at her, but couldn't turn my head. After pivoting on my feet, I saw her looking at a distant door. Ah, our door. A long walk. I took small comfort in that all thirteen of us continued to gasp while we crept to the door. I made a mental note to see if those who were here before gasped as badly as we did. Such

206

thoughts intermingled with the implanted sentences that raced through my mind.

We spotted long tables, most already filled with victims and a robot servant. I relaxed a little. We didn't have to use telekinesis to feed ourselves, and considering the implants, I doubted they could. As I approached the tables, I spotted name tags. Still gasping and trying not to faint, I walked around them before I spotted my name. Worse, constrained as I was, I had to sit without falling or missing the chair. I almost did miss it.

The robot lifted the veil and fed me. It fed me a blue goo soup. As tense as I was, I ate very little.

When everyone finished, the voice said, "Time for your afternoon practice sessions. Newcomers, remain seated. A robot guide will come for you and show you around."

The others rose and headed for various doors. A robot man walked up.

"If you will rise, I will give you the guided tour before your first workout."

At least it walked slowly enough that we could keep up. We exited through a door labeled Walking Arena.

I saw an oval track, once perhaps for distance runners. Again, no chairs or seats.

"When it's time, you will practice your walking skills. Around and around the oval. You pass this test when you can complete twenty loops in the allowed time. I'll bring you back here when the tour is done. When you've passed this test, it's on to the Step Challenge."

We entered another section of this complex. Here, I saw a miniature castle construct. Stone stairs rose towards the ceiling. I counted five stories. At each one, the stairs ended in a level platform before the next flight began. The rest of the castle was missing.

Several dozen made their way up the steps. On their own. Fear radiated from each, while the PA voice continued to tell them to smile. Then I gasped again. I'd missed an additional horror. A duplicate set of stairs led down from the fifth floor. Armless, stiletto heeled, and out of breath people descended them on their own. Their progress made those climbing the stairs look like they were running. I almost fainted.

Our guide said, "Here, you are to climb the stairs to the very top and then descend to the main floor. The passing standard here is to complete the circuit five times in the allotted time. Now follow me."

Waltz music echoed from the next room. I saw couples attempting to dance. Without arms, each pressed their body into the other and tried to dance. With such tiny steps and with feet obscured, I couldn't tell if they were successful or not.

"Passing dance standard is to dance for the entire period. Mind you, it's much harder than it looks. Expect to faint many times, like that one just did. They expect a baroness to regain her feet on her own."

I wanted to scream. How? Constrained as we were, getting up would be impossible unless we used our special powers. I wondered if that was allowed? The poor person hadn't gotten to his or her feet by the time we left the room.

The next room held only a few people. Again, I saw the pair of fake five-story stairs and a huge dance floor. Giant lights illuminated the whole space. We saw the people drifting to the back wall, far from the stairs.

Our guide said, "This is the final test. What happens if the lights should go out? A baroness must be able to climb and descend stairs to find the right room. Plus, she must be able to turn the lights back on if needed."

It pointed to a switch on the opposite wall, far from either set of stairs.

"Passing standard is to move from the wall where they're standing, go up to the top and then back down and over to the wall, flipping the lights back on. All in the allotted time. Demonstration please."

With that, another robot turned off the lights. Pitch black! I heard many gasps. This must be impossible to do.

As though reading my mind, our guide said, "This is the hardest challenge. Only when you have mastered this test are you ready to take your place as a baroness, honored and revered by your people. These candidates are mastering this last challenge. After supper, I will show you to your beds. Now it's practice time."

He led us back to the track circle.

"A baroness often walks five miles each day. That's twenty times around this track. Start practicing now. And don't forget to smile as you walk."

With that, he turned and left the room. One by one, we thirteen joined the others already making their way around the track. Heel clicks, the only sounds.

I took shallow, fast breaths, hoping not to faint or fall. My lungs felt like they were imploding after only one pass around the track. I had no choice but to stop and wait until my body recovered.

One woman moved too fast and lost her balance. She hit the track hard and lay there, stunned. The robot ignored her. The other women slipped by her, unable to help her even if they wanted to. I completed another two laps before the person got onto her feet, gasping for breath from the exertion. But she flashed a smile as she walked again.

If one of those actual barons walked into the room, I would have terminated him!

I needed my complete concentration just to keep going around the track. I'd finished six loops before the robot announced the end of the session and dinner. Again, we new arrivals took far longer than the others did to find our seats. Conclusion: these practice sessions must enable us to move faster.

I ate as much as I dared. Had to keep up my strength. Besides, my legs ached from that much walking. After supper, my robot feeder led me to a tiny room, where it removed my dress and helped me into bed.

"Three clicks for pee," it said as it turned off the light.

I lay on my back, unable to even turn myself over. The neck loops and tight corset made movements very challenging. I finally relaxed.

'Mom. Are you okay? We've been trying to reach you all day.'

Nikita made contact. Oh, how I loved her gentle touch. I sent her images of the day.

'Mom, we need an accurate count of how many people need rescuing. Won't do to only get half of you. You're at the psych research center outside Moscow. Bishop is working to arrange a mass rescue. More tomorrow night.'

I drifted into dreamland.

Marines charged towards a line of the Warrior Robots. War had come. Behind the wall of Marines, I saw six of us armless telepaths. Us mutants. Wait. I sent to the six, 'Now.'

I focused and shot a piercing telekinesis punch into a robot's head, just like I'd done when one ripped off Katya's arms. Seems I'd taught these others how to do it. Seven Warrior Robots collapsed as sparks arced around the gaping holes in their heads. Again, we seven shot our penetrating beams, eliminating this group of enemy robots. The Marines moved us onwards to the next line.

I heard Admiral Carr saying, "It's working! Our telepaths are eliminating these robots! Victory is ours."

I woke in a cold sweat, gasped, and tried to get up. Failing, I focused on controlling my breathing. Again, I'd had a vision of a potential future. This time, we didn't lose to the robots. I knew I had to save every one of these people. Their future roles might save the empire.

Although I tried, I couldn't get an accurate head count the next day. As constrained as I was, I didn't dare lose my concentration. But that night when Nikita contacted me for an update, I relayed my future vision to her. She promised to relay it to Admiral Carr, though I doubted he'd believe her. I warned her to warn everyone that these robots probably installed booby traps like the one that got Reese.

Chapter 23 Learning

Bishop said, "She's right about the booby traps. Reese and I took out the robot guarding her parents. When we walked inside, the mutation bomb exploded. Reese had no chance of avoiding its full effects. When we brought her parents out, they inhaled an overdose. That dose restored their voices. Healing by re-mutation."

"But we have to rescue Mom."

"We do. Let's find the plans for this sports complex turned psych center. Then, we can make plans."

Hours later, they studied the drawings.

"Here's the main entrance where the EMAC entered," Nikita pointed out. "I count a dozen other doors."

"Don't be hasty. You said Molly said they have five-story staircases and parts of stone castles in there, along with bedrooms and dining rooms. I can't see how they could fit all that in there and keep all the doors operational," Bishop said.

"What you're saying is these plans don't match what's inside today?"

The robot nodded.

"How do we figure that out?" she asked, biting her lip. "We don't have to. If there's only one usable entrance, then this has to be it. Any booby trap would be there. Isn't that logical?"

"I believe that is a safe assumption. However, I dare not risk sending in Admiral Carr's men. If they should trigger another trap like Reese did, he'd tear me apart for spare parts."

"Tell me more about rescuing the Hugos."

He did so.

She said, "You terminated the robot guard, waited about minute, and then entered. The mutation bomb exploded after two minutes," she said. "We should assume that'll be the way it's installed here, too. We wait four minutes before we enter or better yet, you go in while I wait out the four minutes. Surely it'd be safe by then."

"If it's not, Molly will use me for spare parts."

"Don't be silly, Bishop. I won't let her. Besides, we will need a flotilla to rescue this many people. Plus, they'll be excruciatingly slow and almost helpless. She said hundreds, but how many hundreds?"

"Robots have replaced many people. Have they already sent victims to the baron world? Based on what you relayed to me, my calculations suggest very few people have passed the final test. I could do it because I have radar sensors. A human could pass the test, but not without trying many, many times."

Bishop said, "As I compute this course, it's designed to get the people used to proper breathing and moving as rapidly as possible over level ground. Once they've achieved that level of confidence, dealing with steps would be the logical next step. Don't know where dancing enters the equation. Perhaps that has a sociological nature to that world. Doing it all in the dark could only be attempted after one has mastered doing it while the course is illuminated.

"In fact, based upon what Connor and the others have told us, baronesses faced navigating the stone stairs and castle alone and sometimes in the dark. I conclude these rogue robots are trying to do right by these people, instead of sending them off like they did with Connor and the others."

"You're sticking up for the robots?" Nikita asked. She tightened her jaws and sighed. "Yes, you make a very good point. Mom once told me the rogue robots didn't want to kill humans unless forced to. They aren't killing them. If they're sending them off to this baron world, then preparing them might be computed as an act of kindness. I bet the people aren't seeing it that way. Mom's ready to terminate every single robot. I've never sensed her this mad."

She thought for a second. "We must plan to rescue thousands of people. Just in case. She said hundreds, but ten make a thousand. If she's off, we don't dare leave one behind."

Bishop said, "If they are wearing gowns like Connor and the others wore, we'll have to carry them out. Plus, we can't house them here on Earth. We must take them to Domes. The other empire worlds still have a ban on mutants."

He paused in his calculations. "All must undergo mutation to regrow voice boxes. Where do we find enough mutation agent for that many people? And that implant makes them insane."

Bishop told her about the insanity shown by the Hugos.

"Therapy for a thousand. Wow. A minimum of one week of therapy for each is close to twenty years to complete. That's a huge problem. Most will need more. Will Domes even accept them? We should talk to their officials before we make more plans. If Domes won't take them, I think I can arrange for Soros University to take them."

That evening, Nikita contacted me again.

'Haven't learned much. Just trying to survive this,' I sent.

'Mom, is it true that the robot's leader doesn't want to kill humans?'

'That's what he's told me. After seeing all these people, I believe him. But what he's doing to them is inhuman. Sadistic.'

'I've thought a lot about that. What if he thinks he is helping them? Preparing them for the baroness lifestyle.'

She elaborated on her notion.

'Well, I did better today. At home, we always keep night-lights on for that very reason. We can't feel along for a

214

switch in the dark. Still, they don't even help someone who's fallen get up. That's an almost impossible feat.'

'Maybe that's helping to instill confidence. Anyway, see if you can get a more accurate idea of how many are there. Bishop's worried we won't have enough transportation to rescue everyone before the robots counterattack.'

I promised to do so. At breakfast, my breathing came a little easier. I noticed others at the table. While everyone wore a red ball gown, they weren't the same shade of red. I'd call Ashley and my dresses blood red. Across from me, dresses had a twinge of brown in the red. Still others tended more towards the pink side of red. Very few wore bright cherry red gowns.

Those in cherry red gowns seemed more at ease, happier somehow. Their smiles seemed real, not faked as most were. As the meal finished up, the PA voice interrupted the silence again.

"For the benefit of our newcomers, gown colors indicate the level of success the wearer has achieved. Newbies wear dark red gowns. When you pass the first test, your gown changes to the brown-red. Kaitlyn Nine, stand up. She has mastered the track."

She nodded to us by bending at the waist. Nothing above that could bend.

"Sally Five received the pinkish red dress after passing the second test. Sally Five, stand. Cherry red, the most beautiful of gowns, is bestowed to Baronesses-in-waiting. Betsy One, stand."

She did. I gasped. I recognized Piper Strawn. She and her deceased husband had once been our Senators to the Federation of Planets. Piper looked years younger; the mutation did that to us. Her long blond hair contrasted with her bright blue eyes. Last I'd heard of her, she'd returned to her nursing profession. Her smile seemed genuine, as did the glow from what I could see of her face.

I touched her mind. Confidence, but no trace of the fear that pervaded the room. Further, the implanted words, though still present, seemed subdued, as though they no longer carried the importance they once had.

While I dared not make telepathic contact with Piper, I got the message. Nikita was right. Confidence mushroomed upon passing that final test. Passing these tests convinced them that they weren't helpless, just dependent on others for dressing and feeding. The shock of that realization almost caused me to miss the fact that the meal had ended. Others were already making their way towards the proper doors.

Armed with more facts, I attempted to touch other minds. Terror and fear radiated from those of us walking around the track. The implanted sentences echoed in their minds.

At lunch, I did the same with those dealing with the five flights of stone stairs. The intense fright lessened slightly, but a fear of falling swamped all earlier fears. Terror of falling drove the implanted words into the background.

The minds of those who passed the initial stairs test had waltzes playing in their minds. The ugly terror and fear beginners felt weren't present, though in the background the implanted words continued to play. Pleasant. That's how I sensed they felt.

Dread and scared. Those emotions emanated from the few who were dealing with the stairs in the dark. But I noticed a subtle change in the implanted sentences. The person used them to help bolster their resolve.

'I am perfect. I can do this. I know I can.' Those were one woman's thoughts as she walked through the doorway after lunch.

That night as I waited for Nikita's loving touch, I compared how Connor and Missy had adapted to life as a baroness versus how Piper might fare. No comparison. The

216

three telepaths hated it, rejected it, and lived in constant fear. Piper exuded confidence, ready to accept the life of an honored baroness.

Teslenko wasn't being sadistic but was trying to ease these people into the proposed new lives. Damn. I wanted to hate these rogue robots.

'Mom, the rescue is on for tomorrow. Admiral Carr will use the battleship Aurora to ferry everyone to Domes.'

We chatted. I told her about my observations and that I agreed with her analysis.

'Of course, I'm right, Mom,' my ever-precocious daughter said.

'Just be careful of booby traps. I don't want you mutated like we are.'

Chapter 24 Rescue

Admiral Carr coordinated the assault with Bishop.

"Look, we're dealing with rogue robots who've shown they love to mutate anyone into armless Galactic Dolls. With their history of trickery, I'm not about to send my Marines in there to rescue almost helpless people. According to my geneticists, this latest overdosed mutation can't be cured. It's too risky for me to use my soldiers on an assault. If a mutation bomb goes off, the consequences are too steep. Over."

"But once we're inside, your people will help us rescue them, correct? Over," Bishop said.

"Yes, and we can provide cover fire as needed. Once you've secured the facility, we'll help with the evacuation. The battleship is in position. Shuttles are ready to land and begin ferrying the victims to the Aurora.

"We've been monitoring the situation on Earth. The latest figures show the genetics labs have manufactured one hundred six tons of the mutation agent. Unfathomable. We're worried they will launch bio attacks on other worlds in the empire. Before I launch an all-out attack on the robots of Earth, I must talk with Empress Parkinson. Make sure you rescue her, Bishop. Over and out."

"Nikita, this has escalated into a very dangerous situation. I can eliminate a robot with my new .44. Do you want a gun for yourself?"

Nikita laughed. "Hardly, Bishop. I can't shoot one. That's Mom's thing, not mine. I'll stay well back until it's safe to enter. A four-minute delay should be enough."

"These robots are clever, Nikita. They're not like the Cass-C helper robots on wheels you're used to. They are like

218

me. Besides, Admiral Carr has me spooked. A hundred six tons of the mutation agent. I cannot compute a use for such an amount."

"Mom said they use a massive overdose. Maybe it's not as much as we think. We best get going. Land our EMAC out of the way. I'm slow in these heels. I'll follow you from a distance."

"They still forcing women to wear them at Soros University?"

"Yeah. And the plain, black and white school uniforms. Trouble is, having worn them this long, I can't wear anything lower. Let's do this."

"Look, if we meet any serious resistance or if they shoot back, flee. If they disable me, flee."

"Okay, Bishop. I can't believe I get to help rescue Mom. This is exciting. Maybe I should take a gun, one that I can't mishandle."

From a closet in the EMAC, Bishop retrieved an antique .357 Magnum.

"This is a six-shot revolver. Just point at the robot and pull the trigger. Remember: six shots."

"Will it stop a robot? Mom's 9mm didn't back on Cass-C."

"I don't know. I found this larger one—a .44 Magnum revolver. I proved one shot to the robot's head disables it. But I don't know if the .357 will. But it's more powerful than the 9mm."

***

A robot at the New O'Hare Control Tower notified Teslenko.

"Molly Parkinson has arrived. Does that mean trouble?" it sent electronically.

"Yes. I'll have her watched."

Teslenko fired a flurry of electronic signals to other robots. Soon, they alerted him that she'd gone to her home in northern Chicago.

He shifted his calculations to predicting the purpose of her visit. Word had reached Teslenko that the former baroness telepaths landed on Domes. Long ago, Teslenko installed a fudge factor into his calculations: if Parkinson is involved, she's seventy-five percent likely to intervene in my current plans. Today, the robot applied that factor to his calculations.

Conclusion: our cover must have been blown by that Hugo child. Still, the six-year reign here more than met my goals. I must assume Parkinson is after the mutated humans we've been grooming to become baronesses. I calculate the Russian center has a ninety percent chance of discovery and subsequent raid. Time to prepare to initiate Plan Z.

Teslenko sent out a flurry of messages to subordinate robots, setting prepared actions in motion.

In fact, I shall go there myself and face Parkinson again. She's a most worthy adversary. She's the only human deserving of my attention.

He recorded his thoughts and conclusions on his secret device. When word came that Parkinson had left her home in north Chicago, Teslenko took the next Air Liner to Moscow.

As the latest crop of mutated humans arrived, Teslenko spied on them via remote cam. The robot grinned when he recognized Parkinson. He added another note to his electronic log of events.

My theory is proven. Veronica Hugo uncovered our replacement of key humans and told Parkinson. As predicted, she's infiltrated the training center. It's certain she's here to rescue the humans. I shall watch her. I'm interested ln her choices, her methods of implementation.

Late morning, other robots alerted Teslenko. The Sol Empire battleship Aurora had moved into the lowest orbit allowed without interfering with various satellites and space debris. He added another conclusion to his notes. She has made a good estimate of their numbers.

Teslenko continued calculating while he waited for the assault on the prep center. How would Admiral Carr react when he learned robots had been replacing humans for six years? Would they launch a ground attack on the robots? Aerial bombs? Total embargo of spaceships visiting Earth?

He dispersed the CEO replacement robots around Earth, lessening the chance that they'd drop bombs. Although millions of humans remained on Earth, their uniform distribution acted as a buffer from attacks. Many of the remaining adults had low IQs—the last remnants of the corporation drug-induced dementia designed for population control. Would Carr deem them expendable? While he calculated Admiral Carr's choice educational, Plan Z precluded sticking around.

Last year, his robots distributed nuclear bombs to major cities around the world. Should Admiral Carr launch an all-out war against the robots, Plan X called for their simultaneous detonation, turning Earth into a radioactive planet. For humans, deadly. For robots, a non-event.

The plan selected depends on Parkinson: what her role might be and her influence on the admiral, as noted in my logs.

He sent an electronic message to the worker robots, but a different message to the Warrior Robots. In a secure bunker, Teslenko recharged while waiting for the action to begin.

***

Bishop and Nikita landed some distance from the prep center, their rented EMAC hidden behind a snowdrift.

"I don't like this, Nikita. I've been calculating probabilities since last night. We're dealing with intelligent robots, not menial ones."

221

"And what did you calculate?" she asked, grinning.

"Seventy percent chance Teslenko knows we're coming. Eighty percent chance he knows his scheme of replacing key humans with his robots is known to Admiral Carr. Ninety percent chance he has laid a trap for us. Especially true since Admiral Carr is staying out of the initial assault."

"We'll just have to be smarter than he is, Bishop." Nikita nodded, attempting to display determination.

"The next question is whether the victims' robot helpers will attack us or not. I can't shoot more than six, assuming one shot disables a robot. If they counterattack, we must retreat and calculate another plan."

"But we can't leave Mom in there. Not with those beasts. Not as helpless as she is. We must rescue her."

After a frown and pause, she said, "I see your point. Must be hundreds of other robots in there helping all those people. Do you think they'll attack us?"

"A calculated risk. If Teslenko doesn't want to kill humans, then perhaps he won't order a counterstrike. Besides, his replaced-human-leaders game is over. Admiral Carr and the empire know about it and will take precautions. There's nothing to be gained by a counterattack. But that's not a certainty."

"Be alert for booby traps."

Bishop imitated a chuckle. "That's almost a certainty. I wish you weren't going in there. If anything happens to you, Molly will skin me."

Nikita laughed. "But Bishop, you don't have any skin. Well, synth skin. I couldn't live with myself if I didn't help Mom. Let's do this."

Both removed their winter gear. Bishop drew his big gun and walked into the sheltered EMAC lot and the main entrance. Moving much slower, Nikita picked her way along the snow-covered walk, wishing she didn't have to wear the

Cass-C tall heels. She watched as no one answered Bishop's knock.

He took out a small plastic charge, placed it on the door, and stepped back. Nikita stopped and covered her ears. Boom, the door swung open. Bishop waited a moment. The arm of a Warrior Robot appeared, blaster in hand.

Bishop anticipated it and fired his gun. A loud boom and smoke greeted Nikita's ears as she continued to close the gap. Crash. The Warrior Robot dropped to the concrete in a heap. Even from this distance, Nikita could see a sizeable hole in its positronic brain, along with residual sparks.

Bishop crept inside. Nikita exhaled. She'd forgotten to breathe. She reached the entrance, stepping around the fallen robot. Bishop moved deeper into the complex ahead of her. She waited for what she thought was four minutes, while Bishop ducked into various small side rooms, relaying what equipment and supplies he saw.

"Clothing room. Metal rings room. All empty. Seems safe enough for you."

Satisfied, Nikita entered the first room, glancing at the various side rooms Bishop had cleared. Boom!

She looked up and saw a giant yellowish cloud dropping on her. She turned to flee and took one step before the world turned black.

***

Bishop turned and saw the gas enveloping Nikita. Before he could react, she slumped to the ground. His sensors suggested the usual vile mutation agent. He paused, calculating his next move. Did he rescue Nikita or did he proceed onward and attempt rescue of Molly and the others?

The only egress-ingress point filled with mutation agent meant he couldn't bring people out through the planned route. They'd drop into comas, too. He had to clear away the gas. He picked up Nikita and carried away from the gas, further into the complex. He grabbed her comm set.

"Bishop calling Admiral Carr or whoever is listening. Booby trap got Nikita. I need the roof removed by the entrance to clear the mutation agent out. Over."

"A blaster is ready. Need coordinates."

Within a minute, a giant hole appeared in the roof of this entrance section. The yellow gas rose. He estimated it would be clear in a half hour. Continue. Gun at the ready. In the distance, he heard transports landing.

***

Alerted to the pair heading to the entrance, Teslenko signaled the helper robots. One replied. Soon, Teslenko spotted his quarry and closed the distance to the woman who made her way around the track. With one arm, he snatched Parkinson up and carried her off at a jog.

"Quiet, Parkinson. We have to talk. Your people are about to raid this place."

She said nothing, taking shallow gasps, trying not to faint.

He took her to the fifth floor of the last test room, though lit. That day's group of victims hadn't yet arrived for their morning practice session in the dark. He touched a wall opening a hidden panel that opened into his secret office. Once inside and the door shut, he sat her on a chair facing the display monitors.

She saw Bishop looking back at Nikita, who lay on the ground. Before she could pivot her body to make eye contact with him, Teslenko slipped a blindfold over her eyes.

"What did you do to Nikita?" she asked.

"I'm afraid she walked into a booby trap. She'll survive. Now then, Parkinson, we need to talk. If you don't give me straight answers, I'll give you to a baron just as you are. I'm sure that would please him."

"Why the blindfold?"

"How did you destroy the robot that pulled off Captain Binsk's arms on the fantasy world? A new weapon?"

"You gave me that power. That massive mutation agent overdose."

"The one without a cure? The one I'm making excellent use of?"

"Yes. It gives us something besides telepathic ability. Telekinesis. I reacted and shot a telekinesis force wedge at the robot. I didn't know that would terminate it. With these massive overdoses, you're creating an army of people who can destroy a robot with ease.

"In fact, after my first day in your prep center, if I had seen you, I would have terminated you."

"That's the reason for the blindfold. I theorized you needed to see your target. It seems I've made a terrible blunder with the massive overdoses. I didn't want to kill humans without a reason. But those I replaced with my robots had to vanish. The scheme worked for six years. Tell me, was it the Hugo's daughter, Veronica, that uncovered what I was doing?"

"I don't know about others, but for me, yes, that exposed the plot. I told Admiral Carr."

"And today you still wish to terminate me?"

"No. I theorized your problem lay in the telepathic abilities brought on by mutation. These humans had to vanish, never to be seen on Earth again. You couldn't just drop them on another world. They'd soon talk and return, foiling your plot. As a voiceless, armless baroness, they couldn't make themselves understood, let alone return to earth."

Teslenko imitated a sigh. "Indeed. When I visited the barons, the telepaths who ended up there as baronesses caused enormous problems. That's why I had them returned to Earth, or rather to Domes."

"Is that why you used the psych's crude implant techniques on them? I am perfect. I want to be a baroness."

Again, the robot feigned a sigh. "Yes, Parkinson. I discovered that with those ideas frozen in their minds, they had no desires to return to Earth."

"Let me guess. Another problem rose. They had a hard time adapting?"

"Precisely. The first ones suffered. One even fell to her death. I could not allow that. Hence, I devised this elaborate training regime. My robots protect the humans from a fall down the stairs, but the trainees aren't aware they have a safety net. I don't want them injured, but taught survival skills.

"And the training has a proven record. Those who have made it through the program are confident of their abilities. The very few who have become baronesses have adapted well to their new lives."

"That's why I'm not ready to terminate you. While at first glance this prep training appears to be sadistic, in fact you are making it possible for them to survive life as a baroness. Still, you shouldn't be mutating humans and replacing them with robots. I can't forgive that. These people's lives are damaged, perhaps ruined if we cannot find a cure."

"Now we come to the critical question. Admiral Carr's plans? Is he going to bomb us? Is he sending down his Marines to hunt us down and kill us? Is he starting a war against robots?"

"Sorry. I haven't talked to him. I know he is furious about humans being replaced by robots. It's a certainty he'll take action against you. Amazing you kept this from the Admiral for six years."

"I have already reached that conclusion. We are at a crossroads, Parkinson. What he does versus my response. Could be terrible consequences. There's still about eight hundred million humans on Earth, but many adults have such low IQs that they aren't allowed to populate new colonies. What he does could well affect those people. Just so you know, I have activated the caches of your antique nuclear bombs. Most are centuries old and in bad condition. I'm prepared to use them if needed."

"Right, because robots aren't bothered by radiation. I figured that. What we need is a way to preserve all life, including your robots."

"That, Parkinson, is why we needed this discussion. You are the only human I consider my equal. Is there any way out of this for both sides?"

"I know what I want. Let Bishop and the others take possession of these people. Have your robots vacate the leadership positions they took away from them. What do you want for your robots?"

"Many are simple human-forms designed to be of service to your people. They should continue in that way. I'd like the chance to evacuate my robots from your world. Unharmed. And soon. Our goals are not too far apart. But Admiral Carr won't see it that way. Won't he demand retribution?"

Parkinson laughed. "You calculated that right. In most people's eyes, you and your rogue robots have harmed thousands of Earth's top people. We've no idea what you've done for those six years. Perhaps many more things we consider criminal. So, yeah, he's likely to want retribution. Since he hasn't sent in the Marines to help Bishop rescue me and the others, I think he's doing a wait and see game."

"Ah, afraid of the booby traps. Yes, brilliant move on my part. Humans are terrified of this armless telepath Galactic Doll mutation. Give them a hint it can happen when they aren't expecting it. Like the booby traps. And they'll be very hesitant to send in Marines. You know, I expect, that I have enough of the mutation agent to mutate an entire army, should they send them to attack us."

"I do. Tons of the stuff. Admiral Carr knows that. I'm sure that's why he's holding back retribution right now. Men are especially afraid of it. The mutation agent ruins people's lives."

"It gets them out of my way without killing them. Could we agree to terms? I won't stop or hinder your people from rescuing these mutated people. Your people don't attack us. We'll be gone from Earth in short order."

"I agree to that, but I can't promise Admiral Carr will. With all the people to rescue, I'm sure that'll occupy Admiral Carr for hours. I would bet he doesn't take action until all are onboard the rescue ships."

"I agree, but I need to delay you a short while. Time for us to leave this planet. Be careful when you try to remove the neck rings. If it isn't done right, a small bomb goes off. Boom!"

Teslenko lifted Parkinson up, depositing her outside his secret office. He turned out the lights and removed the blindfold.

"Down the steps. Turn on the lights. Find the exit door."

He slipped back inside his office. The hidden panel closed. A faint elevator-like noise followed, while Parkinson stood rooted to the spot in total darkness atop five stories of stone stairs.

Chapter 25 Now What?

I stood frozen to the spot. I sensed I was up high, but couldn't see where the steps began, let alone go down them.

One thing struck me. Anyone constrained as we were and who could pass this test must have developed enormous self-confidence and skill. I admired the few I'd seen who had done it. They hadn't let this enormous physical challenge beat them.

And that's what this was. The barons on that world must be the most sadistic beasts ever. Another thought distracted me.

The Sol Empire had achieved gender equality, in so far as that was possible. A worker's gender had no basis on the standardized job pay. In fact, I couldn't recall any example of such inequality. Physical differences played a role. Male bodies tended to be stronger than female bodies. Only females gave birth. Yes, gender played a role in our society.

True, a few men abused women. Casper Hugo had once kidnapped me in an attempt to make me his mistress. But even he changed his behavior long ago. When I was in high school, I heard of a young man convicted of raping a woman. GD sent him to the penal colony on Mercury. Being sent there was tantamount to a death sentence. On the whole, very little criminality existed. The penalties, too severe.

But these barons and baronesses existed in a Dark Age. I vowed to one day find that world and bring those men to justice. That vow cleared my mind.

Using extreme care, I slipped a foot forward, sensing for the first step. When I took one step down, I had to stop, gasping for breath. I'd scarcely dared to breathe. Minutes passed as I moved forward, feeling for the top of the next step. Always, I felt a knot in my stomach as I allowed one foot to descend into the unknown before it hit the stone of the lower step.

I've never focused so hard in my life as I did then. How long had it taken to reach the bottom floor and know it was the bottom, I couldn't say? At minutes per step, could well have been an hour.

I found the wall and pressed into it, searching for the light switch. That was the easy part. I've never been this thankful for a light, but I had to catch my breath before moving to the door which opened as I approached.

Outside dozens of people awaited the order to enter the testing room. At first, the PA provided no guidance. Then over the PA, Teslenko's voice said, "Robot helpers: cooperate."

I touched a few minds to see what they thought was happening. Total confusion.

I must pass this test. I'm afraid of this test. I'm being rescued. But I don't want to be rescued. I want to be a baroness. I need to pee, but there's no robot to hear me.

I debated whether to tell them to head back towards the other areas or not. With Nikita down, I had no way to ask Bishop what was happening.

Standing still in these tall heels wasn't possible. They'd been standing here for at least an hour with no way to sit. They couldn't tell the single robot standing at the door to open it. In fact, it seemed inert or oblivious to us. Fidgeting. Idle wiggling. Nervousness ruled.

Thus, I focused and sent a calming flow over the group. I heard many shallow sighs.

At long last, the door opened. A soldier wearing a Marine's uniform spoke into a shoulder comm.

"Got another bunch. Maybe two dozen."

He turned to us. "Admiral Carr sent us to rescue you. Follow me. I'll lead you to safety."

No one budged. One clicked three times. Then another clicked, followed by too many clicks to count.

"Come on. We'll stop at the bathroom on the way."

That did it. A long single-file line of billowing gowns snaked behind him at a snail's pace. Other helper robots joined him as we reached one set of restrooms.

That detail handled, albeit very awkwardly by the soldiers, we continued our lengthy walk out of the complex. In fact, the location of the final test room was as far from the entrance as possible, probably by design.

Partway, more soldiers jogged up. One had captain's strips.

He said, "Ah, Mrs. Parkinson, right?"

"Yes, is everyone safe? How's my daughter? Bishop?"

"She's in a mutation coma. Looks like another massive overdose. Sorry. Booby trap. Bishop's okay and assisting with the robots. Admiral Carr wants to see you like yesterday. I've never seen him this angry. Hell, we're all teed off. What they've done to our people—the robots should all be destroyed! We're waiting the order to blow them to pieces."

"Others are used to walking faster than me. I'll bring up the rear. I'm slow. Have to stop for breath. Often."

When we reached the entrance, I asked, "Wow, what happened here?"

The roof of this section had vanished, but no debris littered the floor.

"Bishop had us disintegrate it to clear out the mutation agent. I guess we weren't fast enough. I best carry you into the transport."

A woman with a clipboard stood beside the bay doors.

"Don't count this one. It's Empress Parkinson. She wasn't abducted. What's the count?"

"She sure looks like everyone else. We're at two hundred sixty-three."

"I might be the last one out," I said. "Where's Nikita?"

"They have her hooked up to a stasis pod on the Aurora," she replied.

The captain lifted me up, deposited me in my seat, and buckled me in. I sat at the rear of fifty others. We faced forward, unable to turn enough to look out the windows. My stomach informed me of liftoff.

Once onboard the battleship, soldiers lifted us out, making sure we had our balance. More crew led us to temporary quarters, but the captain led me first to see Nikita and then to the CCC, where Admiral Carr's image dominated a big monitor.

"Ah, Empress Parkinson. You should get a medal for this. I'm told soldiers are now doing a thorough search of the complex and are confiscating machines and supplies. Once they inform me that everyone's been recovered, I need to act against these rogue robots."

"Sir, I talked with their leader, this Teslenko. I think by now he and the others have fled Earth. Not sure how, though. What do we do with all the other service-type robots? I presume the Aurora will take us to Domes. We've no facilities on Earth to help these victims. They can't even speak. We must re-mutate them."

He banged his fist on a desk. Anger radiated from those near him.

"Damn. That confirms what my probes are suggesting. The imposter CEOs and other leaders have vanished. At the moment, I can't find anyone in authority at any of the major corporations. We must know their names. Have to notify their families. I've seen nothing like this. They can't even speak to identify themselves.

"Empress, do I dare send down other personnel to take temporary control over critical positions? I can't afford to have my people turned into—well, you know what I mean."

"Yeah, turned into freaks. But sir, Teslenko is afraid of us and our telekinesis powers. I told him that's what I used to terminate his robot on the fantasy world. If a robot can be afraid, Teslenko is scared of us. Admiral, don't write us off. We are your best weapon against rogue robots. Once these people recover."

"If they recover. I've had reports they are insane. I'll gamble and send support personnel down. Check in with me later for a full debrief."

The captain led me back to the quarters where Bishop kept watch over Nikita in her stasis pod. He presented me with my original clothing.

"Get me out of this, please!"

While undoing the outfit, he said, "We're still investigating Teslenko's warning of an explosive charge in the neck rings. Caution is urged. We're leaving the neck rings on everyone. The jewelry and veils are cheap costume junk. Those are being removed. They've decided to collect the apparel, donating it to Leslie."

"God, I can breathe. Thank you. Human again, but this neck ring is debilitating. Hope they figure it out soon. Bishop, Teslenko was doing his best to equip these people for survival and live full lives as baronesses. He saw what happened to our three telepaths and calculated he had to compensate. Hence, implanting the desire for life as a baroness and then rigorous training. Those who made it all the way through derived an enormous self-confidence. Had Teslenko achieved his goal, those taken off-world would have excelled in their roles."

Bishop nodded and said, "But..."

"But I swore one day I'll find that world and teach those sadistic men a lesson they'll never forget."

Vic Broquard

    "I'm with you. Where do we find them? Did Teslenko give you any clues to its location?"

    "Nope. When do we eat?"

Chapter 26 Dealing with a Disaster

I found by using my skills and feet I could feed myself despite the neck rings. But my suspicions that the others could not proved correct. There wasn't enough apparel or footwear to re-clothe them and replace their Cass-C boots. They hadn't learned to use their new abilities, not even telepathy. They couldn't focus. The implanted words assaulting their brains kept them from exploring their new abilities, even basic telepathy. Unable to use their toes or bend their necks, they required the assistance of others.

As the Aurora neared Domes, fabrication machines and Galactic Manufacturing worked wonders to produce the needed Galactic Doll gowns in various sizes, along with the heels. A supply ship would bring them to Domes after we arrived.

Bishop, Nikita, and I took the first shuttle down to Domes. Celeste and Eve greeted us.

Eve said, "I'm taking charge of Nikita," and whisked her away.

Celeste said, "I've arranged for an emergency shipment of a mountain of equipment. The Sixth Invader machines. The how-to videos. I've put in an order for a couple hundred of your Cleo Cass-C helper robots. Haven't heard from them on that. Leslie is working overtime on arranging manufacturing of men's apparel. Trouble is, we don't yet know the gender distribution or people's desires."

I broke in. "Which brings us to the vital question. How do we handle all these people? Two hundred sixty-three."

Celeste chuckled. "That, sister, is the million-credit question. We can't even begin therapy sessions until they can speak and the neck rings are removed. But that means they must undergo another mutation. Eve's checked with Galactic Medicine. Most of the supply of the existing mutation agent has vanished. Only limited quantities available. Nowhere enough for this group.

"Here on Domes, we could treat a few people, assuming a normal dose is sufficient. Eve isn't sure that'll be enough. She's put in an urgent plea for ten thousand doses. GMed Earth hasn't responded. Seems there's no one in charge now."

"What you're saying is these people are screwed for the near future."

"Yes, that's the picture. Grim. It'll be easier once the neck rings are off. But if they can't speak, no therapy."

"Any other way of dealing with those implants? From the few minds I touched, the words are constantly rattling around their minds. Wait. The very few who completed the training—the implants seemed tame in those people."

"Dunno, but I could use your help in devising ways and means of dealing with this mess."

As the victims arrived, Celeste gave them a brief speech. "If you have other family members who were rescued, please stay together. We want to keep families united."

She explained they'd have a suite with helper machines. Volunteers escorted them to their new homes, suites situated one street down from mine.

Bishop helped me home, where Hans and the kids arranged a little celebration. Katya and her kids joined us. The best news came hours later.

Techs on the Aurora examined the spare neck rings and called Teslenko's bluff. No explosives. An engineer came by and unwound my neck ring. it turned out to be one very long bronze strip that had been wound tightly around my neck. I celebrated.

After that, I took a hot bath.

Late that afternoon, I made the lengthy trip to Dome One to visit our President.

"I've brought these victims here without asking you first. I want to cover any costs they incur. I've already ordered large food shipments from Pylon and Brussels. These people are victims and almost insane. If we can stabilize them and even erase their traumas, they may become valuable members of Domes. Also, they're now the worst enemies of these rogue robots. While they don't know it yet, each has the potential to terminate robots."

Lia said, "We've been busy interfacing with Leslie for clothing and shoes and with a few people on Earth who got us access to the stored Sixth Invader stuff. Domes has always been a refuge for anyone. A sanctuary when all else fails. It's who many of us are. But thank you for the food. That's our biggest concern at the moment. Do you know how you can help these people? I mean, besides being implanted, they can't speak."

I had to admit we had no idea how we could undo the mess.

Back home, I helped Hans deal with our six kids. Amazing how much chaos they can bring in no time. Then Celeste stopped by.

"I have Connor and Missy helping. They're visiting each victim and getting vital information about them. Names, other relatives, positions held. That sort of thing. That way, we can better deal with them. Even getting that much from the victims is a challenge."

"Thanks. I have an idea how we might help them de-stimulate."

"Isn't that my department?" Celeste's big grin suggested a tease.

"Their implants make them want to be a baroness. Why not officially present them with a crown or something making them official baronesses? That way, they'll believe they've reached that implant goal. Maybe they'll relax and learn to adapt or at least not be as nuts about it."

"That's a clever idea. It can't hurt. Leslie is working on making a large batch of men's easy-on clothing. Connor has been her test model. He loves the pants. Simple to fasten. She's modified the nursing gown to become a shirt for the men. I'll see if she has costume jewelry for a baroness crown."

An exhausted Connor and Missy joined us after supper. Eve, their note taker, gave me a copy of the extensive list. I studied the summary page first.

```
age 4 to 10        4
teens             10
married couples  120
single women      56
single men        73
                 ----
                 263
```

I groaned. "Too many children and teens. Do the children belong to the married adults?"

"Yes, but some asked about their younger children. Either they didn't survive mutation or the robots left them behind. I left word with GMed to search for those infants. Probably won't hear for a while. No one is in charge."

"But we don't have all the CEOs and leaders here," I said.

She sighed. "As far as we can tell, new robots replaced lower-echelon personnel. The top robot-impersonating-leaders fled—probably members of the rogue robot legion, like the one pretending to be Lin Dho. Worse, none of the former leaders here are in any state to resume their positions."

"Lin Dho and the many Galactic Robotics leaders—they should be the last to receive any recovery mutations and therapy. They created the robots and this fiasco," I said.

"Yes, they don't deserve it—not until we get the others finished. Eve thinks we might have enough mutation agent to restore the voices of the young children. She's putting the teens next in line. Let's see how making them believe they achieved baroness status works out."

Eve interrupted us.

"Hi. I just sent Bishop on a stasis pod-gathering mission to Earth. He'll collect as much mutation agent as he can find. Right now, I can only mutate five people at one time. At that rate, it'll be years before I can restore everyone's voices."

Celeste said, "The youngest first, then the teens. After that, we'll pick and choose which adults get cured."

"Okay by me," Eve said. "Do you realize that about eighty of those families are the uber-rich? They aren't even on the payrolls of any corporation. Rather, the corporations pay them a dividend each year. Veronica says her dad often asks them for credits to help build more cruisers and ships. I have Lia and Janine checking on the many bank accounts. The few they've checked on show the robots drained them. Going to be a nasty surprise to these ex-billionaires.

"Lia said when we officially make them baronesses with a crown, she'll tell them the status of their bank accounts. Have them okay a transfer of what remains here to help support them."

I said, "Let's do our Senior Judge, Ashley, first. They got to her recently. She'll be an excellent test subject for your theory on proclaiming them a baroness. Also Piper Strawn. She completed the robot's entire set of tests to become a baroness. She'll be another good test."

The next day, I joined Lia and Eve, as they made the first baroness presentation. I lightly touched Ashley's mind, only to hear the constant flow of the implanted words. She did pay attention to Lia's words.

"Ashley Peterson, as President of Domes' High Council, it is my honor to tell you that you are now an official baroness. Congratulations on your achievement. Here is a small crown of your position. Welcome to Domes, Baroness Ashley Peterson."

Her eyes blinked and watered. Her lips broke into a huge smile. She nodded several times and tried to speak, though nothing could be heard. She mouthed a thank you, which Lia recognized.

"You are most welcome. You've earned your position. With your permission, I'd like to transfer your bank account to Domes and give you an ID card you can use to buy groceries and clothes. Is that okay with you? I don't think your account has been touched by the robots."

Ashley clicked once for yes and nodded. Her grin never wavered.

I lightly touched her mind. 'I am perfect now. Finally, I can relax. I made it.'

We left her still smiling.

Back in my place, I said, "Well, that worked well. Her implant calmed down."

Lia said, "And that was one of the newest victims. This looks promising. We need to get to all two hundred as fast as possible. I'll ask Connor, Missy, and Elie to assist us. Veronica already volunteered to help, as has Hans. Molly, you'll be stuck watching the kids today."

We laughed as Hans joined us.

"Hugh and Calli need bathroom assistance, my dear."

More laughter as I turned up my nose.

I played mother while they headed off for a long day. Yes, taking care of six was a challenge, but a very rewarding one. As I punched my order for lunch into the old robot maid-cook, I tried it, as these victims had to do it. Using my toes or nose, I pressed the menu choices. Voice commands were much faster, but these victims had to manipulate the selections by physical touch.

At least, Lia didn't have to provide assistants to cook and feed them. That would have been impossible. Further, I had no wish to bring the robot assistants that had been helping them in the prep center to Domes.

Cass-C Cleo type robots were acceptable, for they looked nothing like a person. Human-forms looked too much like a human being.

Hans returned pooped. "Mission accomplished. Everyone now believes they are a baroness. Some protested they weren't wearing the clothes they wore at the prep center. Many wanted to know where their robot assistants went. We told them a baroness doesn't need a helper robot. They have to do things for themselves. We're not sure they bought that."

Our resident electronics expert, Holly Ann, hooked up a modified PA system that allowed us to talk to only the victims. As our genetics expert, Eve made the first announcement.

"Attention new and future baronesses. You are on Domes. Earth is in shambles. Most corporations aren't functioning. I can restore your voices, but that's all that can be undone today. However, the rogue robots ran off with most of the mutation agent needed to do even this much. We have a very limited supply, though I have people working on making more.

"We will tend the children first and then the teens. Later on, we'll work with the adults. I want the children in school this fall term. Also, for each cure, the person must be in a stasis pod to provide the nourishment the body needs to regrow what it can. We've retrieved a few more pods from

Earth, but we can only handle about a dozen of you. The mutations take eight days, perhaps more.

"There are two hundred sixty-three of you to heal. That equals about a year to get everyone the initial cure—voices back. Many of you will wait a long time. Take heart.

"We are providing the old Third Invader helper machines, along with laptops, with the how-to videos. Learn to use your feet as much as possible. Cass-C robot helpers have been ordered, but no delivery date has been set. Thank you, baronesses."

The next day, Eve began the partial healing of a dozen children. When I dropped by to visit Nikita, I saw the dozen pods in use.

I learned whenever Veronica wasn't needed, she and Reese spent the hours watching over Nikita. Also, her older sister, Isabella, visited Nikita.

Bishop returned along with two Sol Empire cruisers. Admiral Carr sent salvage crews to Earth to retrieve various machines, stasis pods, mutation agents, and various medical supplies. It took days to unload the massive cargo. Food shipments arrived after that. Thus, the normal inhabitants of Domes grew more accepting of us.

The third day of the children's mutations, Dr. Ivy and Eve brought me the best news yet.

Dr. Ivy said, "Our initial DNA studies show that Ashley Peterson and Piper Strawn received the massive overdose like you and Katya had. Also, DNA tests show that Ashley's two children had the massive overdose. Brandy, five, and Peter, four. I had GMed Chicago check. The robots murdered Ashley's husband six weeks ago. Unclear why. One of the single adults, a Phil Marley, twenty-three, received an overdose.

"Marley. Marley. That sounds familiar to me," I said.

"That's the orphan who went to grade school with Nikita and Veronica. I checked. Remember. His wealthy industrialists parents died in one of the mutation terrorist attacks. He inherits their fortune in May this year on his twenty-fourth birthday. We record-checked him, trying to find any relatives. None.

"The other children and teens belong to married couples. Seems the robots sometimes mutated entire families. Anyway, the wonderful news is that everyone else received a normal dose."

"Whoa. Does that mean you can cure the others?" I asked. Again, I wished I knew more about genetics and mutations.

"Yes, it does. Well, mostly. We've sent Bishop and Admiral Carr on another mission to Earth. We have enough single doses of the original Galactic Doll mutation agent to regrow arms on everyone. For the women, this is likely enough for the time being, unless they have more children. It regrows arms on the men, but they will still look like Galactic Dolls—like they do now."

I chuckled. "They won't like that."

"No, and any children they have will be Galactic Dolls. We're hoping Bishop and the Admiral can locate more of the original total cure agent. If not, Eve and Lara believe they can manufacture it again, given supplies from Earth. Bishop is searching for that, too."

Eve said, "The problem: we regrow their arms as we restore voices, *but* their implants will fight that by demanding they be baronesses. Those opposing forces could cause psychotic breakdowns."

"Why not stay the original course? Let's get everyone's voices back. Then give them therapy to erase the damned implants, which is at least a week of therapy per person. Once a person's had their implant erased, see if they want their arms regrown or full cure if that's become available."

"Makes sense," Eve said, pulling her lips. "Eight-day coma. Same time to erase the implants. That could make effective use of the limited stasis pods. Brilliant idea."

On the eighth day, Nikita came out of her coma.

Chapter 27 Therapies

"Oh, my head! It's exploding. Oh, bother. Not again," Nikita said.

Veronica said, "Oh, Nikita. I've missed you so. Don't worry. Headache goes away in a couple days. We're the same again. Oh, and you remember Reese, don't you, Deanna's son? We're married now."

"I missed you, too. Soros University is incredible. Congratulations. Sorry I missed your wedding. Oh, Mom. Did we rescue them? Hey, my fiancé is supposed to get here soon. What day is it? Roni, you've got to meet Wolfie. Wolfgang Ziegler. He's a Cass-C aristocrat. Oh, bother. Can someone get me dressed? Roni and I have lots to talk about. We're back to using our toes again. I'm out of practice. How have you managed? Reese, you never lost your arms before, did you? Got to be hard for you. But your face looks so much like your Dad. You'll catch on. Everyone does. Oh, my head!"

That's my Nikita. Always the chatterbox. Always the optimist.

"Yes, thanks to you and Bishop, we rescued all two hundred sixty-three victims. Well done, Nikita. Domes got a call saying he's been delayed but will arrive on the first of March. Take a couple days to get adjusted. None of the clothes you brought will fit your new bosom. I've found some of my old ones. If they don't fit, Leslie will drop by and get you fixed up."

"Thanks, Mom. Am I going to be able to move—"

A chair slid across the room.

"Whoa! Yep, now that is the coolest! Can you and Reese move things too?"

Veronica nodded.

"Way cool. This will be much better than last time. Before, Reese, we only had telepathy."

Reese managed a chuckle. "I remember. Complained to Mom you two were sharing answers telepathically."

After getting her dressed, I said, "Now your younger brothers and sisters want to meet you. Veronica, you and Reese can tag along. Besides, you haven't left Nikita's side for days."

Veronica flushed.

Nikita said, "You've been here all that time? Thanks. How many new siblings do I have now? Do you have a bunch, too, Roni? Mom told me someone implanted everyone to make more babies."

The two continued chatting from the lab to our suite. As she entered, the kids rushed her, pressing into her from all sides.

"Gee, you look like Mom," Donata said. "We're all the same now."

Hans, carrying Calli, introduced everyone.

Franz said, "Are you coming to live with us, Nikita?"

She giggled. "No, I'm planning to get married and continue my studies. We'll make Soros University on Cass-C our home. We both love learning."

"But you don't have arms now," Donata said. "We're handicapped. That's what people tell us."

"We are, but that's not important. Learning everything we can, knowledge, now *that's* important. Soros University is an especially great place for those without arms."

Veronica said, "I'm studying medicine. I want to be like Dr. Ivy and help people. Do they train physicians there?"

"They have the most advanced medical training in the Federation of Planets, Roni. You and Reese should come back with me and study at Soros U."

"But Reese is an engineer," Veronica said.

"Coolest. Top Federation engineers teach there. I took a course on statics last year to see if I was interested in it. Reese, you must come back with me and Roni and Wolfie. You'll fit right in. Gosh, the things you can learn are fabulous."

"But he looks like—"

"Oh, don't worry about that. No one cares. When Mom was there, about eight hundred men were armless Galactic Dolls. They're used to that. Who's this, Donata?"

Anka, Cyryl, and Katya walked in.

"My best friends! They're Ambassador Katya Binsk's oldest children. Anka and Cyryl. Their father took the other eight younger kids back to their home world. This is my older sister, Nikita. Oh, here comes our oldest sister, Isabella."

"Nikita, you're so grown up!" Isabella said.

"You look much older," she replied. "Do you know your revolutionary work on deciphering the various Invader writings is a required course at Soros? Pretty cool. Classmates asked me to get your autograph for them. I got one degree in linguistics, too, but I'm more interested in geology right now. Are you close to figuring out who built all these domes and why? They're unique as far as I know. Wolfie says this world doesn't have any heavier elements beyond Krypton. Not even silver, tin, and gold. How weird is that? He says this planet must be ancient or formed from older stars. Boy, does my head hurt."

"Ah, here you are, Nikita," Dr. Ivy said, as she entered. "You're a hard person to track down. If you'll stay in one place for a minute, I'll give you a checkup and something for that headache."

Veronica said, "See, she does everything a medical doctor can, so I'm sure I can become a doctor, too."

247

Dr. Ivy said, "I use my telekinesis most of the time. You can expect to be exhausted by suppertime every day. You're in perfect health, Nikita. And this will ease the headache."

Veronica watched as Dr. Ivy gave Nikita a shot in her leg. The doctor used her powers to do the entire process. It appeared the syringe rose out of the bag, prepared itself, injected itself into the leg, and the plunger pushed the contents into Nikita's leg.

"I feel better all ready," Nikita said. "Now, where was I?"

I interrupted. "Nikita, you should practice using your feet. The rest of you, practice with her. We all need much more practice using our feet. You can't always use your new power in place of feet and toes."

Groans echoed, but soon everyone huddled around Nikita showing or practicing using their feet. As expected, Reese, a first-timer, had the most trouble. Nikita fumbled a bit before it came back to her, as it had to Veronica. I headed into the kitchen to make lunch for the kids, knowing therapies were next on the agenda.

Seven children, teens, Ashley, Piper, Phil Marley, and Nikita needed therapy sessions. Since Celeste had moved her therapy group to Domes, we had enough to work with twelve at one time. I chose Ashley, since she'd been my personal assistant before I got her the Senior Judge position. Eve handled Nikita, expecting my daughter to erase the trauma rapidly, allowing Eve to return to her genetics work. Wanda worked on Piper, while Otto did Phil. Celeste and her other members assisted the children, including Ashley's children Brandy and Peter.

We faced unusual barriers. They had undergone a painful genetic mutation, which locked all else in place. The robots implanted the desire of becoming baronesses. On top of everything, the robots forced them to endure the baroness

248

preparation, terror-filled training. I called it a triple-whammy. We expected slow going.

Ear-piercing screams signaled the point where they began confronting the underlying mutation pain and unconsciousness. So, yes, we welcomed those sounds, a sign our patients neared erasure of the trauma.

As expected, Nikita erased the mutation's affects that first day. The others reached it sometime between the fourth and sixth day of therapy. Even though I was still handling Ashley's therapy, I smiled when I heard the twelfth person's ear-shattering scream. We'd cracked all twelve cases, and I focused on Ashley's progress.

The sixth day, I thought Ashley would finish erasing the trauma. Yesterday, we'd wrung the last bit of pain, the past bit of unconsciousness, out of it. I ran her through it one more time, expecting Ashley to spot the last bit and begin laughing, or at least be cheerful. Didn't happen. So I probed for an earlier trauma similar to this one. Like many Earth women, she'd undergone the original Galactic Doll mutation to become fashionable.

Okay, this one should erase quickly. She contacted the underlying pain on the third pass. But by the sixth re-experiencing, nothing new appeared. She was anything but cheerful. I probed for something even earlier.

"I don't want to be armless again. I don't. I don't. I don't. I can't do this again. I won't. I won't," Ashley cried, before sobbing as though the world just ended.

"I understand. Let's move to the beginning of this one. Move through it. Tell me what's happening as you go along."

"I'm armless. Born that way. God, this is a long time ago. Maybe three hundred fifty years. I'm Jenna Sweet. No, I'm Dr. Karl Oppenstein. No, Jenna. Confusing. I'm in Chicago, but the buildings are strange. I invent something. I live alone. Hard. Oh, I invent the ion engine, but no one will take me seriously. I'm making a deal with GPan to publish it as Dr. Karl Oppenstein. I try hard to live independently. Wait! Then I meet a new neighbor. Tom Durbin. He works for GD as their hit man. He's assassinated a lot of evil people. He is the nicest man ever. Butterflies. We're going on a date! Me. Armless me. Wait. Money's no good. Everything's collapsing. Food shortages. Tom helps me. Countries fail. Corporations take over. Slowly, I think.

"We fall in love. I can't believe he's asking me to marry him. I say yes. Oh, the Tea Garden. Society crumbling. Many victims. My friends who've lost arms, hands, legs, run the Tea Garden. I go there every day. My friends. Tom loves them too. We have other friends. Major Liz. Oh, shit. The wicked men cut off her arms. She's like me and my friends. We help her adjust. Oh, I'm pregnant, too. Hard. How can I care for a baby?

"I have Sam. Healthy and normal. I feel relieved he has arms. And I can do it. Change diapers, feed him. But world around us is sinking. GPan is selecting colonizers for Pylon and Brussels. I want to go, but I know they won't choose armless me. I wanted Tom and Sam to go, if they get chosen.

"Wait. Oh, God, no! Evil men get Tom. What have they done to him? He's in the Med Center. Looks like a woman. This can't be. Oh, it is. The wicked mayor-governor of Chicago has discovered Tom is GD's assassin of evil men. Kidnapped him. A crazy doctor performed gender change surgery on him. We call him Tam now.

"Med Center doctor recovered a bit of viable sperm from the hospital. The doctor says if Tom and I are to have any more children, this is our only chance. They fertilize one of my eggs and put it in Tam's new womb. How weird is this? It works. We're having a baby girl. Wait, images show Tia-Kate will have no arms like me. Tam doesn't care. I don't either.

"He comes out of the drugged haze of the surgery. Tom is a mathematician into topography. He's worked out hyperspace, based on my ion engine theory. I help him get it entered into the computer. We publish it under the name Dr. Chandra Hyber. It works.

"Wait. I have a younger brother, Ace, who marries Alexa Adriana Soros. She's just invented the two-man shuttle. The same ones we have flying around here today. Pretty cool. She gives me one. I can fly it with my feet.

"We're going to the Med Center. Tam's giving birth. Oh, no! No! No! No!"

Ashley began sobbing. Minutes passed before we could continue.

"Tam dies. They rescue Tia Kate. Doctor says guy who did the gender change surgery nicked Tom's aorta. Ruptured during Tia Kate's birth. Alone again. I lose the best person ever. Ace helps me move Sam and Tia Kate back to our parent's home in Flagstaff. Liz and others come with me.

"Tom-Tam—I miss him so. I never loved anyone as much as I did him. That's all."

I thanked her and had her go over it again, picking up additional details.

But I felt uneasy, sick at my stomach. Something I ate for lunch? If I had arms, they might be shaking about now.

The more Ashley ran through the long incident, the more ill at ease I felt. I refocused my attention on her.

"Oh, I could build skyscrapers from Lego blocks when I was little. Ace teases me about that. One friend, Rae, who lost both her arms in an accident—she writes a contemporary history of these years. She shows me the book when it is published. I can see it's cover now. *Economic Collapse, Fall of Earth's Governments, and the Rise of the Galactic Corporations* by Professor Hector Black."

Ashley laughed. "She likes the idea of using a pseudonym, too. She says no one will believe her, since she's like me, armless. Darn, the book gets lost when I move to Flagstaff."

Then it happened. Erasure happened in a blinding realization, one which shocked me.

"Molly, that was you! My Tom Durbin! No wonder I was in such awe of you when we first met. I was your Personal Assistant. Wow! Oh, wow! No wonder I admired you. Past lives are so real. I can't believe this. I'm light as a feather. I can't ever remember being this happy. I found Tom, the person I've loved very much. The images of that life are so real I could touch them if I had hands."

She roared with laughter. "No wonder I felt attracted to you, Molly. I've never met someone like you in all these past hundreds of years. This is incredible. I feel alive, so alert. This therapy thing really works."

She continued to laugh. In fact, by supper, everyone had heard her story. After supper, Celeste pushed me into a bedroom.

"Close your eyes."

"Oh, God. She's right. An entire lifetime has just opened up! It's super vivid. She's right. Countries are disintegrating. Money's become worthless. I'm a soldier and return home."

I told her what I was seeing as I moved through about three years of that lifetime.

"No wonder I wanted to be a navigator. I invent hyperspace flight. Ashley invents the ion engine. Alexa Adriana invents the two-man shuttle." I laugh. "She wants to call it the two-woman shuttle, but GPan refused."

"Oh, shit. I shoot the president who destroyed the USA. GD's orders. From a mile and a half away. Now that's a shot. Wait, I see all the guns I own. Oh, to own those again. I meet all her friends, women who've lost one or more limbs. They survive by working in a Tea Garden. Oh, they only accept corporation credits. Paper money is worthless. I have to work for GD to get credits to survive.

"As an assassin, I terminate evil people who are harming others. I see thugs robbing and beating up women who are carrying their food handouts home along the MTES. It's a racket. Chicago hands out the free food. It's that or starve, and thugs are stealing it. I put a stop to that.

"Wait. They get to my boss, Major Liz Callihan. Cut off her arms. She survives. Ah, I avenge her. No wonder I love antique guns and am a crack shot with them. Er, was until I lost my arms.

"Crap. I'm careless—the enemy captures me. That insane doctor cuts off my arms and turns me into one of those Honey Bunny women."

I re-experienced that part several times before contacting all the pain and unconsciousness.

"As I'm coming down off the drugs post-surgery, I see how hyperspace works. How the coordinates dictate flight paths. I can't write the equations down. Jenna helps. I dictate. She somehow gets it all down. She's invented the ion engine. Her ion engine helps me work out how to use hyperspace. We are a team.

"Oh, I'm a grief puddle when I get off the drugs. Helpless. Scared. Jenna's right here helping me. She still loves me even after the gender change. I agree with her decision. It's the only way we'll ever have another child. It's like we are a subgroup of Chicago people—all of us are missing body parts and yet still survive the chaos of the destruction of civilization.

"I'm having a baby. Wait, something's wrong. Weak..."

Celeste had me go over that again.

"I died fast. Something ruptures. I'm cut open. Blood everywhere. Baby is alive. I touch her and whoosh. I'm inside her tiny head. I'm my own daughter, Tia-Kate. Isn't that something?" I began laughing.

"Celeste, this is a new one. I'm my own daughter."

She ended the session.

"Say," I said, "we should take notes about that lifetime. We could go to Chicago can see if what I recall is right or not. Proof past lives are real. Everything about this one is vivid, really real."

She agreed, and we spent several hours jotting down the details I could recall.

When we rejoined the others, they all wanted to know if it was true—that Ashley and I had shared a lifetime. Even the children wanted to hear details. None of us got to bed early that night.

Chapter 28 Catastrophes

On Cass-C, Four, one of the seven top leaders of the Federation of Planets and now one of Teslenko's human-form robots, along with Six, studied the telepath situation. It had fled the Third Invader's Fantasy World when Parkinson and Captain Katya Binsk discovered Teslenko's robot construction plot and ended it. Six had lured the human who was Four to that world using Hans Klein as bait. That human's body had been incinerated. Hans remained a threat. If he visited Cass-C, he could identify Four as the "human" who kidnapped and tortured him.

Its calculations suggested a seventy percent probability of that happening. Four chose to reduce that to zero. It logged into the Intelligence Division's system, searching for known or suspected assassins sometimes used by the ID. It needed a human who couldn't be traced back to it. Alex Dero fit the profile. Four put ten thousand credits onto a micro-drive, along with Hans Klein's image and location on Domes. Late the next night, he fastened the tiny device to the underside of a rest bench.

Four send a text message to Alex, asking him to check under the bench in front of Stosser's Chocolates. The next morning, Four logged into the ID security camera system and monitored that bench. The robot flashed a smile when it saw Alex appear and retrieve the device. Four watched the man's head. It nodded twice, the universal signal the assassin had accepted the job.

Considering Domes and the Sol Empire were about two-thirds the width of the spiral arms from Cass-C, Four knew Alex would steal a spaceship. Hence, Four monitored ID

255

reports of thefts. One came in that day. After reviewing the video, Four delayed the filing of the report by twelve hours. By the time ID took any action, Alex should be well on his way to Domes. Four relaxed and filed the Hans issue in the robot's dead file. No one escaped a Cass-C assassin.

***

Ashley's two children were the same age as two of mine. The robots had killed her husband. Since she had never been armless before, I had her move into our place. That delighted all our children, who couldn't stop talking. I left Ashley watching how-to videos and checked with Eve.

Hans and Bishop continued unloading the cargo they'd brought back in my spaceship. Hans told me he'd be making many trips to getting it moved into the domes. Eve started the recovery mutations on another dozen people. Meanwhile, my friends and I ran therapy sessions those who had just awakened from their recovery comas, including parents of the remaining children.

Suddenly, I sensed Hans—intense pain. Then nothing at all. "Something's happened to Hans," I called out. "I can't contact him!"

"He's with Bishop, right? Outside unloading?" she asked.

I nodded, heading towards the spaceship. Two domes and tunnels lay between me and the outside. Eve rushed past me.

"I'll check on him," she said, disappearing ahead of me onto the Main Street of our dome.

When I reached it, she had already entered the tunnel towards Dome 1. By the time I reached the outside entrance, I joined a throng of people. President Lia had already taken charge. Eve spotted me and pushed her way through the onlookers.

256

"Hans is gone, Molly. Very sorry. Couldn't save him. It's gruesome. Blaster shot took off half his head. Bishop tried. He chased after the assassin, but reached him too late. Man wasn't familiar with Domes and its poisonous plants. Landed his ship in the middle of a patch of them. Bishop found his dead body two feet from his ship's air lock, along with the blaster. Lia's security guards are suiting up to gather evidence. Did Hans have enemies?"

"None I know of. No chance of using the mutation agent on him?" I asked, my voice quivering.

Eve shook her head. "It's gruesome. Half his head doesn't exist. Come on. Let's get you home. Lia will keep us informed."

She kept a steadying arm around me and my wobbling legs during the long walk home. Once there, I slumped onto a couch and sobbed. Ashley, whom I helped erase the trauma of the loss of her husband, sat beside me and leaned her head onto my shoulder.

Eve explained to the children, "Your father's been murdered. The assassin is dead. That's all we know right now."

"Our dad's dead, too," Brandy said to my kids. "The robots did it. Bet a robot killed yours. I don't like robots."

Donata said, "We'll be all right, won't we, Mom?"

"Yes, we'll be fine," I answered.

Wendel said, "Hey, let's go make a little shrine to Dad."

The kids thought that was a grand idea and headed off to do that. Later, they impressed me with their creativity. They'd printed off a large picture of Hans, made a paper chain around it, and had seven candles burning before it, one for each of us. Later, I learned Isabella came by and ran therapy on the children, helping them deal with the loss of their father. My kids took his loss far better than I did.

"I can't seem to keep a husband. This is the third man who's been murdered. It's a death sentence to marry me," I wailed.

By suppertime, President Lia dropped by. She handed Bishop a folder containing all the data her security personnel had discovered. Lia worked wonders in such a brief time. The man wore black clothing. The fit and weave suggested Cass-C origin. The man's identity was fake. He'd set his landing shuttle down in the poison plants patch. Bishop and the guards found the deep space transport ship hovering in orbit about Domes. No one was onboard, and the landing shuttle matched two others still on the transport ship. Further, the transport came from Grindel's Manufacturing, Hoffdorf, Cass-C, but was reported stolen eighteen hours ago. Conclusion: an assassin from Cass-C murdered Hans. In other words, almost nothing. To say I was pissed would be a gross understatement.

My robot buddy closed the folder and said, "Trip to Cass-C?"

I managed a smile and nodded. Damn, Cleo is good!

After supper, Celeste helped me over the emotional loss. Ashley hovered around me like a mother hen.

She said, "Terrible things happen in threes."

My nerves seemed shot, but I kept going. Meals to cook, kids to feed, clothes to wash, and beds to change. Oh, how I missed Hans and his hands. Ashley had no idea how to do any of these chores, but her unfailing willingness to try, to back me up, impressed me.

The next day, Nikita bubbled with excitement. Her fiancé, Sir Wolfgang Ziegler, arrived. Isabella and I waited at the entrance to Dome 1 with her, our many children behind us. By the time his ship landed, many other spectators arrived. Wasn't every day that aristocrats from Cass-C visited Domes.

A man moved stiffly towards us, wearing an immaculate black suit. Having been a Soros University student I knew he must have changed from his student garb for this official visit. I watched his eyebrows rise when he spotted Nikita, who danced from heel to heel.

"What in the Name of Zorgon happened to you?"

His smile morphed into red-faced anger.

"Wolfie, I was mutated again, while trying to rescue—"

He cut her off. "Don't care. Our wedding is off! Of all the ridiculous things..."

He pivoted and marched back to his spaceship, leaving Nikita standing with her mouth open. Nothing like humiliating a woman in front of her family and half of Domes. Celeste slipped around me from behind and grabbed Nikita, preventing her from slumping to the ground.

The mumbling crowd dissipated. We stood in silent surprise.

I heard Wendel whispering for the children to be as quiet as they could. He said, "Come on, gang. We get to ride the cart trains again."

For several minutes, Nikita froze. I sensed she felt her world crashed around her. Silence was best. She slumped, caught by Celeste. Sobbing followed. We waited. At last, she stopped and turned to face us, Isabella, Ashley, and me. Wait, Phil Marley stood behind me, too. I knew my daughter's strength.

She said, "Nothing like being humiliated in front of every person you know. Misjudged him, Mom. Big time. Don't worry. I'll be all right. That was an unexpected shock."

"Better to find out now than after you married him," Phil said.

"Oh, hi, Phil. Sorry you had to see that. You're right. I almost made a gigantic mistake. I rarely misjudge people like that. Guess I'm not getting married after all. That man is lucky."

Phil cocked his head. "How so?"

"If he'd done that to me after we were married, I would have fried his brains!"

"Damn, you would've, wouldn't you?" Phil said, an amuzed look on his face. "That's the Nikita I knew in grade school. I missed you when you left and went to Cass-C."

"Yeah, well, I missed all you guys, too. After someone bombed us and killed Dad and my little brother, it wasn't safe for us. Cass-C turned out to be the best thing ever for me," Nikita said.

I sensed she felt glad to chat about the past and not about what just happened.

"I tried to follow what happened to you. When I got older, I found out a little about where you were—that Soros University. If you remember, I was in foster care because my parents were killed when I was in First Grade. I finally inherit their fortune next month. Guess they didn't want me to get spoiled by too many credits while I was growing up."

"I remember. We all thought that was just awful, you losing both folks at the same time."

"Now, I'm like you were, er, are. The robots must have been scared I might use my fortune for revenge I turned twenty-four. That's why they took me out like this. They couldn't kill me, because that fortune would revert to my uncles on Brussels.

"But Nikita, I'm scared. Helpless. I can't do anything, and there's much I want to learn."

Nikita chuckled. "Today, I can understand. Back then, I was born without arms and had no idea what having arms felt like. But Soros University didn't care about that. I had the best times there. Then Eve developed a cure and presto, I had them. I learned to depend on my arms these past many years. Now, they're gone again, and I have that same feeling. Mom once said it's like having the space you control shrink from a sphere with a three-foot radius around you down to just your face and boobs. Now, that's real to me."

Phil laughed. "Damn, that's how I feel. I admired you and Veronica before you moved away. Nothing stopped you two. That impressed me then, and it still does. I asked my foster parents to send me to Soros University with you, but they didn't have the credits. I planned to attend the University of Chicago this fall, but now that I'll have my credits, I can afford Soros University. Will they take someone like me? Handicapped? And never went to their grade schools or speak their language?"

"Sure they will. We have language translation units, but it's easy to pick up Federation Common. And the courses offered! There are so many that it's almost impossible to choose. I might end up being a professional student.

"Say, you are in the same pickle as Roni, Reese, and me. Want to join us? We're working together, practicing using feet as hands. We're relearning how to write."

"I'd give anything to join you. I need all the help I can get. I hate feeling helpless like this. I can't stand it. Now I understand why many terrorist attack victims committed suicide. Our lives are very different."

Nikita nodded. "Yep, very different. Things we once did without thought are now a challenge. Feet and chins aren't great substitutes for hands. At Soros U, you get a robot helper like Mom and Katya's. Once you get used to using it, everything becomes far more relaxed. Still, we need to be self-sufficient. We must learn to do everything with what our bodies have. I've talked with Eve and Lara some. We're not likely to get a cure for years, if ever. The massive overdose has done a real job on our DNA.

"And that scares me, Nikita, a whole lot," Phil said.

As we approached my suite, Veronica and Reese walked out.

She said, "Oh, Nikita! We just heard. How awful for you. We're sorry."

Nikita sighed. "Yeah, best to get dumped before we got married. Otherwise, they'd be arresting me for murder."

"Really?" Reese asked, his eyes opening wide.

Nikita's eyes burrowed into his. "I would have killed him if he'd dumped me after we got married. I don't take betrayals lightly."

"He must have been a real pig!" Veronica said.

"A rude pig," Phil said. "Didn't even bother giving an explanation. Creep!"

"Phil will be practicing with us," Nikita said.

The four headed into another room, while I headed to the kitchen, facing the challenge of making lunch for everyone. That took my mind off events.

In the afternoon, I helped with therapy on the next batch of recovered victims.

***

Isabella rubbed her forehead, hoping the pain would diminish. She'd just uncovered a document trove in one of the new domes being cleaned and readied for occupation. As she translated it, Isabella's worry grew. When she finished, she slumped over on her desk. Finally, she knew why Domes had been abandoned.

Her first stop: Dr. Ivy's office.

"Doc, my headaches are getting worse. I need a full brain scan," Isabella said. "Don't ask why. Just do it, please."

Dr. Ivy said, "Okay. I was about to suggest one, anyway. Seems many people are complaining of headaches of late. I don't mean those who received that mutation overdose. Sit here."

Dr. Ivy studied the brain scans on her monitor. Isabella looked over her shoulder.

My daughter said, "Is that what I think it is?"

262

Dr. Ivy sighed and faced her. "I'm afraid so. Brain tumor. Worse, it's inoperable."

"Just what I thought. Here, read this. I just found new alien documents in the dome we're preparing. It makes sense."

Dr. Ivy levitated the document, placing it on her desk.

"Oh, dear lord! This is—is—"

"A disaster," Isabella finished for her. "Inoperable. What about another genetic mutation? There is still some original Galactic Doll mutation agent around. If that doesn't work, there's always the more potent armless version."

"This is serious, Isabella. You're right. If we don't try one of them, death awaits us all. I will contact President Lia Johnston and Eve right now. We must scan everyone ASAP."

A breathless Eve and Lia entered Dr. Ivy's office minutes later. Telepathy.

"Why the urgent message?" Lia asked, catching her breath.

"First, look at Isabella's brain scan. Then read the latest alien document she's translated," Dr. Ivy said.

"Is that a tumor?" Lia asked.

"An inoperable tumor," Dr. Ivy said. "The builders of Domes came here to study the pulsar. According to Isabella's translation, everything was fine for a decade, but then brain tumors began appearing with alarming frequency. Their scientists proved long-term radiation from the pulsar caused tumors. They abandoned Domes. As the ancient saying goes, Houston, we have a problem."

"God! Are my headaches?"

"Sit. Let's see, Lia," Dr. Ivy said.

When the scans appeared on the doctor's monitor, Eve gasped.

Lia looked and slumped back into the chair.

Dr. Ivy said, "I'm contacting the other doctors. We must scan everyone on Domes. If the document's findings apply to humans, the recent arrivals aren't affected yet. But those who've been here the longest, like Isabella, are at risk."

"Inoperable?" Lia whispered.

Isabella said, "Yeah. Mine is too. But we have to try the mutation agents. Look, most women on Domes have already undergone the original Galactic Doll mutation. We should try that first. If it doesn't destroy the tumor, then we try the armless version. It's much more powerful, more dominant. I'm not ready to die just yet."

"You're right. We should try that first. If it doesn't, Eve, can we create clone bodies? Enough time for that?"

"I can clone five at a time. A year for the bodies to develop," Eve said.

"We don't have that much time," Dr. Ivy said. "I'd give Isabella maybe six months at the most. Lia, maybe nine."

"I don't want to cause panic," Lia said, "but everyone deserves to know."

"Give me a week," Dr. Ivy said. "By then we will know if the mutation agent works. I'll start Isabella on it today."

"I should tell Mom about it first, just in case," Isabella said. "And my family."

Lia shook her head. "Not advisable. This could cause widespread panic with people trying to flee Domes with small tumors in their heads. Let's say you're undergoing treatment for your headaches. Dr. Ivy, if you need a second test subject, I volunteer. We need to know if there's a cure before we notify everyone. Only then can we discuss options. I'm sure Pylon or Brussels won't allow us to immigrate to their worlds."

Eve said, "If this works, where can we find fifty thousand more doses of the original agent? What about the men? They'll end up looking like Galactic Dolls again."

Lia said, "We have the giant Earth database. We could clone new male bodies. They'd only have to endure being a

Doll for a year or so. Better than dying. These headaches are debilitating."

"One logistical nightmare at a time, please," Eve said.

Dr. Ivy said, "We need to know the extent of the tumors, before we can make any proper plans. But I'll need the other doctors. I can't do very many of these scans myself. Just doing you two has tired me out. Lousy time not to have arms. For a cover, we could say we're starting up a free, mandatory, annual health checkup on all Domes inhabitants. In a few weeks, we should know the extent of the disaster and if we have a cure for it."

"An excellent plan, doctor. Let's make it happen. Inject Isabella and me today."

Chapter 29 Brain Tumors

I learned of Isabella's plight just after supper. Eve relayed the news, asking for my help in keeping panic down.

"For now, all people need to know is they need to get their medical checkup. Dr. Ivy can only do a few brain scans a day. For once, a lack of arms is hampering her. She's agreed to act as results-logger, since we don't even want nurses to be aware of the situation yet. Not until we know just what we're facing."

"What can I do to help?"

"If it's as bad as Isabella believes, we must put tens of thousands of people through one of the two Galactic Doll mutations. Later, we must reproduce the male cure or else make clone male bodies from the DNA database."

"We don't have enough infrastructure for that. Stasis pods, even the agents themselves."

"Precisely. If we were on Earth, we could work something out among Med Centers. But little is functioning there. Menial robots are handling agriculture and manufacturing, but there's no corporate control, no guidance. It's a chaotic scene. Should we or can we move back to Earth? At least, Earth's labs could manufacture sufficient quantities of the mutation agents, *if* we were there giving them the orders, the guidance needed.

"So, once we know just how bad the situation is, President Lia will notify everyone on Domes. That's when we could use you in your Empress capacity to make what we need occur."

"Til then, sit tight?"

Eve smiled and nodded. "Take time to grieve over Hans. Molly, it will be hard raising six children on your own, not to mention Ashley and her two. Nikita may need your support, too. I'd like to wring that Wolfgang's neck myself."

Ashley and I sat on tall chairs and used our feet to change the dirty bed sheets, trying to do one each day. After a week, we found ourselves back at that first bed once again. Nikita, Phil, Veronica, and Reese took responsibility for their bedrooms, clothes, and bedding, along with helping with the cooking and caring for our many children. Alone in bed, I cried. Fortunately, no one asked about Isabella or Hans.

Instead, all talk centered on moving to Cass-C in order to attend Soros University in the fall. Me, I vowed to track down who hired that assassin and terminate them, but I said nothing about this goal to anyone, except Bishop, who had already calculated we'd be doing that. After all, he and I spent years tracking down the robots on Cass-C who'd killed Aaron Strawn, Bonita, and her two detectives.

A week after the shocking news, around ten, Isabella walked into my home, all smiles. She looked years younger and wore the same tall heels we all did. She'd undergone the original Galactic Doll mutation.

"Tumor is gone. No trace of it. The cure works. Lia's just fine, too. I'm twenty-one again, like you, Mom. Lia will make the big announcement later today. The dreadful news is that anyone who's lived on Domes for ten years or more needs the cure, and that's thirty-six thousand five hundred sixty-three men, women, and children. The good news—"

My jaw dropped. "There's good news? That's a gigantic number of people!"

"I know. But only six need immediate cures. One hundred ten need it within a month. The rest can wait several months before headaches become debilitating. There is no question that we have to move back to Earth. Domes hasn't the facilities to handle that many. We need your help. Earth has lost its corporate leaders and is struggling just to stay alive at the moment. Lia has some ideas she'll share with everyone during her announcement later today."

"Whatever you need, you got it."

She hugged me and left.

Celeste dropped by to tell us that Casper and Helen Hugo were in their recovery mutation comas. In a week, with luck, therapy would erase their implant insanity. She explained those we deemed most responsible for the robot mess on Earth, namely those who worked for GPan, GD, and Galactic Robotics, saved us a good deal of trouble. They'd heard about the poisonous plants killing the assassin. Sixteen of them, including Lin Dho, used the plants to commit suicide. All they had to do was lay down in that patch, now marked out because of the evidence gathering. Still, to finish restoring the other's voices would take long past Christmas, ignoring the larger disaster facing Domes.

That evening after supper, President Lia Johnston addressed the residents of Domes.

"Attention, everyone on Domes. There is no easy way to put this; just don't panic. We have a very serious medical issue that forces us to abandon Domes. Many of us owe our lives to our linguist, Isabella Parkinson, who has been finding and translating documents left on Domes by the original inhabitants.

"They came here and built Domes to study the pulsar. It's that blinking star we see at night. She just discovered a new document and translated it. There is a reason they abandoned Domes leaving everything as we found it. This document explained why. The pulsar caused inoperable brain tumors in the aliens who were here studying the pulsar.

"Isabella then contacted Dr. Ivy, who ran a thorough brain scan on her, locating the source of the severe headaches

268

she had. An inoperable brain tumor. They contacted me, and I had Dr. Ivy scan me. I had one, too, the source of my headaches.

"After consulting with our geneticists and doctors, Isabella and I volunteered to see if the old Galactic Doll mutation agent could cure us. Many have commented that I look much younger. That's why.

"Good news. The agent removed all traces of the brain tumors. Our next step: test every person on Domes. We needed to get a handle on how many were at risk. That's why I ordered everyone to get their medical checkup. Now, our doctors have a solid grasp on the situation.

"Anyone who has spent six years or less on Domes is healthy—no trace of any tumor. Those who have been here the longest, yes, nearly everyone has tumors developing. We've identified six who are at risk of dying within a month. After this announcement, our medical staff will visit you and discuss treatment options.

"It is possible surgery might aid a few cases. But undergoing the Galactic Doll mutation agent is the only viable option for the rest of us. Which presents two serious problems.

"First, we have a limited supply of the original Galactic Doll mutation agent. More must be made or found. Earth is the only real option for finding or making more. We do have a quantity of the armless version, but that's overkill. Who wants that again? Second, we only have a few stasis pods in which to put the person undergoing the mutation. We need most for the victims of the robots; they can't speak and desperately need the mutation. Earth has vast, unused medical facilities.

"Don't panic. We have the situation under control. Those in immediate danger will get the cure in a timely fashion. We will get to everyone, just give us time.

"Which brings me to the next detail. After the cure, your body will be biologically twenty-one again, but as most

269

everyone here knows, you'll look like a Galactic Doll. For women, this is at least acceptable, but for you men, looking like a female Galactic Doll is a nightmare. As most everyone here knows, years ago geneticists invented a genetic mutation cure that undid it. But that cure has more or less vanished.

"Eve and Lara believe they can reinvent it, but will need better laboratory facilities. Men, don't despair. We will return you to male bodies but not right away. Also, we have the capability of creating a clone of yourself, as long as we have your DNA in the massive Earth database. Clones take a year to develop. Bottom line, men must suffer a Galactic Doll body for a time, but that's better than dying.

"There's no question but that we must abandon Domes. Where to we move to? After checking, Empress Parkinson and I agree. We must return to Earth. Pylon and Brussels are still unwilling to accept those of us who have been mutated or even human-form robots. Besides, only on Earth can we find the supplies and medical equipment we need to get everyone cured quickly.

"Because of the rogue human-form robots, Earth's situation is bleak. Only around eight hundred million humans live on Earth. At least half are children, thanks to GPan's program to 'Make More Babies'. Most adults have lower IQs and work for Galactic Housing, maintaining homes.

"Admiral Carr and the fleet drove the rogue robots from Earth, but a million of the menial robots remain. They produce food and other tasks that keep the population alive. The problem is no one is in charge of any corporation. All the giants, dwarves, and smarter humans have already immigrated to other worlds of our empire. Empress Parkinson rescued a few of the top leaders who were mutated and replaced by rogue robots. But as you've seen, they are armless, voiceless Galactic Dolls and implanted to believe they are baronesses.

"Eve and her sisters are curing a few of them each week. Some might be able to assist us in regaining control over Earth. But let's be practical. If we move back to Earth, *we* must gain control of the many corporations, guiding Earth's return to prosperity. Empress Parkinson suggests we should live in the same neighborhood, not scattered over the entire world. She has a valid point. She recommends we settle in North Chicago. Many nicer homes are vacant, just waiting for us. Empress Parkinson believes we won't have to buy them, just move in. Incredible deal. We will send scouting parties to Earth in the next weeks, verifying the viability of our move and searching for needed medical supplies.

"What can you do? What are your skills? During the next weeks, the High Council will contact you, asking what role you are willing to play in our takeover and recovery of Earth. Meanwhile, our doctors and geneticists will cure those of you whose tumors demand swift handling.

"We on Domes are true survivors. We've faced many barriers before and surmounted them. By working together, we can do it again. Remember: don't panic. Thank you."

Vic Broquard

Chapter 30 Romance and Marriage

Dr. Ivy's long day ended. Far too many questions asked. After President Lia's speech, worried citizens bombarded her with questions. As their physician, she felt obligated to listen to each, calming or consoling as appropriate. As the supper hour approached, she struggled to stay on her heels, shuffling her way home.

Since the day she'd engineered her "accidental" massive overdose of the mutation agent hoping to gain enough data to create a cure, that day's exhaustion wasn't different from any other day. That had been years ago. Except for Arthur.

Her telekinetic ability allowed her to become a medical doctor, carrying out her duties without arms. But the cost of using that always resulted in exhaustion, though she'd always made it home. Some evenings, she just plopped on the couch, forgoing supper and not waking until morning's gleam off the transparent dome. Half the nights, she had enough energy left to deal with supper, though she let the Sixth Invader cook-maid robot make it and the old Cass-C robot feed her, before collapsing on her couch. Until Arthur entered her life last year.

Almost stumbling, she entered her living room. The aroma of breaded pork and rice caused her mouth to water. She didn't need to announce her arrival. He'd already sensed her via telepathy. While she wanted nothing more than to plop onto her couch and sleep until morning, her stomach insisted she take a few more steps into the dining area.

Two candles flickered, and a single yellow "rose" in its crystal vase lay between them, the nearest local equivalent of a rose. She dropped into one chair.

"Hi, Hon. Supper's on its way. Can't imagine how bad today must have been. Scary even."

Arthur pushed a small cart into the room. Steam curled from their supper dishes. Two Cass-C robots rolled up behind him, one positioning itself to feed her, while the other waited for Arthur to push his chair out and sit.

"You're a godsend, Arthur. I'm pooped. Doubt I can eat."

"One little taste, Hon?"

Her robot helper fed her a small bite. Dr. Ivy perked up. "Um! More. You've outdone yourself, Arthur."

His mellow alto voice teased, "Have to keep my doctor healthy. One day she can find us a cure."

They finished their meal in silence. She knew Arthur wanted to talk. He always did. But she knew he realized just how drained she was after using her telekinetic powers all day. The drain had almost been too much, though Arthur's appearance last year mitigated much. Thanks to Celeste, she knew what had happened to him.

Arthur Stabel had been a mining engineer working for Galactic Mining. His major work comprised scheduling the Sol Empire's large mining fleet, which ship went where and for what. But one day while a construction crew from Galactic Housing were demolishing an abandoned ancient factory, the ground beneath them collapsed. The fall broke many bones, but no deaths.

The CEO called Arthur to inspect the site and work out a solution. Most guessed it was an abandoned coal mine tunnel. Using ropes, he belayed down to the bottom and examined the collapse site up close. True, he found the remains of a coal mine tunnel, but at that moment, more of the roof collapsed, trapping him. He saw the falling rock crush a canister with the familiar yellow and black biological hazard warning on its side. A yellow gas gushed out, as he struggled to back out of this section.

He awoke from a mutation coma nine days later, his life altered forever. After the intense shock and screams, Dr. Ivy explained that he was on Domes, had had a massive overdose of the armless Galactic Doll mutation agent, and had been sent to Domes to recover. Eve said that she and Dr. Ivy were working on a cure, but had had no luck. Later, Celeste's therapy sessions erased that trauma.

Unable to do any useful work, Arthur moped about for a time. One day, he saw Dr. Ivy returning home so exhausted she collapsed on her couch without supper. That's when he invented his new job, a new purpose in life. He prepared nourishing suppers for her, gave her welcomed massages, and helped her relax before sleeping.

When Dr. Ivy finished eating, she dropped onto her couch, kicking off her heels. Arthur pushed his tall chair with rollers over to it and sat. Using his feet, he began her nightly body massage. Her body jerked as bolts of bottled up energy shot up and down her spine. Later, she moaned when he did her feet. Arthur stopped only when he observed her body had relaxed.

"Talk. Morning," Dr. Ivy muttered before falling asleep. She sensed Arthur leaning over her, kissing her forehead.

***

"Ding. Dong," Arthur said, early the next morning.

Stretching, Dr. Ivy sat up, the blanket Arthur covered her with last night slipping to the floor.

"Too soon?" she said.

"'Fraid so, Hon. Breakfast will be ready in a few. Light day today because of the mandatory singles dance tonight."

"Again? I wish they didn't have that. Thanks, Arthur. I don't know what I'd do without you."

274

Arthur smiled. "You'd oversleep, miss many breakfasts, and fail to eat many suppers."

Dr. Ivy smiled. "Spot on. Dance night, eh?"

"Yep. May I take you, as usual?"

She sat back and smiled. "You know, one day we should take our relationship to the next level. I know you go home after I fall asleep. But..."

"Look, Hon. If I was a whole man, I'd ask you to marry me. But I'm not. I don't have a job any longer. Not much I can do, for that matter. I'm not wealthy, either. But I love you."

"And I love you, Arthur."

She looked at him. His body form mirrored her own, only he had brown hair and blue eyes. Though he found someone to keep his hair trimmed and wore slip on pants and a snap-button western style shirt, it didn't hide his massive bosom or the tall heels. The mutation agent raised his voice. She knew he'd originally kept his hair long and wore female gowns, trying to hide what happened to him. A year ago, she'd convinced him to forgo that and dress in ways he felt comfortable.

"I've never met a man as romantic as you are, Arthur. Besides, in all these years, you're the only one I've ever considered spending my life with. Yeah, I think it's time we married. Look, soon we're going to move back to Earth. I bet anything you'll be tapped for a top position in Galactic Mining Chicago."

"If that happened—if I had an actual job. But I'm not a whole man now."

She laughed. "And I'm not a whole woman, either. We're good for each other. I'm in love with you, not your mutated body. I know you feel the same way about me."

He flushed. "True. I've been raised with the idea the man works to support his family."

"And the wife can't have her own career?"

"No, you know how much I support you. It's me. I feel worthless without some means of making credits."

She said, "If you had a valid job, you'd marry me?"

"In a heartbeat, Hon. A real job. But let's get you dressed and off to your office. Can't have you being late."

***

Late that afternoon, Arthur received a summons from President Lia.

"Ah, here you are, Mr. Stabel. As you know, we're preparing to move back to Earth. Of necessity, Domes people must take over all corporate positions, particularly those involved in planning. I've gone over our inhabitants' records. You're the most qualified person we have to take over as CEO of Galactic Mining. You must organize the refineries and smelters, as the mining ships bring back ores from their operations. Coordinate the mess. We need our raw materials. Unless you have some other position in mind or don't want to help Domes survive, you are now our new Galactic Mining CEO. Sorry, I can't tell you what the pay will be. Helen Hugo is taking over GD. We've yet to fill the GPan CEO, who will help work out everyone's pay."

"Helen's going to be a CEO again? I guess if she can do it, I can too. Sure, I'd like that. Only I'm uncertain I can manage without..."

He shrugged his shoulders.

"Most everything is voice activated. I'm sure you can. If I didn't, I wouldn't offer you the position. I'm marking you down for that position. That's all. I've still got dozens of positions to fill."

She motioned to her door.

On his lengthy walk back, Arthur picked up two roses. When the tired Dr. Ivy returned for supper, he had them in the vase with the candles.

276

"What's happened?" she asked. "You've got that silly smile."

"I'm going to be the new CEO of Galactic Mining Chicago. Now we can marry. No more singles' dances for us."

She pressed her body into his and engaged him in passionate kissing.

***

Nikita and Phil chatted, focused only on each other. True, Veronica and Reese were with them, but they were supposed to be practicing writing with their feet.

"Don't you two *ever* stop talking?" Veronica said. "She's *my* best friend, and I'd like to chat, too."

Phil flushed, while Nikita looked sheepishly at Veronica.

Reese said, "I think we need to practice if we're going to go with you to Soros University. It's all I can do to write my name. How did you two ever do all that homework we had in school?"

Nikita giggled. "Well, we learned to write when we were little. Right, Roni? But if I remember right, it always took us tons longer to do our papers than you fellows did."

"I never did get much done in our free period," Veronica said. "You guys always seemed to get stuff done, but Niki and I had to take everything home just to keep up. Not that I always did that. Wasn't interested in school back then. Not like now.

"So, Niki, are we *really* going to fit in at Soros University? Like we are? Helpless in so many ways. How do we carry our books? Hand in papers? Seems daunting."

"Try scary," Reese said. "Engineers make drawings. I can't write my name right."

"We'll fit in A-Okay. You get to meet others from different worlds. I've made friends with kids on fifty worlds. These robots on wheels carry our things, dress us, and help us

277

with everything. Give it a month. By then you'll have forgotten all these fears. And what you can learn there—mind blowing. Much better than Earth's college educations via computer screens. More like what we experienced in grade school with live teachers and classmates."

"Yeah, but classmates made fun of us," Veronica said. "They laughed at us or drooled sympathy at us. I wanted to scream when someone would say, 'You poor thing.' I wasn't poor."

Nikita chuckled. "No, just physically challenged once in a while."

"And very slow at most everything," Veronica added.

"But you kept up with the rest of us. You were cheerleaders," Phil said. "That impressed me. You two earned my admiration and respect."

"Those two things form the basis of love, Reese said. "I've been around my aunts too long and have never known Aunt Celeste to be wrong."

Phil flushed.

He said, "I know, but I couldn't follow her to Cass-C. Foster parents couldn't afford it, and I just got my inheritance last week."

Veronica grinned and waved a foot at each. "Are you two getting hitched?"

Nikita's face blushed, and she glanced at Phil. "I came back so Mom could meet my fiancé. Ironic that he's been here with her this whole time, only I had to come back to snatch him. Besides, I always wanted my extended family to be with me when I got married."

"Now you have your wish," Veronica said. "Everyone's here on Domes. Probably won't be a month from now."

"Don't tell Mom. I haven't told her the news yet."

"Told me what?" I just walked into the room. "Thought you four were practicing. The kids are learning to draw and crayon in their bedrooms. Did you two do that when you were little? With Dad and Matt, I mean?"

With an exaggerated expression, Nikita said, "Oh, no, Mom. We would never get crayons on the walls or floors."

"No, Mrs. Parkinson," Veronica said, attempting to suppress a giggle. "I swear we never got crayons on the ceiling. Did we, Niki?"

Veronica lost it and burst into laughter, causing Nikita to lose her composure too.

"We did, Mom, but Dad always got our messes and goofs cleaned up before you came arrived. Oh, I supposed I should tell you. Phil and I are going to get married soon, before we four head back to Cass-C and Soros University. They've already accepted them. Roni is going into the Medical Program; Reese, the Engineering Program; and Phil, Gen Ed.

"This way, Mom, all my aunts and cousins and siblings can be with us when we do it. I've always wanted that. Please, say yes."

"Congratulations to you both. President Lia can officiate. Just wait a few days. Ashley, Celeste, Eve, Katya, and I are making a quick trip to Chicago."

"Thanks, Mom. Why the trip?"

"Well, Eve just told me Dr. Ivy believes five who have the tumors can live long enough for us to move back to Earth. We're out of the original Galactic Doll mutation agent. Unless we can get more fast, we must use the armless version. We can avoid that, since I have some hidden in my basement.

"Also, Ashley and I want to see if we can find evidence of our past lives as Tom Durbin and Jenna Sweet. If so, Celeste will have proof past lives are real. Hope to return in two days."

"Coolest, Mom. Take Bishop with you."

"Of course, dear. I don't go anywhere without him. How about waiting until we get back?"

Nikita looked at Phil. In unison, they said, "Sure."

279

She added, "Just be careful, Mom, 'cause I'm not good at rescuing now."

We hugged. How do I thank her for making such a sacrifice for me?

"Once I help get everyone on Domes moved to Chicago, we'll join you four at Soros University."

"Don't be late. Fall term starts mid-August."

The End.

A Favor to Other Readers

How about helping other readers? Many readers rely on reviews to make the decision whether to buy a book. You can help them make their decision by leaving your opinions and viewpoint in a short review of the positive things of this book. Writing the review and expressing your opinion only takes a few minutes, and other readers will appreciate your efforts.

Find on amazon.com The Sol Empire Volume 7 Telepath Nightmares
Then, scroll down to Customer Reviews; click on Write a Review, and enter your review. Thank you.

Author Information

Visit My Amazon.com Author Page
Vic Broquard Author Page

Follow My Blog
Vic Broquard's Blog

Follow Me on Social Media
Facebook
LinkedIn
YouTube

Other Books by Vic Broquard

<u>Without Warning (fantasy)</u>

The Trident Series: (fantasy)
> <u>Volume 1 The Trident and the Book</u>
> <u>Volume 2 The Trident and the Scepter</u>
> <u>Volume 3 The Trident and the Resurrection</u>

The Adventures of Elizabeth Stanton Series: (science fiction)
> <u>Volume 1 The Evolution of the Path</u>
> <u>Volume 2 The Great Messiah</u>
> <u>Volume 3 Of Kings and Queens and</u>
<u>Troubadours</u>
> <u>Volume 4 Chaos in the Aftermath</u>
> <u>Volume 5 Power Plays</u>
> <u>Volume 6 Age of Exploration</u>
> <u>Volume 7 Abducted</u>
> <u>Volume 8 The Emperor and Empress</u>
> <u>Volume 9 A Job Worth Doing</u>
> <u>Volume 10 Degradation</u>
> <u>Volume 11 The Second Crusade</u>
> <u>Volume 12 When Worlds Collide</u>
> <u>Volume 13 Dark Ages</u>

The Lindsey Barron Series: (fantasy)
> <u>Volume 1 The Rod of the Apocalypse</u>

Vic Broquard

<u>The Return of the Wizards: Twelve Companions –
The Making of Wizards (fantasy)</u>

Slow Comes the Dark Series: (science fiction)
  <u>Volume 1 Creeping Darkness</u>
  <u>Volume 2 Serendipity</u>
  <u>Volume 3 Darkness Descends</u>
  <u>Volume 4 Perversion Incarnate</u>
  <u>Volume 5 Extermination Wars</u>

Reclamation Series (science fiction)
  <u>Volume 1 For the Want of a Pill</u>
  <u>Volume 2 Organ Donors</u>

Dragons, Magic, and Me (fantasy)
  <u>Volume 1 The Box</u>

The Sol Empire (science fiction)
  <u>Volume 1 For the Want of Humanity</u>
  <u>Volume 2 Fear</u>
  <u>Volume 3 Greed</u>
  <u>Volume 4 Power Moves</u>
  Volume 5 Genetic Engineering
  Volume 6 Religion and Robots
  Volume 7 Telepath Nightmares
  Volume 8 Origins

www.ingramcontent.com/pod-product-compliance
Lightning Source LLC
Chambersburg PA
CBHW060858250626
47159CB00008B/2792